M000093330

The Stone of
DAVID

MATT
DOSS

Copyright © 2013 Matt Doss
All rights reserved.

ISBN: 098976091X
ISBN 13: 9780989760911

Library of Congress Control Number: 2013915029
Matt Doss
Huntsville, AL

DEDICATION

For Phil Fowler, *my uncle, mentor and friend
whose support, encouragement and collaboration
made this book possible.*

Thank You

And for my daughters Madison *and* Margot;
*be faithful to whom your heart calls you to be
and then live passionately into that calling.*

Go, return not die in war

– Pythia, Oracle of Delphi

TABLE OF CONTENTS

1

There were times when it seemed he'd never lived at all, stretches of time that were some kind of white noise at most. Yet, as he watched her graceful form carving through the waters of their private lake, he realized in fact he had lived, felt, and even tasted every moment of life since they'd first met. Rather than lingering here though, he needed to get up to the cabin and complete the final chapters of his latest novel, a notion with which his editor would whole heartedly agree. Perhaps more than that though, he needed to live for just a few moments more in this place, to dwell upon the miracle that was taking her morning exercise right before his eyes.

The air was calm with just a whisper of morning fog dwelling in their cove. Laura emerged from the lake with a smile, a shiver and an inquisitive look on her face, a look he'd seen a million times that said, "you're about to tell me what's on your mind." Without drying off she hopped into his lap and thoroughly soaked his freshly donned clothing. The sensation of her warm body and the cool water gave him a start as she flashed a devilish grin and used him as a human towel. "What?" she said in a lilting and falsely innocent tone.

"Oh, nothing." he replied, holding up a towel still warm from the dryer "So glad I brought a towel for you to wrap up in after you've dried off."

"No..." She nuzzled his neck then playfully bit his earlobe, "I mean what are you thinking so intently about?" With her index finger, she stroked the furrow just above the bridge of his nose.

He could manipulate his editor, he could effortlessly massage a confession out of the most stalwart of people, go toe to toe with anyone, anywhere and be on equal if not superior footing, but not her and not ever. Like no one he'd ever met before, she could play him like a virtuoso plays a violin. Fortunately, she loved him deeply and madly and only used her power over him for good, at least insofar as she was concerned.

About the time he was going to make a half-hearted effort to avoid her question, a most unusual and somewhat disconcerting sound came from up the hill on the other side of the house, a car door. People rarely made the journey to their mountain retreat, and normally called before they did. Alexander turned to look over his shoulder and as he did, the blood drained from his face. She saw a flash of rage in his countenance right before composing himself. Unusual for him and not perceptible to anyone but his beloved Laura, but there was no mistake, it was rage she had seen.

Walking toward them was a man that appeared to be in his mid to late 70s. He wore a dark suit and shoes that were obviously not suited for the sloped and rocky terrain. He carried himself as one far more accustomed to paved culture as his legs met the ground uneasily with each step. Laura swiftly reached for the towel and wrapped herself in it as she inquired, "Do you know him?"

Without any discernible expression he simply said, "I used to."

As the man approached, Alexander stood and put himself between the unannounced guest and Laura. Halfway down the hillside the man stopped.

"I contemplated wearing a bullet proof vest before coming to see you." A nervous smile and chuckle seemed to be hiding just behind the man's words.

"Some mistakes in judgment often prove fatal." Alexander's words had no indication of a smile, nervous or otherwise. Laura could sense a tension growing in him that she'd never witnessed. It was as if she could hear the magma of a volcano bulging just beneath his veneer of calm. Much like a domestic animal encountering the intrinsic danger of a wild animal, this unexpected visitor sensed the same thing and took a step backward.

"Why are you here?" Again, his words were as solid and void of emotion as the cold blade of a sword and they imbued the intended effect. Alexander took a step toward the man while dropping his right hand to his side.

"If I know you at all," the man nervously replied "and I'm sure I do, I suspect that your hand is now resting on that favorite little snub-nose revolver you've always carried, and as much as I wouldn't blame you for wanting me dead, I assure you what I have come to say is worth far more to you than my life."

Though it was a cool morning, sweat had broken out across the man's forehead and he was obviously frightened to be there. "I know you blame me for Hongkou and I understand, but I wouldn't have come all this way and risked you following through with your promise to kill me if you ever saw me again if I didn't know I had something that would change your life."

"You've already changed my life once, and it cost me everything except my life and it very nearly did that." Almost as if he were stalking his next meal, Alexander began a slow measured pace toward the man. "The kindest thing I will do for you is to let you turn and leave and forget that you ever showed up here."

Laura had never seen this side of him and she was in somewhat of a daze. Right before her eyes a part of his life with which she was obviously and completely unaware was unfolding in a most unpleasant manner. "What is this about?"

Before she could follow with another question or Alexander could respond, the man spoke again, "Who do you think got you released from Tilanqiao Prison?"

Alexander's face flushed into a violent shade of red at this comment, "Leave... NOW!"

3

The man took several steps back stumbling somewhat as his leather soled shoes failed to gain purchase on the uneven ground. "OK, I'm leaving. I'll be in town at the bed and breakfast for two days." His voice shook and faded with each breathless word. "I have it Alex. I have it with me." The man turned to leave but not without some trepidation. He'd seen Alexander in action several times before and knew all too well what he was capable of doing to his foes.

It was an exaggerated length of time after the car sped off down the long road away from their place before either of them spoke. Just beyond the tree line to the west, in the opposite direction the car and its jittery driver had gone, a twig snapped. Alexander had spent most of his formative years in the forests of the Deep South and knew the precise difference between the sound of an animal and that of another human presence. He was also wary enough not to allow that most dangerous of mammals know he'd discovered their presence.

Somewhere between annoyed, frightened and shocked, Laura measured Alexander's countenance for just a moment more and began, "Um...OK? Who's going to start?"

Almost imperceptibly he directed his eyes in the direction of their watchers, then said, "Let's go inside, this is going to take a while."

2

Once inside their stone cabin, a place Alexander had dreamed would hide and protect them from the very world that had just once again engulfed him; he very calmly asked Laura if she would care for a cup of tea. Of course, he had anticipated her exasperated response to this extension of civility in the face of such an interruption to their peace, but he needed her to be exasperated and frustrated as he led her nowhere near the kitchen or the kettle.

A 1992 Olympic silver medalist in the Biathlon, recruited by both the NSA and CIA right out of law school, a collection analyst for multiple acronym agencies including the National Reconnaissance Office, Laura had navigated some hair raising journeys without so much as a twitch of her nerve. This was different. Her heart was involved and the man she'd given it to had evidently been keeping some rather large secrets. She was unnerved and was letting Alexander have it with both barrels, so much so that she hardly noticed as he effortlessly and silently pushed their 300 year old cherry bureau to the side.

Alexander knew the snapping twig had caused the human element to withdraw from the area whether they thought he'd discovered their presence or not. However, he also knew the technology being employed to observe him at this very moment would be shocking to even the vaunted National Security Agency and horrifying to the average citizen. Miles Alexander Kilpatrick was no ordinary citizen though and he was neither shocked nor horrified that their every move, every breath, every heartbeat and synaptic impulse was currently being monitored. Which, is why he needed Laura to continue her focused tirade.

Everyone has those things that set them off, for Laura it was lying of any kind. The more she trusted you, the higher her expectations and the lower her tolerance for lies. Soft, loving and accommodating in every way, but lie to her and the dismantling of what might've been a pleasant day will be intense. As she lit into him, he almost laughed at the thought of their watchers trying to analyze the synaptic activity of her brain on their monitors at that moment. However, as being provided with a brand new double-wide asshole was sufficient for him at the time, Alexander chose to keep his laughter to himself.

He ushered Laura down the narrow steps right at the moment her surprise at the freshly gained knowledge of this hidden room exacerbated her anger. He was beginning to consider a return to Tilanqiao Prison as a more pleasant alternative than facing her once they were sealed in his safe room together. Once inside though, nothing they said, thought or did could be observed or detected in any way. Alexander had constructed this room himself and it made the soundproof rooms of Langley seem like damp cardboard boxes.

This was no post-apocalyptic survivalist prepper's bunker though. Except for a partially consumed bottle of Laphroaig and a bag of low-sodium almonds there were no provisions. The furniture consisted of a WWII era rolling desk chair that had belonged to his grandfather and a dove stool that he'd had since he was twelve years old. There was no weapons cache either, no AK-47s loaded with 30 rounds of armor piercing bullets, no .308 sniper rifles, not even a butter knife. There were no computers, no phone lines, and no aerial antenna arrays connected to it, not a single line of plumbing or wiring running to it or from it.

Alexander built his cabin in absolute secrecy making an offer on the land it sat on after it was complete. It was a bit risky, but he'd researched the history and ownership of the land well in advance. The roughly 200 acres in the mountains of North Carolina was picturesque but was not suited to much else but being viewed. It belonged to a group of squabbling heirs that were happy to trade it for the amount of cash he'd offered them. To the estranged family members of the original owner the cash was a windfall that would be blown on new pickups, mobile homes and multiple trips to the casino in Cherokee. To Alexander, it was a place to retreat from his former life, write his novels and poetry, and if necessary protect the one thing his pursuers wanted most, his knowledge. This room was designed to do precisely that. As Laura would soon discover, the technology used to construct the room defied conventional logic in some senses and utilized materials that leading scientists and engineers couldn't even comprehend. Instead of thick layers of heavy, sound deadening materials, the key to the room's secrets was in one thin layer of micro-engineered fabric capable of absorbing and storing energy. Essentially, any wavelength or particle of energy directed into or out of the room was immediately absorbed and held in perpetuity in a sort of sonic stasis. The bottom line on this particular morning was that the ass-chewing going on within in its walls would never be heard by anyone other than Alexander, nor would the explanation that followed ever be heard by anyone other than Laura.

"I'm not sure where to begin..."

"At the *beginning*!" Laura was not prone to raising her voice but at the moment she was willing to make an exception. "And what did he mean that *he* was the one that got you out of Tilanqiao? I seem to recall working *very* hard and making some next to impossible promises through some *very* shady diplomatic channels to get you out of there. Was he the one pulled off of every other assignment he was working on to go get some priest accused of espionage out of a Chinese prison?"

"Some priest?" Alexander began with a bit of an indignant air.

"Look Ace, parsing my words ought to be the last thing you're worried about right now."

Right then he knew it was going to be a long day and night. When she started calling him "Ace" she was at the top of her tolerance scale. As cathartic as most people found it to be, Laura simply did not use profanity. At just over six feet tall with the build of a competitive athlete and the classic beauty reminiscent of Grace Kelly, she rarely needed words to intimidate. The first time he'd ever seen her he thought

7

he really may have died and was seeing an angel. For all intents and purposes she might as well have been an angel on that day nearly five years prior.

At the time, Alexander was indeed an Episcopal priest and he had in fact been charged with espionage, but the reason he was on the verge of spending the rest of his life locked away in one of China's most brutal prisons had nothing at all to do with being a spy. That was only the official and documented reason. In fact the Chinese government was not truly behind his incarceration at all. They were simply the ones being handsomely rewarded to facilitate it. Alexander and the 11 others like him were the most unique individuals on earth. None of them were especially wealthy, they had no specialized training, nor were they connected by nationality, religion or any other particular allegiance. In fact, most of them disliked each other intensely. The one thing that bound them together was knowledge.

Alexander planted himself on the woodland camo canvas seat of the dove stool leaving the better of the two seating options for Laura. At six and a half feet tall and weighing in at 240 pounds, it was somewhat comical to see such a large frame perched on the small folding stool. It was a subtle attempt to elicit Laura's maternal instincts and get her to soften a bit. By this point however, her professional training and mental acumen was in overdrive, she stood her ground solidly and ignored the open chair. Her weight was on her left leg and her arms were hanging by her sides cocked slightly forward. He would've much preferred arms folded and weight shifted to the right leg. That at least would've given him some wiggle room for what he was about to have to tell her. Her current disposition clearly indicated that every single syllable and nuance was about to be thoroughly analyzed by that genius level brain of hers. He knew before he began that he was about to place her in more danger than she'd ever been before in her life.

3

"**L**aura, there's so much that you don't know."

"Yes, I see that... And wait a minute, what is this room? How is it that I'm just learning of this room after three, no...four years?"

"At this very moment, there are people trying their very best to learn what I'm about to tell you. When I say 'trying their very best' I mean they have likely allocated several million dollars, focused at least three satellites and have no less than two dozen people working on this one discussion we're about to have. When I constructed this room, it was with this in mind, that one day such a conversation would have to take place."

Alexander stood as the immense gravity of what he was about to have to do flooded his mind. The memory of a similar conversation between Walter Trowbridge and him so many years ago beneath All Saints' chapel at The University of the South now felt as fresh as the day the unbelievable words were spoken. His countenance was morphing into compassion and a bit of dread because he knew once they emerged from the depths of the earth, her life would no longer be her own.

"This room was designed to prevent anyone or any technology they may employ from hearing, seeing or sensing what is spoken here."

The look of skepticism was growing on Laura's face. "Alexander, in case you've forgotten, I happen to have worked for an agency that has proven itself to be quite proficient at hearing what they want to hear and when they want to hear it with far less allocated assets. Forgive me if I seem unconvinced." Though her blood pressure had returned to normal, her anger was still at an unquantifiable level. The thought of her sweet-natured parish priest turned author that she'd rescued from the torturous underbelly of a Chinese prison speaking of the elements of her world was somewhat humorous and more than a little annoying.

Without a word Alexander reached down to the dove stool he'd just vacated and unzipped the pouch underneath. He handed Laura what appeared to be a four inch square piece of material. In the palm of her hand it felt lighter than a piece of tissue paper and looked like a series of tiny metallic dust mites holding hands. "What is this supposed to be?" Laura inquired.

Producing a keychain laser pointer from his pocket, Alexander focused the beam on the material causing it to suddenly contract and Laura to gasp. Instead of reflecting off the surface or dispersing as a laser will often do against a similar surface, it seemed to be consumed as if the beam had been aimed into the night sky. Which was fascinating enough to Laura, but even more so was the unanticipated and unbelievable result that followed. As soon as the bright red dot had melted into the material, thousands of undiluted laser dots had simultaneously decorated the dimly lit walls as well as Laura and Alexander. Though everything within her informed her that what she was seeing was impossible, there it was. The little piece of material was reproducing the laser light from every open edge of its perimeter.

"It's an engineered micro-fabric, a technology that won't be made available to your former employers for another 50 to 100 years." Alexander had to resist the urge to smirk though he didn't know why he bothered. He knew his chances of having sex that night had completely disappeared when only moments before, the Reverend Dr. Trowbridge came walking down the hill behind their house and back into his life.

Laura was not quite as amused as Alexander but not because of his smug demonstration. It was the implications of what she had just seen that steeled her nerves.

Before taking an early retirement from the spy game, Laura had earned legendary status for cleaning up messes that normally had their genesis with Presidents of the United States. Her razor sharp wit, unnerving mental acuity, Hollywood beauty and athletic prowess quickly made her a superstar amongst the highest level operators around the world. Her reality made fictional spies and covert operators seem like shoe salesmen with vivid imaginations.

The final verses of this chapter of her life began closing from the moment she saw a swollen and bruised Alexander Kilpatrick being escorted out of Tilanqiao prison and into her custody. Of all the reactions to being released from Hell she'd ever seen or heard, his was the most unusual and strangely endearing. With eyes still adjusting to the bright sunlight and in a weak, raspy voice he spoke his first words to her in front of both the Chinese and American officials: "Were all the ugly spies on vacation?"

"Rev. Kilpatrick, my name is Laura Wells. I'm the temporary diplomatic aide to the American ambassador here in Shanghai. Welcome home." Her words were intentionally direct and brief. The previous 90 days had been a furious maelstrom of negotiations, threats and bribes to get her to that point. Weirdo fundamentalists and Bible thumpers were always getting themselves into hot water with various "non-Christian" countries and being charged with anything from sedition to espionage. She was initially a bit surprised and frustrated with this assignment but she had grown accustomed to the *sine qua non* of that particular administration to swat flies with a sledgehammer. Now, standing several meters underneath their mountain cabin in a safe room made of seemingly impossible materials, it was becoming clear that his had not been a simple case of a bumbling preacher who'd taken his rhetoric too far with an unsympathetic government.

Alexander discontinued the beam but the light show continued for several seconds following. He reached over and removed the fabric from Laura's hand and zipped it back into the pouch underneath the dove stool. As he did so, she finally took a seat in the vintage desk chair. With her anger now completely dissipated, she watched silently as he took a seat next to her. "Laura, before I begin, you need to know my deepest desire was to walk completely away from the life I'm about to describe. I was an arrogant fool to think that I could."

She reached over and took his hand. If anyone understood how a previous life could suck you right back in to where you didn't want to be like an angry rip current, it was she. The trajectory of her life had been such that she'd never had much of an opportunity to fall in love until Alexander. Over the last five years that love had only grown and strengthened. "Whatever life that was or is, it is now a part of me, a part of us, and that's how we'll proceed."

"The man that visited us today," Alexander paused for a moment, still trying to find the most appropriate place to begin. "He's a retired seminary professor... kind of."

This was another first for Laura, seeing him at a loss for words. "This is going to be like trying to describe the color red to a person born blind." He continued. "William Trowbridge is a retired seminary professor but he's also one of a small group of people that walk around with the world's oldest secrets." Laura's expression, normally stoic in such situations, was now nonplussed as her head tilted forward and her eyes rolled upward toward him.

"The world's oldest secrets?" she said with obvious disbelief.

"How well do you know the Bible?"

"I know where they keep them in hotel rooms."

It was now his turn for a look of impatient exasperation.

"Sorry...couldn't help myself. As you know, I didn't grow up in a very religious household. My father was a disillusioned Baptist and my mother was a disinterested Catholic. We spent most of our Sundays on the lake. As for the Bible, I briefly studied it as literature in college."

Alexander pressed forward "There are four enigmatic verses in Genesis that most people tend to gloss over and generally speaking with good reason. It doesn't seem to fit with the rest of the story and as far as most people are concerned it has no bearing on one's life, religious or otherwise. It's the first four verses of chapter six, "When people began to multiply on the face of the ground, and daughters were born to them, the sons of God saw that they were fair; and they took wives for themselves of all that they chose. Then the Lord said, 'My spirit shall not abide in mortals forever, for they are flesh; their days shall be one hundred twenty years.' The Nephilim were on the earth in those days—and also afterward—when the sons of God went in to the daughters of humans, who bore children to them. These were the heroes that were of old, warriors of renown.'"

Laura was listening but having a difficult time seeing what this had to do with their strange morning of mysterious guests, unbelievable technology and secrets her husband had been keeping from her over the last five years.

"Immediately following those verses, the flood narrative begins. God becomes angry with the sinfulness of humanity, regrets creating them and decides to destroy them. So you can see how the preceding verses might be lost on most readers of the Bible." Based on her current facial expression, Alexander could see that this was going to take longer than he'd anticipated.

"OK, look...I know how this sounds." Alexander went straight to the point, "The Nephilim, the offspring of the sons of God and humans are real." There was an exaggerated pause between them as Alexander waited for Laura to respond and as Laura waited for the punch line. Though concern for his sanity began to flicker to life within her, she decided to stick to an age old interrogation technique, just keep quiet and let them talk. Alexander knew what she was doing and continued.

"'Bene Elohim' or 'sons of godly powers' is actually a more accurate translation and honestly a little more acceptable to our modern sensibilities. The Biblical narrative is full of allegory and myth, but that doesn't make those stories necessarily untrue. It simply means that some truths are too profound for literal interpretation and

13

some truths are described in terms that to the authors of ancient texts seemed most reasonable. Look at it this way, if you were a five-foot-two Jew in eleventh century BCE Palestine and you came across an eleven foot tall Philistine named Goliath, wouldn't you assume, given your complete lack of knowledge regarding genetics that this individual must be some kind of super-human or said another way, a god?"

He allowed his question to hang in the dank air of the subterranean safe room for a few moments. The silence gave her time to understand there would be no punch line, that in fact he was completely serious.

"Imagine inviting a professional basketball player and a jockey over for dinner and then trying to explain that both are fully grown adults to a six year old in terms they could comprehend. In the jockey, they'll see someone not much larger than they are, but in the basketball player, no matter how hard you try, they're going to see a giant."

"So the giants in the Bible are just big people that scared all the small people?"

"Well, that depends on your definition of 'people.'" This was not the response she'd anticipated. "We know that several hominid species lived in parallel over various periods of time. Currently, except for the occasional Big Foot sighting we assume homo sapiens is all alone in this category. Is it that difficult to imagine the intertwining of the hominid gene pool at some point in history?

Laura pondered his question. "The Nephi-whatever are real? Giants are real? They're just genetic anomalies?"

"Not anomalies Laura, far from it, but that's not the most important information right now. What I need you to accept even if you can't wrap your mind around it quite yet is that there is an ancient race of people called the Nephilim. They've been amongst us for a very long time and their history is intertwined with ours in ways that would take years for me to fully explain. It's going to take long enough to explain how their history and existence is intertwined with mine."

Her senses were beginning to adjust to the outlandish information Alexander was sharing. "OK, so why don't you start at Tilanqiao and go from there." Her senses were adjusting, but she would withhold judgment for now as to whether Alexander had lost his mind or not.

"Well, like I said this room is designed to keep secrets." He scanned the room as he said this almost as if he expected there to be a stenographer hiding somewhere taking down his every word. "Old secrets...secrets that have kept humanity in a delicate balance between life and oblivion for millennia. I was arrested under false pretenses and imprisoned in China to keep me out of the hands of a group of people willing to go to just about any length to obtain those secrets, people who would think nothing of igniting World War III just to get what they want." Alexander looked once more into the innocent eyes of the one person he cherished above all others. After this moment, she would become a part of something that would swallow her life as it had his. "Laura, the Nephilim, Jews, Muslims, Christians and all manner of people connected to these groups all want one thing, the pursuit of which has engulfed nations and the world in warfare over and over again. They want the Stone of David, the one he used to slay Goliath."

4

T heir conversation had lasted into early evening without as much as a single
break for sustenance. "There's of course so much more to this," Alexander
went on, "but for now that will have to do."

Laura was as exhausted as he was; the ground of everything she believed and
thought she knew had been removed from under her feet. "Before we go upstairs,
you need to understand that you can never speak openly about what I've just told
you, in fact keep even the thought of it pushed from your mind. Now that that
jackass Trowbridge has led them here, they'll be watching your every move and
listening to your every word."

Her mix of emotions and the rapid fire processing going on within her was too
intense to allow a response. She nodded slightly then turned to ascend the stairs
into a world that now seemed alien to her. Alexander followed close behind and
embraced her as they entered their bedroom from beneath the old bureau. "I love
you, Laura." It was all he could say at this point and it was honestly all she could
hear. Without another word they laid down on their bed exhausted, though it
would not be a restful night for either of them. Alexander would lie awake con-
structing his plan for moving forward and Laura would lie awake putting the pieces
of a three-dimensional, six sided jigsaw puzzle together trying to reconcile the history she thought she knew and the new reality before her.

Sometime just before dawn and as he'd told her he would, Alexander rose and got
ready to go into town. He knew for a fact that Walter didn't actually have the

stone, but he would have to find out exactly what the old man had risked his life to share with him. After a quick shower and shave, he threw on a pair of jeans, a crisp and heavily starched white button-down and his well-worn hiking boots. Within 30 minutes of getting out of bed, Alexander had his old Jeep Grand Wagoneer directed towards town and within an hour he was walking up the wooden steps and into the only accommodations in their small mountain village, a Victorian era home thought to have been constructed by George Vanderbilt as a temporary residence while he built his famed Biltmore Mansion. The current proprietors loved advertising that while he never actually lived there, it was rumored that his lover had, which is why there was no clear connection to the 19th century billionaire.

He could smell the brewing coffee as he entered the large foyer but was pleased no one was around to greet him on this somewhat surreptitious visit. Taking two steps at a time, he bounded toward the upstairs guest rooms. Walter hadn't told him which room, but the two out of state vehicles in the parking lot and the rental that Walter had driven to their cabin told Alexander there were only three guests currently lodged at The Willow. The newspapers outside the doors of the two downstairs guest rooms indicated that the out of state guests were occupying those rooms. Walter would've already been up and have read his paper by now. In fact, it was almost certain he would be on his laptop conducting his daily correspondence when Alexander knocked. However, as he reached the door Alexander realized immediately something was amiss as it stood slightly ajar.

He edged the door open with a sense of dread filling his chest, a feeling that was validated as his mind began processing all that his eyes were taking in. The chair at the desk adjacent to the fireplace was pulled out and slightly askew. A laptop sat open with the screen still displaying the Associated Press website and the heavy, ornate bed curtains had been closed only on the side facing the door. Though he knew very well what he would find on the other side of the curtain, he eased his way around the side of the bed anyway. Death, he had learned long ago, leaves an unmistakable aura in a room. It was a feeling neither good nor bad, just distinct. The confirmation of his perception was the lifeless body of Walter Trowbridge lying in repose, fully dressed for the day ahead. On the bed next to Walter's hand was an item that chilled Alexander to his core. The antique syringe case lay open; its black velvet compartment was missing the nickel and glass implement it had most certainly contained only moments before. It wasn't the stone Walter had brought with him, it was data; encoded amino acid sequences carried as inert proteins within his bloodstream to be specific.

With great dispatch and very little concern for decorum, Alexander lifted Walter's torso and stripped his suit coat off in one motion. Before the coat could even hit the floor, he ripped at the French cuff of the corpse's right sleeve so violently that the gold link went sailing through the air and hit the wall behind him. At the crook of his arm in the triangular area known as the cubital fossa was the telltale little pucker he was looking for. No sign of blood told Alexander the fluid had been drawn postmortem, a situation he was very much hoping to avoid for himself.

His instincts spurred him into immediate action. There was nothing he could do for Walter now and the amount of noise he made from this point forward would be of no consequence. Alexander tore across the room, slammed the laptop closed and held it tightly against his body like a football with his left arm while throwing the bedroom door open with his right. At the top of the stairs, he took hold of the rail and leapt halfway down, his hand keeping him steadied in mid-air. With a resounding thud, he landed and propelled himself over the last few steps, across the foyer and out the front door. Completely ignoring his Jeep in the parking lot off to the side of the house, he ran as fast as he could across the front lawn and around a large stone fountain. It was about there that he felt the concussive blast of the explosion that knocked him off of his feet. The laptop went flying as he tucked inward in preparation to absorb the shock of the fall.

Consciously he knew none of his bones were broken and he was fairly certain he'd sustained no serious external wounds, a minor miracle given the amount of shrapnel that had flown in every direction. At the moment, he was simply attempting to regain the breath that had been knocked out of him upon his landing. Alexander often marveled at his own ability to remain calm in some of the direst circumstances. It wasn't a practiced or cultivated talent; it just seemed to come naturally to him as if within the force of the storm was where he preferred to be. Willing his diaphragm to be equally as calm to resume drawing air into his lungs was another story. His lungs were now searing from the momentary lack of oxygen and he struggled to get to his feet. However, the burden of standing suddenly eased abnormally as he felt himself being lifted off of the ground.

The ringing in his ears and disoriented senses had prevented him from observing the approach of the two men who were now on either side of him, their arms hooked under his as they dragged him along. The possibilities of what was happening to him were too myriad to fully consider and he doubted very much that the unwelcome assistants would give him an answer even if he inquired. The men carried him with purpose and ease, not an easy task given his size. Alexander knew it wouldn't be long before he was spirited away in a vehicle without a trace of his having been abducted. With just the slightest and unobserved motion, he drew his hands closer together at his abdomen and quickly slid his wedding band off allowing it to drop to the ground in a place where his feet would instantly drag across it. Within seconds he was hoisted to his full height then pushed forward into a waiting van that sprayed gravel from its rear tires before the door could be completely closed.

"You realize you've just started World War III don't you?" The air had returned to his lungs sufficiently to give voice to this mocking yet quite sincere question.

The two men who had escorted him to the van sat on either side of him giving him very little room to maneuver, which was not really an issue. Ordinarily he might have taken out three or four of them before they subdued him, however under the circumstances that might not be the wisest choice. They had already killed Walter and almost certainly set a chain of events in motion that would lead to military strikes in the Middle-East. He surmised it would likely be stray rockets fired from Syria into Israel this time, since Gaza had taken their turn last time. Allowing this to play out was his best tactic for the moment. They needed him alive or he would already be dead, this much he knew and it wasn't his status as an untouchable keeping him amongst the living. Walter's death was an order of magnitude that his group of captors probably couldn't comprehend. On the other hand, there was almost certainly a group of people, namely those running this little operation, just learning of the situation and were breaking into a cold sweat as he was being carried to an as of yet unknown location.

"Trowbridge's death was an accident." A voice spoke from the darkened corner in the very back of the black Mercedes cargo van now serving as his temporary prison.

Alexander's eyes had not yet adjusted to the interior of the vehicle so he directed his response in the general direction of the speaker, "And you obviously believe that will suffice as a reason for your neighbors not to strike back with extreme prejudice?" Though he had a pretty good idea, he wasn't precisely sure which group had perpetrated this act. All of them were capable but only one group currently had enough reason for concern to make such a bold move. The Persians (as he still liked to call them) were getting restless and the Israelites were tense to say the least. Their trigger finger had gotten really itchy right after the changing of the guard in the U.S. As soon as it became clear the traditional ground of support from their Western allies was beginning to crumble they'd elevated their defensive footing. "Like I said, you've started World War III whether you realize it now or not. The last time this happened it was an Archduke in Sarajevo and in case you've forgotten, that didn't go so well."

The gravity of the situation was obviously settling in with the faceless voice at the rear of the van. For a moment there was a shift in the feel of the occupied space. It was a discernible shift from that of the expedience, adrenaline and excitement necessary to complete an operation spiraling out of control to that of the realization the spiral was becoming a hurricane.

"The neural scan was not working; his ability to control his thoughts was nearly unbelievable. We gradually increased the intensity..." The man's sentence was interrupted by Alexander.

"...which then induced a stroke." His remark contained no small amount of disdain for their incompetence. There were moments over the last five years that he'd

21

considered ending the old man's life himself, but that was personal. This was a matter of pure stupidity, just like every other event that had ever led to war, pure stupidity.

"Yes...I'm afraid so." As difficult as it was to imagine there might've been something of sadness in the man's voice. Perhaps he realized the immensity of the morning's events after all.

"The empty syringe case..."

"We got what we needed."

"I sincerely doubt that. If you'd gotten all you needed, I wouldn't be here now."

The man in the dark was quiet. During the last few seconds of the conversation, Alexander had failed to notice the more modern syringe that the guardian on his left was now palming in his left hand.

Alexander considered the situation for a bit more then laid bare the painful truth for his captors. "You have what you need, but you have no idea what to do with it. Do you?"

"Goodnight, Mathias."

The needle sank into his neck as did the sudden realization of what the man had just called him. "Oh fuck..." It wasn't really clear to him whether he'd spoken the words or simply thought them before fading out under the influence delivered by the mega dose of sodium pentathol. Either way, it was an entirely appropriate response.

5

Laura heard the blast waves of the enormous explosion reverberating throughout the surrounding mountains. All of her training and intuition told her that this was no coincidence. Fortunately, Alexander had taken his Wagoneer, a relic from his college days held together with duct tape, Bondo and a kind of love that she really didn't care to understand. That left her with the BMW M3, an indulgence for herself when she left the Agency and one that would propel her reliably and with lightning speed to the site of the disaster. She hoped beyond hope that she was wrong. However, as she worked through the 6-speed transmission powering out of every curve, and putting every bit of the growling 414 horsepower to use, the feeling in her chest told her she was not, that and the fact that her persistent calls to his cell phone were going unanswered. This never happened. No matter where he was or what he was doing Alexander always answered her calls.

By the time Laura arrived, the volunteer firefighters from the Laurel Ridge community were working furiously to keep the area clear and the flames suppressed. The Black Mountain firefighters were in route and she knew she would have to conduct a rapid investigation of her own before they arrived. The locals knew her and would give her some latitude but without the credentials of her former life, the B.M.F.D. would undoubtedly keep her at bay.

"First gas explosion in over 30 years." Caroline Lanter, Laurel Ridge VFD's fire-chief and proprietress of the only local grocery managed to inform Laura in the midst of shouting orders to her crew.

"You're sure that's what it was?"

"Has to be..." she cut her own explanation short as she shouted into her radio. "Don, tell Corbin and Jack to get some damn water on those cars before they're our next problem." She looked back toward Laura, "Christ almighty, if I wasn't their mother I'd shoot both of them. This is a bleeding mess, a damn tragic, bleeding mess."

"Survivors?"

"Hell hon, we don't even know yet how many were in the house, it'll be..." she stopped short, looked back toward the parking lot and then again at Laura. Her command voice shifted to one of sudden realization and concern. "That's Alex's Jeep, isn't it?" Laura simply nodded in response.

"Don...what's the word on those boys from Black Mountain?"

"Just turning off 40."

After hearing his response and realizing that her time was limited Laura began making her way toward the house across the front lawn. Caroline was about to warn her back when the north side of the house next to the parking lot collapsed sending her boys scrambling backward. She lifted the radio to give further direction, but before she could, the guys working on the front of the house immediately redirected their lines toward the newly collapsed section of the building and her two sons rushed back toward the burning ruins. Amidst the cacophony of the roaring blaze, the cracking timber and beams of the old house, the diesel pump of the fire engine, and the running engines of the various sheriffs cars and rescue squad trucks, Laura couldn't hear Caroline's shouts, not that she would've heeded her protestations anyway.

The heat from the conflagration intensified with each step toward it. Laura stopped just short of the street side of the fountain. The debris field, an odd mixture of scorched, charred and splintered detritus, was scattered up to about 20 feet from the other side of the fountain. Most of it was smoldering and unidentifiable. It was taking every bit of her fortitude to ward off the sense of fear and dread that was attempting to buckle her knees and hurl her to the ground. One's imagination can run wild at times, ideations of recovered remains, the funeral, what life will be like after, but such thoughts would have to wait. "Not today, and not like this Miles Alexander." She thought to herself.

This was as close as she could get to the debris field without protective gear and that would just have to do for now. She began mentally cataloging each bit of debris, creating an imaginary search grid in her field of vision. It wasn't much, but it was a start. Grids containing easily identifiable items would be 'blanked out' in her mind. Grids that contained items worth a closer look would be given a number in ascending order from North to South and West to East. With her visual search plan established, Laura took a step back to stand perfectly clear of the large ground level basin of the fountain. As she did, her right heel caught the edge of something hard. It was a black laptop computer, un-singed and seemingly undamaged on the other side of the fountain. As she squatted down to make an observation regarding its possible trajectory of having landed here, a hand reached down and touched her shoulder. The din of noise and her intense scrutiny had prevented her from noticing his approach. Instinctively she whirled her body around remaining low to the ground and had the Black Mountain fire chief by the ankles before he knew what was happening. They were mutually surprised but for very different reasons. Laura released her grip and rose to her feet.

"Mrs. Wells, you're going to have to clear this area, I'm sorry." Caroline had obviously told him who she was and she knew arguing wouldn't change the results. She simply nodded and turned slightly back toward the computer. "And you'll need to leave that laptop there." Laura could've easily convinced the man that the laptop was hers, but he was not her adversary and though deception had often been part of her job, lying to the good guys was not her style.

"I understand." was all she said, which was fine because that was about all she could manage without the flood of emotion overwhelming her.

The fire chief waited just long enough to realize he wasn't going to have to escort her to a safer distance. Laura turned back toward the fire engines on her own volition even though her greatest desire was to rush headlong into the fray and pull him to safety. A fantasy at best. "Anyone in that building at the time of the explosion…" she put the brakes on that line of thinking and started toward the perimeter, her thoughts shifting back to the computer. The laptop had not landed there as a result of the explosion. It was on the ground on the west side of the fountain. The debris field ended at least six meters short of the fountain on the east side. The force and trajectory required to propel the device that far would have broken it apart on impact. Someone had placed it or dropped it there. Either way, it had something to do with this whole affair, and she wanted that laptop. Getting her hands on it would take some doing.

Laura was not prone to tears. It was not a matter of pride or conditioning, they had simply never been close to the surface for her. The events of the past 24 hours and certainly of this morning had her right on the verge. She'd spent so many years wondering if she would ever fall in love. There had been many suitors but between her training, athletic career, school and life in the services the aperture for anything long-term or serious had been quite narrow. Finding Alexander, strange as the circumstances were at the time, was exactly what she'd thought falling in love would be. He understood her and that was no small feat. He was even capable of picking up on her mood or understanding the underlying motivations for her communication via text messages without trying, it was uncanny. She definitely would not claim to believe in soul-mates, the mere term made her retch, but if there was something that caused others to believe in them, it must feel like this. Whether it was genetics, pheromones, oxytocin, or some other sub-atomic science she wasn't sure, but the one thing of which she was certain, he complemented her as no one ever had. On the other hand, Alexander would say, "Your brand of madness simply doesn't conflict with mine." For someone who could be so romantic, he could also be an absolute imp.

These feelings, and that's more of what they were rather than thoughts, swirled within her intermingling with her investigative sensibilities, distracting her and pulling her toward a part of the inner self rarely encountered. Compartmentalization was never really an issue before love. Now head and heart were in absolute combat. She needed to keep a clear mind and combine all she'd learned over the past day to identify and find those responsible. Her heart however, just wanted to cry out in agony.

Nearing the roadway where the emergency vehicles were arranged, her chest expanded with a sudden gasp and the tears burst forth in abundance. She dropped into a low squat and her crying intensified. Her hands rested momentarily on the ground as if to steady herself. Caroline Lanter, having relinquished command to the Black Mountain boys, came to Laura's side and placed her arm around her sobbing neighbor as she knelt. In three decades of working with the volunteer fire department, Caroline had seen enough lost homes, dreams, pets, and loved ones to know that the best thing, the only thing she could do at the moment was be present with Laura in her grief.

After several seconds, they rose to their feet. Caroline kept her arm around Laura as they stood, still not a word was spoken between them. Laura kept her head down, her shoulder length hair forming a veil on either side of her face hiding the smile through which she was crying nearly inaudible sobs of joy. She pressed Alexander's ring deeply into her palm as if she were trying to make it a part of her very being.

Looking back across the lawn she could now see what she'd missed before. Mixed between the shifting hoses and the ground that had been turned and trodden by the heavy boots of the firefighters was a distinct indication that someone had been dragged from the fountain to the roadway. At the very end of that line was the shining beacon that let her know he had survived the blast and had made it out, albeit not by the means of his own choosing.

"Why don't you come on down to the store? You'll be close enough by to get word quickly and I can..." Before Caroline could finish, Laura pulled away slightly.

"Oh, Caroline you're so kind...but...I can't... I just..." The words were not forming for her. Her brain was too busy formulating the strategy and tactics necessary to find her husband. "I'll be fine; I just need some time to process." Not waiting for another word from the woman who rarely took 'no' for an answer, Laura made a beeline for her car and was blistering the asphalt road back toward their cabin within seconds.

6

A lexander reached for the nightstand and his bottled water and in the process nearly tumbled out of his bed, or at least he had experienced the sensation of falling out of bed. In reality, he hadn't even budged. His mouth was dry, his brain was in a fog and his muscles were unresponsive. The light given off by the illuminated trim around him was gradually increasing giving him a better perception of his whereabouts as he emerged from the induced catatonic state. The straight and modern lines of the furnishings were softened by the use of exotic woods in a striking combination of dark and light hues. A small buffet sat across from the bed. On it was an assortment of fresh and dried fruits, dark chocolates, bottled water, a carafe of coffee and a crystal pitcher of juice. Judging by the extravagantly appointed surroundings and the perfectly pitched singing of the jet engines this was certainly not a military transport nor was it one of the lumbering commercial crafts constructed solely for the maximization of revenue. Whomever it was that had decided to liberate him from his peaceful existence in the mountains of North Carolina, they were definitely well funded. There were only two groups that would both want him in their possession and simultaneously have the kind of financial wherewithal to imprison him in such grandeur. As each of his senses flickered to life, he noted that Itzhak Perlman's interpretation of Vivaldi's "Winter" was playing softly through the overhead speakers. "Well that cinches it." he said just under his breath, "the Israelites."

The brightness of the lighting continued to increase and the volume of the music ticked up gradually. His hosts may have acted treacherously in putting him to sleep, but they obviously intended to rouse him gracefully from his slumber. Alexander slowly shifted his weight and rotated his body in order to get his feet on the floor. In doing so, he now realized he was only in his boxers and undershirt. On the actual nightstand, rather than the imagined one of his groggy state, was a silver valet with his wallet, keys, pocket knife, and strangely enough his Smith & Wesson M&P 340. "That was ballsy of them." he thought as he retrieved it. "Or not." as he opened and closed the cylinder now missing its five rounds of 125 grain hollow points. The only things that seemed to be missing at this point were the remainder of his clothing and his iPhone.

The padded wool carpet felt luxurious beneath his bare feet as he made his way over to the buffet and cracked the seal on a bottled water. After quenching his immense thirst, Alexander realized he was hungry and began picking through the victuals so elegantly displayed for him. Within the first few sips of the piping hot coffee, the words that had jolted him just prior to succumbing to the drugs came rushing back to him, 'Goodnight Matthias.' The effect of their return to his conscious mind was nearly as shocking the second time around. It had always been a Chess game with these people and the knowledge of his code name was a startling move on their part. The actual names of the 12 was not a tremendous secret, however their code names linked them to specific pieces of information. Each was a keeper of particular knowledge and the code name was more of a title or indicator of which piece of the puzzle they possessed. The fact that they had his code name told him they'd gained way more knowledge than they ought to have.

"Good afternoon, Alexander." The voice was that of the faceless man from the van and remained faceless as it was now emanating from the intercom.

Without missing a beat Alexander replied, "*Erev Tov.*"

There was an unnatural pause, then "You speak Hebrew."

"Let's not waste time with inane chatter. I know who you are, you obviously know who I am...what do you want?" Alexander's mood was far from amicable. They knew very well that he spoke Hebrew as well as German, Spanish, French and now prison yard Chinese.

"The same thing we've wanted for over 2000 years."

"Oh, well...why didn't you just say so? I could've saved you the time and trouble of these extravagant travel arrangements. Why don't you just come on in, pull up a chair and I'll lay it all out for you?"

"Now who's being inane, Alexander? Besides, we both know it doesn't quite work like that. However, I very much would like to have a conversation. We have a favor to ask."

"A favor?" Alexander's tone remained slightly terse.

"Yes, but for now that can wait. I'm afraid I must deal with another pressing matter. In the meantime, please make yourself comfortable. You'll find suitable attire in the closet next to the lavatory and a warm meal is being prepared for you. If you need anything, please don't hesitate to inquire."

"I don't suppose you'd know the whereabouts of my phone?"

"Actually I do, but as you might suspect I can't return that to you just yet."

"No, I suspect not."

The music gradually faded back in, making it clear the conversation was over for now. Alexander suspected the pressing matter had to do with Walter Trowbridge's death and the resonant effect it was most assuredly having behind closed doors amongst some of the most powerful people around the world. If that was indeed the case, then Alexander had incredible leverage in this situation and was a pretty good indication of why, though a captive, he was being treated so well. As talented as they were, this group of operatives had ultimately failed to get the information they needed and had killed an untouchable in the process. They needed him, but why and what leverage could they possibly use to motivate him to perform this favor? It might have been Laura, but based on how they were behaving that seemed unlikely. No, the favor had to be something that would be of interest or benefit to the 12 and something that only they could affect. Alexander hit a button next to a bank of windows and the shades automatically lowered revealing a plain of clouds painted a golden orange from the fading sun as their progress took them further eastward. Staring out into this ethereal vision, comprehension slowly unfolded before him and a smile spread across his face.

A soft chime sounded at the door followed by a most pleasant female voice over the intercom. Her words were completely void of any accent, "Mr. Kilpatrick, I have your meal if you are ready to dine." Taking the smooth Egyptian cotton robe from the lavatory he approached the door. To his great surprise it was not locked. On the other side of the cabin doorway stood a young woman in her mid to late twenties impeccably dressed in a charcoal pinstripe dress suit. Her features indicated that she was almost certainly Jewish and of Greek descent. She was likely Romaniotes, a relatively scarce population of the Diaspora living in Greece for just over 2000 years and very nearly wiped out during the Holocaust. It was widely believed that after the dismantling of an enormous energy deal by a Nephilim interest in Greece, one of the world's most famous billionaires and shipping magnates on the losing end of that deal formed a secret alliance with the Romaniotes. Alexander's current surroundings definitely lent credibility to this theory.

The young woman was bearing a rolling cart that held a shining stainless steel food service arrangement complete with a vase of tea roses. Alexander stood aside as she wheeled the cart past him stopping just short of the buffet. Working in complete silence, the young woman locked the cart into place then opened the middle drawer of the buffet and drew a hidden table top from within. After securing the table with its supports, she procured a chair from the nearby desk that was obviously intended to serve both as a desk and dining chair as it met and mated perfectly with the table. Continuing in silence and efficiency the woman set the table and then removed the domed cover from his plate as her final act. "Bon appétit Mr. Kilpatrick, do let me know if you need anything further."

"Oh, I'm certain this will be fine." Alexander watched as she left and pulled the door closed behind her. The door may have been unlocked but they obviously intended for him to remain isolated in his cabin. Before him was a meal of broiled whitefish, mixed vegetables, roasted figs, goat cheese, hummus, olives and flat bread. A small carafe held what appeared to be Chardonnay though he was in no mood for alcohol. Instead, he reached for his unfinished bottle of water then sat to dine. Breaking his fast earlier with the fruits and chocolates had diminished his ravenous appetite. This, coupled with his heightened sense of nerves and awareness, caused him to merely pick at his meal.

Leaving the table, he decided to get dressed. Sure enough, in the closet was a wardrobe sufficient for what appeared to be several days. Everything was new including an exquisitely tailored suit that caused Alexander's eyebrows to rise a bit. It was unmistakably a Nino Corvato that, even though he'd never visited the bespoke shop, seemed to be tailored especially for him. A five-thousand dollar suit was not his typical attire and it was a clear indication that a high-level meeting was in his future. For the moment he would opt for the linen lounge pants and silk shirt hanging next to the suit.

After about an hour the door chime sounded again followed the now familiar voice of the faceless man, "Alexander, I would like to have a moment of your time if I may?"

"By all means." He wondered to himself how they would react if he simply cold cocked this son-of-a-bitch as he came through the door. Granted, it wouldn't accomplish much but it sure would feel good.

The door opened and once again the girl with the cart was standing there. She came in and just as silently but with greater expedience set about clearing the table and buffet. After completing her task she went to the door, opened it and stood by as a

33

distinguished looking man entered. He was less than six feet tall and trim. Though he was evidently over 50, his perfectly coiffed hair had obviously gone silver many years prior. His dark olive skin, jet black eyebrows and rimless eyeglasses in contrast gave him an unusual and unforgettable appearance. This man was definitely not a field operative as his striking features made him far too memorable.

"Alexander, I am Ephrem Goldman. We have much to discuss." His manner was elegant and precise.

"How long till we land in Rome?" Alexander's comment momentarily unbalanced the man.

Recovering, his perfectly white teeth flashed into a genuine smile, "Your reputation for extraordinary powers of perception and reasoning has preceded you. This conversation may be of greater brevity than I imagined."

The young woman pushed the cart through the door, parked it and came back through with a chair matching the one at the retractable buffet table. Once the chair was in place at the opposite side of the table, Ephrem turned toward the departing woman, "Thank you Ana."

"You provide exquisite service on this flight." Alexander watched as Ana cleared the doorway.

"Ana? She's one of our finest operatives." They both took a seat at the table. "We weren't entirely certain of your disposition and thought you might respond more favorably to her than to Mitri or Asa. Of course, I pity anyone who would tangle with her including Mitri or Asa."

"I take it Mitri and Asa are the ham fisted buffoons who helped me into your van." Alexander's tone was derisive. Actually he wouldn't have classified them as being 'ham fisted' but there was always a certain joy of rubbing salt in the wounds of an adversary.

With a look of reflective disappointment in his crew, Ephrem responded carefully, "Yes, I'm afraid so. We did not anticipate such an occurrence and were unprepared for your involvement. Whether you believe it or not, I am appalled by the events of earlier today, and there is no need to remind me of the implications."

"You were unprepared for my involvement, but once you realized you were woefully lacking the technology to decipher the information carried by Trowbridge you had to make a last second decision to abduct the only other person who could either do it for you or personally deliver the message to our friend."

Ephrem held his hands outward and aloft just above the table in a gesture of somewhat false admiration, "Again, your powers of perception and reason... remarkable." He reached for a water, opened it and filled a glass before continuing. "Simon, or 'our friend' as you call him, is out of control and putting the entire world at risk. We have every reason to believe Trowbridge knew this and was coming to you with proof. We just wanted that proof and the opportunity to get to Simon first."

"Because you wanted him to know precisely who it would be taking him down?"

"That, and so he would understand just how precarious his situation truly is."

Alexander rose out of his chair and walked to the bank of windows. Evening was burgeoning on the horizon as they continued their eastward journey. "And just how precarious is that?"

Ephrem now rose from his seat and joined Alexander at the windows. The two men stood silently for a while. The only sound in the cabin was the roar emanating from the Rolls Royce jet engines propelling them through the air at a swift 480 knots.

"Walter Trowbridge's death is regrettable. It was an accident." Ephrem repeated this for effect. "The Pope's will not be."

7

Laura whipped her car into the pea-gravel drive of their cabin. She bolted from the car with the acrid metallic odor from its brakes trailing behind her and the noise of the cooling fan punctuating the otherwise peaceful morning air. Alexander's ring was still clutched in her left hand. She'd even held it between the steering wheel and her hand as she carved up the winding mountain road to their home. It was the most tangible symbol of his having survived the explosion and simply feeling it gave her both peace and determination.

She needed to think, and where better to think than the newly discovered underground lair of secrets. Laura entered their bedroom and pushed at the cherry bureau, but nothing happened. She might as well have been pushing against a solid concrete wall. Alexander had moved it as if it was made of papier-mâché. She ran her fingers along and down the sides looking for a release mechanism of any kind, then closed her eyes to recall where and how he'd stood as he moved the piece. One handed, he'd moved it one handed with his left hand at the top. Reaching above her head with her left arm she ran her fingers along the top and discovered a slight indentation. Laura went to the kitchen, grabbed one of the chairs from table and placed it next to the bureau. "Great..." Her exasperation came at the discovery of a biometric fingerprint scanner. "Just great, Alexander." Though she was certain it would serve no purpose since she hadn't been privy to its installation and therefore had not programmed her own fingerprint into it, she scanned her left index finger. Nothing. "We are *so* going to marriage counseling after this..." As she vented her frustration, she simultaneously slid her middle finger across the scanner. There was a hiss, a click and the bureau slid effortlessly to the side nearly taking Laura with it. "How did he...?" She allowed her exasperation to fade. Too much to do to think about that now.

Once downstairs, the feeling of hopelessness tried to creep into her consciousness. She couldn't quite determine what good it would do her to be down there. She immediately threw a block against such despair and took a seat on the rolling desk chair and closed her eyes. Laura was determined to work her way backward, step by step through the events that had led to this point. Then, if nothing turned up that might be helpful, she would run the events forward and continue running that circuitous route backward and forward until a piece of evidence showed up that gave her an indication of the way ahead.

The first pause in the rewinding of events was the laptop. That computer would likely answer several of her questions. Getting the information off of it would be easy. Getting her hands on it would be a different issue all together. Evidence rooms were not the simplest places to get authorized access to, especially in a small town. Everybody knows everybody, so bluffing her way in was not an option. But enough on that for now, she thought. Access to the laptop would be a top priority.

The room she now sat in was of significance. Alexander had access to incredible technology, incredibly expensive technology. The cost of the research and development alone for the fabric he'd shown her would've been beyond the economic capabilities of most countries. She'd never seen anything remotely close to it and his remark that it wouldn't be available to Langley for at least half a century indicated that it was a privately funded project and production. The kind of capital necessary for such an enterprise narrowed the field considerably. Disguising that level of wealth was not easy, however making the connection between the funds and Alexander would likely prove daunting. Hiding the possession of tremendous wealth may not be simple, but how such people direct and layer that wealth is an unimaginable labyrinth, one that she'd encountered often enough to know how deadly it can be to go snooping around in such matters.

Laura leaned forward in her seat toward the dove stool, unzipped the pouch and took out the mysterious little square. A reactive, micro-engineered fabric with the ability to store energy, she held it out in front of her eyes like some kind of alien exoskeleton. She'd never been a conspiracy theorist but this was enough to make one think that the Area 51 nutters might be right after all. Leaving off the extraterrestrial theories for now, it was obvious that a team of metallurgists, energy engineers and textile engineers had been employed with extraordinary funding for a facility that was on no one's radar. The loose thread for scientists though was their ego. Laura knew she needed to find that loose thread and pull; somebody somewhere was talking or writing about these achievements. Whether it was in an obscure university paper or via an alcohol fueled rant in a dive bar, these were the high school geeks that never got the girl and they craved the validation. Once the technology finally surfaced on the consumer market, they would want the affirmation and credit for having developed it, and honestly she couldn't blame them. Nearly every masterpiece is signed by the artist and this was an absolute masterpiece as far as Laura was concerned. Finding and pulling the loose thread would require calling in some favors.

The laptop would possibly reveal who had abducted Alexander and the creators of the fabric would likely reveal who would want him back. Laura leaned forward once again to put the material back into the pouch. This time she noticed a business card lying in the bottom of the canvas stool. "JOHN B HOOD 110112-1" was all that was printed on it. The good news was that Laura had seen this kind of thing before and knew exactly what it was. The bad news was that she didn't have the two phone numbers required to get in touch with one John B Hood. Mr. Hood was likely a handler or an operative for Alexander. In her former life, such people were like lifelines. The field operative would dial the first phone number and wait for a busy signal, then dial in the ID number from the card. Once connected, the second number would be dialed followed by a prearranged variation of the ID number. During this process the caller's location would be triangulated via satellite and the connection secured with a rolling code encryption.

Finding the card meant that there were definitely people who could help but she didn't have the time to pursue what ultimately might turn out to be a dead end. It was time to start calling in favors. Laura wanted to continue scrutinizing the events leading up till now, but getting some wheels turning took precedent. Without a single bar showing on her phone, Laura bounded up the steps and back through the secret door dialing as she went. As soon as her head hit the opening she hit the 'Call' button. It never rang. Instead there was a click and a response, "What's up?"

"I need a favor."

"Go."

"I need the names of the leading: metallurgical, energy and textile engineers of the past decade, everywhere they've studied, categorized by places of employment in order from those who've fallen off the radar to those employed by the Fortune 100s. Subcategorize by personal wealth and further categorized by off shore assets. I also need the names of the Bilderberg Group categorized by members associated with each of the annual meetings over the past decade, subcategorized by known dummy corporations and religious affiliation."

"Religious affiliation?"

"Religious affiliation. Do the same for the 100 wealthiest individuals eliminating duplicates from the Bilderbergs."

"Timeline?"

"Yesterday."

"Always."

"Yep. Thanks."

There was a pause and a softening of tone, "You OK?"

"Not really. I'll explain as soon as I can. No immediate danger to me."

"Well at least that. We're shorthanded due to cutbacks but I'll have this to you in a couple of hours."

"You're awesome."

"As are you, dear."

Laura ended the call, made sure the doors were locked and that the alarm was set. She was about to descend the steps once again into the safe room but paused for just a moment and turned toward their walk-in closet. Pushing her hanging clothes to the side revealed the door of a built-in gun safe. After a quick manipulation of the dial Laura opened it and drew her Heckler & Koch 45 out, hit the magazine release, checked the load, drove it back in with the palm of her hand and racked the slide. After de-cocking and flipping the safety up, she put the rather sizable pistol in the waistband at the small of her back. She didn't know with whom she was dealing but then again, neither did they.

Grabbing an apple and a protein bar as she passed through the kitchen, Laura made her way back down into the safe room. Regardless of its amazing properties, there was something comforting about being in the recesses of the earth while ruminating on her plans. Though spartan, it gave her a feeling of being surrounded by Alexander's strength. She was far too competitive to ever tell him she felt weaker than him, though she was certain he knew. Most of the men in her life had been insecure and often attempted to cover it in ridiculous ways. Some tried to show her how much better of a marksman they were than her. They weren't. Others would try to outsmart her. They couldn't. A few prima donnas tried to match her sense of style or her fitness routine. Hopeless. On the other hand, Alexander was smart, talented and funny but more than anything he possessed inner strength the likes of which she'd never seen. On the flight out of China as he was being tended to by a physician and two nurses, a casual observer might have thought he was returning home from a vacation. By the time they landed in Frankfurt he had the entire

41

flight crew, diplomatic ensemble, and medical staff eating out of his hand feeding them one hilarious or harrowing tale after another. At one point, she'd considered recruiting him into the services. Anyone that could convince a group of otherwise highly intelligent people that he was now the marital property of a Shaolin monk imprisoned for rigging table-tennis matches would be an incredibly effective field agent. This particular memory caused Laura to laugh out loud but it was short-lived. The emotion was overwhelming and she burst into torrents of sobbing cries.

Laura was angry that this part of his life had been concealed from her; she was horrified that he was missing, she was furious with his as of yet faceless captors, and perhaps worst of all was the disappointment in herself. Her increasing complacency since leaving the services had caused her to miss a mission critical element: always establish or provide back-up. Five years ago she would've insisted on going with Alexander to meet Trowbridge. Failing that, she would've simply followed him and covered his backside. Whoever it was that had dragged him away would now be crossing the proverbial bar and the two of them would be redefining the term "full disclosure."

Laura took a few minutes more to internally lament the situation, then composed herself and got straight back to work. For the following two hours she examined every detail beginning from the moment she emerged from the lake on the previous morning to the lightning fast trip back home just hours earlier. She alternated rolling each scene forward and then backward in her mind as if going through a film editing process. All of the information thus far brought her to some intriguing realizations. Ultimately, the world's wealthiest and most powerful people were engaged in a power struggle with ancient roots. Global upheaval, warfare, murder, kidnapping, extortion, corruption, it was all there and all for the sake of a rock that was as meaningless as any other chunk of stardust until someone sanctified it as a holy relic. At the moment, the love of her life was at the epicenter and she wanted him back.

Her stream of intense thought was interrupted by the realization that it was time to check in with her friend at Langley. Because of the signal blocking attributes of the room, she once again headed upstairs and keyed a long sequence of numbers into her phone then hit 'Call' and waited for a confirmation tone. Within a second of hitting "End" an encrypted email appeared in her inbox. Laura downloaded the attachment and deleted the email. "Michael, you truly are an angel." She spoke her gratitude into the air, but would be sure to properly thank her old compatriot once the mission was wrapped up. "Now...laptop."

A quick shower, some clothes with a sufficiently revealing neckline just in case, the HK in an oversized bag designed for a cross side draw and a S&W .38 snubbie on her ankle, Laura was ready to head back into town and track down that computer. Reaching into the fridge to get a bottled water, the images of Alexander's cup of tea ruse suddenly rushed through her mind. There was no snapping twig, just the tingle at the back of her neck that developed over years of training and field work. She was being watched.

Laura took a sip from the bottle then put it in the recesses of her cavernous bag and casually took out her phone and dialed a number. "Alice, I'm headed your way right now. I'm so sorry that I'm running this late."

She closed the refrigerator door and headed for the front door where she set the alarm for away. "Right, right...I know. Well the timing couldn't be better." Keeping the phone sandwiched between her left shoulder and head, she pulled the front door closed behind her and faced it to lock the deadbolt. "Honestly I couldn't be happier with the results."

Laura spun around to her right, the phone dropped to the ground and she swept the gun aimed at her from the man's grip with a round-house followed with a front kick to his solar plexus. Her aggressor was taken completely by surprise and was still in the air as she launched toward him with the .45 auto at the tip of the spear. He landed with a thud; Laura squared his center mass in the sights and scanned her perimeter. "DON'T MOVE!"

The man flinched ever so slightly and almost as if her reflexes were hard-wired to his movements she put a bullet in the ground mere inches from his left ear. "I said,

DO...NOT...MOVE." The man was struggling for air from her full frontal assault but he was now doing so with more grace and as little movement than was thought to be humanly possible. "Roll to your stomach, hands stretched above your head." Her orders were coming in staccato succession as he followed each of them. "Cross your right leg behind your left. Place your right hand on your head, now your left and interlock your fingers." She continued to scan the surrounding area, backed toward her bag and withdrew some flex cuffs. Laura knelt into the small of the man's back with her right knee and put the barrel of the gun at the base of his skull with some force. The man grunted. "Slowly rotate your left hand back toward me. Breaking the speed limit *will* get you killed." The man complied by moving his arm carefully and slowly back toward her. When his arm reached its full extension she slipped the first loop of the cuffs over his hand and with one motion zipped it tight and pulled his arm to the top of her knee. "Now the right hand at the same speed." He began the same measured process with his right arm. "I don't know who you are, but you're about to tell me that and more."

The man had regained his breath and as Laura securely zipped his right hand into the plastic restraint he managed to speak, "John B Hood."

8

"I'll need my phone." Alexander formed his words insistently and as non-negotiable terms.

"We no longer need the precise information carried in Walter Trowbridge's blood; we simply need you to inform the Pontiff that we possess the information." There was an underlying current of disdain in Ephrem's voice. "I'm sure that will be sufficient in getting his attention."

"You may no longer need that precise information, but I'm afraid I do. If it is verifiable, then we have something to discuss. If not...well...then you might as well turn this lovely jet around and deposit me back into my life because the discussion will have at that juncture concluded."

Ephrem's eyes narrowed. Without looking away from Alexander he spoke seemingly to no one in particular, "Bring the phone and the syringe." The intercom was obviously active which meant their conversation was being overheard by other and as of yet unidentified interested parties. The cabin door opened without the usual preceding chime. Ana once again entered the room with a large metal tray containing the phone, the syringe, sterile gloves, a pipette, microscope slides and cover slips.

"This is going to take some time, so feel free to leave me to my work." Alexander didn't expect them to take him up on his offer.

"That's quite alright, Alexander. Both Ana and I are great fans of the sciences, it runs in our family."

Alexander looked at Ana and then back at Ephrem.

"Ana is my daughter. Ana Goldman, I would like you to meet Alexander Kilpatrick."

"We're old friends." Alexander was of course referring to her polite and gentle meal service, but there was something else. He couldn't quite nail it down yet, but he could always tell when there was something else. Ana simply nodded and allowed a faint grin to briefly appear before placing the tray on the buffet.

Without further delay, Alexander went to work preparing to scan and translate the encoded data explaining each step to Ephrem and Ana. "Before we transfer the fluid, every other aspect of the process must be ready, especially in this environment. The proteins will degrade rapidly so I have to work quickly. I will need to dial into a database and keep the line open until I'm ready to scan."

"You can route the call through our onboard communications system." Ephrem volunteered this as if he would take him up on the offer, but the tilt of Alexander's head and the look on his face indicated otherwise.

"That won't be necessary." Alexander held the phone aloft, "I've got it covered." He then began dialing a sequence of numbers presumably connecting with the database. First a telephone number and then after hearing the busy signal he dialed 110112#1. There was a click followed by a dial tone on the other end. "I'm connected."

Before he could dial the remaining phone number and second code, Ephrem's body language and facial expression told Alexander he was about to lose the phone. He quickly depressed and held the volume down button and keyed in a three digit code causing the screen to fill with binary code at the precise moment Ephrem snatched it from his hand. "What the hell are you doing? You're not dialing into a database."

"Well actually I was, but if you'll look at the screen it's of no use now. You tampered with this phone didn't you?" Alexander was feigning anger and bluffing like crazy. "You tried to scan the material yourself. Didn't your Imah teach you to leave things alone that you don't understand?"

"Of course we tried, just as you would have." Ephrem was fuming. "What do you *mean* it's of no use now?"

"That phone might as well be a saucer for your teacup now. When you made your attempt to access its data, it locked up on you didn't it? It locked because it was loading all of its data into a nice neat little digital package. When I accessed it just now it wasn't connecting to the database I wanted. Because it had been previously tampered with, it was set to automatically dump its contents the next time it was accessed. We discovered a long time ago that people like you will torture others to get what they want. If there's nothing to obtain, it tends to cut down on the torture rate." Alexander looked at Ephrem for a few seconds in silence. "I'm truly sorry. And now if you'll turn this plane around and get me home, I have a lot of explaining to do. Oh, and some more of those figs would be nice..."

"Fuck you!" Ephrem threw the phone against the cabin wall. Amongst Alexander's many talents, pissing people off was perhaps his greatest. It was normally a very helpful attribute inasmuch as when people are angry they rarely think clearly. Leaving the phone with him, unceremoniously or not, was Ephrem's muddle-headed mistake in this instance.

Ephrem stormed out of the cabin as Ana turned quietly toward the door. Alexander wasn't certain, but he might've seen a smile on her face. Perhaps she enjoyed seeing someone getting the old man's goat, but he doubted it. Something else...there was something else.

As he retrieved the undamaged, specially designed phone from the cabin floor, Alexander realized they must be getting close to landing in Rome. Between the possibility that Ephrem would return for the phone or the syringe and the time

47

it would take to extract, scan and translate the data he would have to finish his distress call later. For now, he needed the data that Trowbridge had risked and ultimately given his life to transfer to him. Ever since this Pope was elected, there had been stirrings of discomfort in the secretive world Alexander inhabited and in that world, stirrings of discomfort often led to very bad things.

There was actually no need to dial into a database but the lack of a more powerful processor would slow the endeavor considerably. Alexander methodically prepared three slides and deposited a drop of Trowbridge's blood onto each. One sample would normally provide all of the information necessary; however, the program would overlay each of the three samples adjusting for any degradation in the samples. The probability that the same protein sequences would be degraded across all three samples was extraordinarily low. It would take a little longer to process, but seeing as how the life of the Pope was in the balance, getting the most accurate information possible seemed to be the right thing to do.

Holding the phone perfectly still over the first slide, he allowed the optical reader to do its work. He did the same for the second and then the third. Once the data collection was complete he returned the phone to the floor where it had landed after hitting the wall. Alexander cleaned the slides and placed them back into their original packaging. If Ephrem returned, he wanted it to appear as if nothing had changed. Depending on the quality of the samples it would take anywhere from one to three hours for the data to translate. Alexander was hoping for the lesser of these times.

While the phone sat on the floor processing, he decided to take a shower and dress. It was likely going to be a long night ahead and he would face it more ably with a clean body and fresh clothing. The lavatory, though small, was as well appointed as the rest of his cabin. He stepped into the cylindrical shower stall where multiple, digitally controlled shower heads were waiting to reinvigorate his aching body. "Damn it!" The hot water hit an abrasion on his forehead that until now had gone unnoticed. Must've happened in the explosion he reasoned.

Once the pain subsided, the one thought he'd been keeping at bay since waking up on the plane now came rushing into his consciousness, Laura. She must be out of her mind with concern yet simultaneously planning how to torture and kill him if he survived this. She had done way more than simply rescue him from Tilanqiao prison. Being in a Chinese prison was not the worst thing that had ever happened to him. He grinned at this thought. Laura came along and rescued him from a life that had robbed him of his identity. With her, he was rebuilding a life that was more faithful to his core and the essence of whom he truly wanted to be.

Being tapped by Walter Trowbridge as one of the 12 had been both exhilarating and devastating. At first it was intriguing if not surreal. Learning that he was part of a genetic lineage dating back to families whose origins predated Judaism was heady stuff. As with most of the newly recruited, it had taken him several years to fully adjust to his new identity. Within five years though, the constant and often unexpected travel, the uncertainty of how long he had to be gone and the extraordinary secrecy surrounding his work ultimately destroyed his first marriage of 17 years.

Over the generations, there had been those who thought it was better for the world to know the truth about the Nephilim than to allow them to continue manipulating world events. Once he'd lost everything else that mattered to him, Alexander became one of those. Their power, reach and influence were staggering, occasionally corrupting even those amongst the 12. Bishops, priests, Imams, rabbis, monks, and lay people over millennia had caved into whatever weaknesses the Nephilim exploited. Politicians, potentates and despots were the easiest marks for them. Whatever the currency of corruption of the day happened to be, they could provide it in overwhelming supply: power, wealth, empires, and armies. They traded in everything and everyone and Alexander was doing his best to bring them down. The multiple attempts at bringing attention to their existence and global influence through interviews and exposé articles had only served to cast him as a conspiracy theorist amongst the general public.

Having lost just about everything that was important to him, Alexander was preparing to declare all-out war on the Nephilim, a modern day David and Goliath.

The problem was that he was about to disappear from the face of the earth before he could even load his sling. Trowbridge admired his fierce determination and sheer courage that often looked a little like a death wish, but Alexander needed to be saved from himself. He conducted an operation to have Alexander abducted and hidden in Tilanqiao prison until things could settle down. The Chinese were being paid handsomely to hide Alexander in a place the Nephilim would never look. Not that the Chinese would allow them to do so anyway. The Chinese power brokers had despised the Nephilim since the 1962 Sino-Indian war. The Himalayan Nephilim was keeping China out of India. The British Empire, a construct of the Nephilim, had grown to a point that it was beginning to bite the hand that fed them, so in the 1940s the Nephilim began pushing back and nowhere near as 'non-violently' as history has recorded. India ended up being one of the Nephilim's greater successes and they intended to keep other aspiring empires from taking it over again. Not to mention the Himalayas were a perfect place for them to remain hidden where the rural religious culture of India helped keep their reality a myth.

By the time the dust that Alexander had kicked up settled, Trowbridge had arranged his extraction from Tilanqiao by an unsuspecting Laura Elisabeth Wells. Little did he know the two of them would fall madly in love on the journey home and that Alexander would pull completely back from his obligations as one of the 12. He'd done an outstanding job of dropping off everyone's radar for five years. During that time Laura had reintroduced Alexander's heart to the kind of love that heals one's soul and he was tenaciously guarding that gift.

Unfortunately, the current Pope's activities were on the verge of tipping an uneasy balance. His lifelong anti-Semitism was well known and if he was indeed in league with the Nephilim and the Persians, he would have to be stopped, and soon. This was why Trowbridge had gone to such great pains to get this information into his hands. Just as each member of the 12 held information specific to their title, they also held certain responsibilities and authority. In Alexander's case, it was that only Mathias could effectively remove Simon. This authority was a relatively new institution since the Western Schism of the 15th century that had been so messy. It now seemed clear, even without having seen the evidence yet, that for the first time in history a Mathias was going to have to unseat a Simon. There would be push-back, but once it was seen that the Israelis had him zeroed and in their crosshairs, the results would be the same regardless of the protestations. The Pope had to go.

9

"What did you say?" Laura had heard clearly, but wanted him to repeat the name.

"John B Hood." The man was still winded and was grimacing as Laura's knee bored into the base of his spine.

"What's that supposed to mean?"

"Honestly I was hoping you'd know."

Laura pushed a little harder into his back and drove the barrel just a little deeper into that tender cove where the skull meets the neck. "Five...Four...Three..."

The man could feel the subtle shift in the pistol's disposition as Laura began applying pressure to the trigger. "Hey! Hang on! OK! I got a call... Actually I got a partial call...from a number associated with a friend named Alex."

"What do you mean a partial call?" Laura hadn't yet released the tension on the trigger in the slightest and the man knew it.

"Alex and I used to work together, we were friends. Whenever he found himself in a tight spot he would call me on two different numbers. The first call told me it was him; the second began a process of triangulating the origin of the call via satellite. Today, I only got the first call...then nothing. So I got on the horn to my former employers. I'm retired now. They didn't know anything about it but asked me to check it out. They gave me these coordinates and..."

Laura interrupted, "How long?'

"What?"

"How long have you been retired?"

"Seven years, why?"

Laura pulled the pistol away from the man's head and without a word got to her feet. The evidence was building that Alexander was alive. She went to her purse, retrieved a pair of Scarab cutters, put the .45 in her waistband and then severed the heavy plastic cuffs off of her unannounced visitor.

"John, you have no idea how happy I am to meet you. I needed to know if you'd retired before or after I came into the picture, before or after Tilanqiao prison. If you'd said anytime in the last five years...well, we wouldn't be having this conversation right now."

"First of all you have a damn strange way of showing gratitude." The man got to his feet, but with his core still aching horribly from the straight kick she'd landed, he kept his distance. "And secondly my name's not John."

"I'm Laura Wells, Alexander's wife."

"Wife? A man goes off grid for a few years and the next thing you know everybody he knows is getting crazy and married and who knows what else." The man flashed the first smile between them and held out his hand. "I'm Robert Cox."

Laura accepted his hand and returned the smile. "I'm sorry for the rough greeting."

"If I wasn't so impressed, I'd be pissed."

Laura gave him a withering look, "Why, because a girl took you down?"

"No, not at all. That he met you before I did." Robert gave her a broad smile and a wink.

"Nice save."

"I thought so."

"So who's John B Hood and why are you sneaking around here with a gun?"

"Alex. Alex is John B Hood. It was his codename when we worked together, my little joke. John Bell Hood was a Confederate general that no matter what they threw at him he kept coming back. Even with the loss of use in one arm and one leg, he would have his men strap him to his horse so he could ride into battle."

"Sounds like a brave man."

"No hon, hot tempered, reckless and tenacious as a pit bull would be more accurate."

"Well that's not Alexander."

Robert looked at her with something of disbelief in his expression. "Hmmm... maybe not with a woman who could obviously kick his ass, but there was a day when your boy would take on Hell and half of Georgia before calling for back-up."

Laura really couldn't conceive of Alexander in this way and she wasted no further thought on it. "And the sneaking around here today?"

"With half a distress call from Alex I just assumed he was in trouble. When I saw you, I knew he was." They both laughed.

Laura abruptly cut her laughter off and scanned their surroundings. Though Robert didn't know exactly why, he followed suit and looked for anything out of the ordinary. "Hear something?"

"Not here." She said this while continuing to observe their surroundings.

After a couple more seconds in silence, Laura tilted her head in the direction of the front door, "Let's step inside." She really wanted to get her hands on that laptop, but Robert's unexpected arrival meant a temporary change in plans. Given that he'd worked with Alexander as what was known in the services as a 'handler', having him on her team was something of a boon. He would very likely fill in some vital blanks left empty by Alexander in his haste.

They entered the front door, Robert ahead of Laura. She locked the door behind them and set the alarm. "Grab a couple of waters from the fridge and then join me in here." She said this as she passed hurriedly through the kitchen and into the bedroom. Laura believed he was who he claimed to be, but she wasn't taking unnecessary risks. As he was getting the water she slid her middle finger over the scanner at the top of the bureau and moved it to the side once again. He was not far behind her yet didn't look the least bit surprised to see the opening in the floor. Laura gestured politely with her hand for Robert to take the lead down the steps. With his hands full and in front of her descending the steps, if he wasn't who he claimed to be she would have the advantage.

With the door now closed behind them they were safe to speak more freely. Laura kept her distance from Robert and remained standing as he took a seat on the dove stool and put the two bottled waters on the floor beside him. "Trust is earned Laura. I get that, and you're obviously not the average homemaker. I'll tell you everything I know and you decide how much you want to tell me, if anything at all. Alex must be in some trouble if he called that number and since he wasn't able to complete the process, I'd say he's in more trouble than he cares to handle alone."

"I believe you Robert, but as one of our presidents famously said, 'Trust...'"

"But verify" he said, finishing the quote for her. "I don't know if this will help your feelings at all but I happen to know Alex has a tattoo.

Laura's eyes widened. Alexander hated that tattoo and so did she, another relic from his college days. He never told anyone about it.

"It's a bat on his upper left thigh."

"While not conclusive, that certainly makes me feel somewhat more trusting of you. I hate that stupid thing."

Robert opened a water, took a long drink and winced a bit as he shifted in his seat.

"Sorry about that." Laura knew both his torso and ego were hurting after their encounter. Robert seemingly ignored her apology. Acknowledging it would mean acknowledging the take down she'd so effectively dealt him just moments earlier. "Ah the male ego," she thought to herself, "Can't count the number of times that's been the weakness I've successfully exploited."

Almost as if he was reading her thoughts, Robert pressed ahead rather than acknowledging this embarrassment. "I was recruited out of the Secret Service by a group of people whose identities I've never known. At the time I was on the president's detail. Normally that's the rung we all strive for in the Service, but I was miserable. He had the morals of an alley cat and we were spending more time and energy keeping his dalliances out of the public eye than we were keeping potential assassins at bay. When he lost the biscuit, that was the last straw for most of us."

"The biscuit?"

"Nuclear codes. Every president has a card with the nuclear codes required to initiate a launch. The commander in chief is supposed to have that card, or 'the biscuit' on his person 24/7. In the event that a nuclear launch is warranted, a briefcase called 'the football' carried by an aide is opened and the procedure begins. Without those codes, nothing happens. Well, nothing except if we're truly in a nuclear war we watch as our country and her allies go up in radioactive flames."

"Seems like I remember hearing about that." In actuality, Laura knew a great deal about it but wanted him to keep going.

"As you can imagine, asking for a transfer off of the most cherished post in US law enforcement tends to be a career killer and unless you screw up, the assumption is that you'll serve as long as the term allows. Most of us wanted the hell off of that detail. It was like guarding a frat boy with an unlimited expense account." He paused reflectively for a moment, took another drink of water then continued. "Anyway, I got a call from the director one day that I was not to report to work the next day, that one of my colleagues was covering for me and that further instructions would follow. I was baffled but I didn't even have a split second to think about it. As soon as the director clicked off, a different voice caught me before I could end the call. It was a man asking if he could meet with me. I asked when and he said, 'right now' and my doorbell rang. When I looked through the peephole there was a woman standing there. I opened the door and she told me to pack a bag." Robert took another drink of water as Laura sat in the rolling desk chair beside him and now opened her water.

"For the first 24 hours it was all very cloak and dagger type moving around from place to place and never with the same person twice. A day and a half later I'd accepted an assignment I knew virtually nothing about. My entire Government Service record was wiped out as if I'd never worked for Uncle Sam a day in my life. I eventually learned that there were four more just like me assigned to Alexander and an equal number assigned to each of the other 11. We were strategically placed around the world each with a different task all directed toward keeping tabs on him and making sure he had everything he needed to do his job."

"That's what I don't get Robert, how is it that a rock, though admittedly of profound historic significance, is at the root of so much violence?"

"Well, what would you prefer: oil, water, gold or land perhaps? Thoughts, ideas and philosophical nuance, those are the things over which we go to war, Laura. You know that. Take Jerusalem for instance. What makes that land valuable to Abraham's squabbling children? Instead of claiming a covenantal responsibility for one another as fellow human beings, they make a covenantal claim on a piece of land. It's a covenant that was written by human hands, supposedly given to their prophets by an invisible god. It's all connected. Every war, every empire, every shipping lane of commerce every election and assassination, the very way we are has its roots in this philosophical struggle and the Nephilim who promote the strife. Only two groups have ever stood above it."

"Two groups?"

"One is the group of 12 of which Alexander is one."

"And the other?"

Robert paused for a while simply looking into Laura's inquisitive eyes. "Where were you headed today?"

Laura was not accustomed to people avoiding her questions but she would play along for now. "A man named Walter Trowbridge came to see Alexander yesterday morning. Until then, I had no idea about any of this. After Trowbridge left, he brought me down here," Laura looked around the room then continued "and told me as much as he possibly could over several hours." She stood from her chair as her nerves began working on her again. She wanted to get going. She wanted to find him.

"Alexander left here early this morning to see Trowbridge at the bed and breakfast. There was an explosion. I went to investigate and found the place in flames. While there I discovered two items of significance, a laptop sitting on the lawn in such a way that I'm convinced it was not propelled there by the explosion and Alexander's wedding ring at the edge of the roadway lying just ahead of a line in the ground made by someone being dragged. I was on my way to get my hands on that laptop."

"Was it his?"

"The laptop? It wasn't Alexander's but my theory is that it was Trowbridge's."

"Where is it now?"

"I'm not sure. By now it's probably in an evidence room in Black Mountain."

"So who's driving?"

"I am!" Laura said this with a little too much defiance.

"I know..." Robert grinned. "So let's get going."

Laura returned the grin, "Sorry, it's been a really bad day."

They returned to the upper level through the doorway. As soon as Robert was standing in the bedroom his phone dinged. He looked at it, punched in a code and then, looking at the illuminated screen smiled from ear to ear. "Got him."

"Got who?"

"Alex. He's in Rome."

"ROME? As in Rome, Rome? Rome, Italy Rome?" Laura was incredulous.

"Got a passport?"

10

The phone finished processing the data just as they landed at Fiumicino airport. Alexander wasted absolutely no time. He transmitted the data to a secure database then dialed the appropriate numbers for his old friend Robert Cox, locked the device and put it on the tray with the syringe. As he did so, the pleasant door chime sounded followed by Ana's voice, "Mr. Kilpatrick may I enter?"

Instead of responding, he simply opened the door and greeted her, "Ana."

"Good evening Mr. Kilpatrick..."

"Please, call me Alex."

She seemed to ignore his familiarity though not uncomfortably so. "If you'll pardon the intrusion we will get you packed."

He then noticed Mitri and Asa standing just outside the cabin door. Mitri, the one who had stabbed him in the neck with a hypodermic had a rather large piece of custom leather luggage in tow. Alexander stood to the side and allowed them to enter. Asa remained outside the door and once he'd placed the suitcase on a retractable luggage rack, Mitri rejoined him. In her usual demure way, Ana began neatly packing the clothing and accessories from the closet.

Once the packing was accomplished, she left the room without a word. Mitri reentered and retrieved the suitcase while Asa followed to collect the phone, the tray and its contents. Just as they cleared the doorway, Ephrem entered. "Ana, Mitri and Asa will accompany you to a safe house for the night. I suggest you get some rest." His tone and disposition were cold and it was something more than the embarrassment of having lost his temper earlier. Alexander was guessing the failure to obtain the encoded data had not gone over well with Ephrem's superiors and the overnight stay at a safe house was probably an unwelcome delay in the ever shifting plans since Walter's death. This however was not the time to gloat.

"I assume you won't be joining us there." He was almost sorry for the man as he said this. Ephrem was no doubt going to face the music of having been in command of an operation that took the life of one of the 12 with nothing to show for it. To make things worse, they had kidnapped him which, ultimately was an additional effort in vain. The storm brewing somewhere in Israel was going to be intense once it hit, and poor Ephrem was going to be the first casualty.

"No, I'm afraid I won't." Again his words were devoid of emotion and his countenance was that of a man adrift in deep thought. He looked around the room as if he was looking for something, but nothing in particular and returned his gaze to Alexander. "The complexities of our world often bring us to unfortunate junctures, crossroads if you will that force us into decisions we would have preferred not to make."

"I understand."

"I know you do more than most, Alexander. As you certainly intended, we lost track of you several years ago. It wasn't until Walter showed up at your door that we even knew if you were dead or alive. Your attempt to cripple the Nephilim was valiant, if not misguided. We were of course all for any damage you might have inflicted on them but knew all too well the end result would be your demise. When you disappeared, that was our assumption. You resurfaced momentarily though, coming out of Shanghai then gone again for years. It was all rather difficult to follow. You wanted out, didn't you?"

Alexander could tell that Ephrem was attempting to bring closure to his own narrative. His future was uncertain given the stark nature of the situation that he had brought upon the entire world. "You know Ephrem I did, and would still be happily out if Walter hadn't shown up."

"Does it not bother you that one of your own, the Pope no less, has direct ties to the Shoah and is funneling billions of dollars into Iran's nuclear program for the express purpose of attacking Israel?" The tenor of his voice remained surprisingly even as he posed this question.

"Those are very serious allegations, Ephrem."

"Allegations you know to be true."

"I've yet to see the evidence that they are."

"Damn it, Alexander!" His veneer of calm was shattered. He slammed his fist on the buffet hard enough to cause Mitri to jump up and look in on them. "You know damn well that it's true, and you know that's why Walter came to you."

"And now you want me to flush him out so you can assassinate him, bring the evidence to bear against him in the aftermath thereby exposing the Vatican's inextricable ties to the Nazis, the Holocaust and the Persians. Those are *your* tactics Ephrem, not ours. We operate very differently and take a much broader view of history."

"You speak of history and yet for my people the Shoah remains very much present. These are not scars that we bear, they are open wounds. We've never been the hunter Alexander, always the hunted." He rubbed the underside of his hand where he'd hit the piece of furniture, and then straightened his suit coat as a means of regaining his composure. "When we induct soldiers into the IDF we swear them in at Masada where two thousand years ago less than a thousand of my people held off an entire Roman legion for three months. When they complete their basic training, we take them to Yad Vashem. There they are surrounded by throngs of tourists checking off an item on their bucket list, but to them, to us, to me..." His chest began sinking and swelling with emotion. "This is not merely a museum, it is a window that peers into our reality."

Arguing any of these points would serve no purpose. For one thing, Ephrem was proving to be a zealot and there was actually enough validity to his claims that it would require hours of engagement ultimately resulting in nothing. He was suddenly reminded of why he'd dropped out of sight for so many years and that his solitary objective now was to obtain his freedom and once again seek peaceful anonymity. Ephrem and his entourage could chase demons on their own time, he was finished and there was nothing they could do to compel him to further accommodate their purposes.

"Your reality?" Alexander couldn't restrain the mocking tone in his question. "Here's some reality for you. You're going to engulf the world in war if you haven't already. Taking out Simon, especially without the benefit of the evidence you need, will destroy everything you've worked for thus far. You should be concerned with repairing the damage done by Walter's death and forget about Simon for now, that situation will take care of itself."

"What Alexander, wait for him to die of old age? I don't think so. In the third century one of your most prominent theologians, Hippolytus of Rome declared that it was not appropriate to even baptize a soldier because of the brutality required of an individual combatant. Now, seventeen centuries later you've elected a Pope who participated in history's most brutal, methodical and devastating genocide. Now he's plotting anew with the Iranians, but this time instead of marching us one at a time into the ovens, they're going to unleash a nuclear holocaust." The calm and professional demeanor had returned but his rhetoric was obviously charged with an undercurrent of incredible energy.

Though he hadn't had the opportunity to review the information on his phone, whatever evidence there was, Alexander couldn't believe that it was a nuclear option. On the other hand, Iran would certainly be the first to want to hit Israel and murmurings of reclaiming Jerusalem had been part of the Roman Catholic underground since the last Crusade. "Well, I think now that you've pretty much destroyed any opportunity of obtaining the information you need and as we sit on the brink of global war I'm fairly certain your strategy has shifted dramatically."

"Alexander, I have much to do and I'm sorry things have turned out this way. Yes, our strategy has shifted somewhat as you say, but our objective remains the same. Israel cannot afford to take Simon out, but my people like yours, have typically worked more effectively in the dark, around and behind the official channels anyway. We can and ultimately will hold him accountable. He's a war criminal in our eyes and he continues behaving as one today. His time has come." Ephrem turned toward the door to leave.

"Surely you know I will do nothing to help you accomplish this madness."

Ephrem stopped at the doorway and turned his head slightly back toward Alexander as if he was going to say something more but righted himself and continued out the door. "Goodbye, Mathias."

Alexander watched as he went, sensing a condemnatory tone in his farewell.

11

Before taking off on their commercial flight to Rome, Laura made a call to Langley. She may not have had the same autonomy in her travels as before but she still had enough clout to obtain a diplomatic package that would accompany her. Inside this package was an assortment of tools that might prove helpful should they find themselves in a tight spot. Anyone willing to snatch Alexander and haul him off to Rome most likely had the ability to create tight spots.

"What exactly was in that box?" Robert's curiosity was killing him but he'd waited until they were seated on the plane in their first class seats to ask.

"Oh, just a few toys that may be helpful."

"That's what I thought. You have any idea what will happen to us if we get caught with those kinds of toys without the papers that go with that diplomatic package?"

"As a matter of fact, I do. So here's my best advice...don't get caught." She winked and smiled as she said this, but was also being very sincere.

Robert shook his head slightly. "And what's with first class? CIA retirement must be a hell of a lot better than the Service."

"I once dated a rather high level executive with American. He loaded me up with more frequent flier miles than I could ever possibly use. Back then I never knew when I could get away from wherever I happened to be in the world or when I would suddenly be called away when we were together. Kills a relationship."

"Tell me about it."

"It was his attempt to remedy a perpetual conflict, but in the end it still wasn't enough. After we broke up I got to keep the miles."

"Not a bad parting gift."

Laura smiled, "Tell me about it."

Though the spacious seating and dividers provided ample privacy, Laura lowered her voice, "So any ideas about Rome?"

"Would've been helpful if Alex could've given us a sit-rep but apparently he was unable. Probably took some doing just to get the call out." Robert was stating the obvious mostly because he frankly couldn't imagine why Alex was in Rome and he was still processing all of the information. "Honestly Laura, I don't know why he's there. He dialed from Fiumicino, so he could be just about anywhere."

"Did you two ever work Rome together?"

Robert's eyebrows rose at this question, "Not really." There was obvious hesitation in his demeanor. "The thing is the most famous of the 12 lives in Rome."

"Are you serious?"

"Dead serious...and they can't stand each other."

"You're talking about the..."

"Yes."

"And they can't stand each other?"

"Right."

She let this sink in for a moment. "Robert, this 12...they're obviously somehow based on the 12 disciples aren't they?"

"The only way I can answer that question with any integrity is: yes, no and I don't know."

"When Alexander was describing this group to me he said that religious affiliation was not a factor, that there had been members of just about every known world religion as well as Atheists and Agnostics over the centuries."

"That's true. The only religiously consistent member and the only one that is not necessarily born into it is the Pope. Everyone else has some kind of genetic lineage that predates all three Abrahamic faiths."

"So why the Pope?"

"He's supposed to be kind of like the Switzerland of the group. Also, the Vatican is a really great place to meet in secret, to hide things you don't want found and to disappear when necessary. It is after all a sovereign state, a status that allows the Pope an extraordinarily high degree of autonomy."

"To hide things you don't want found. This stone, is it really worth going to war over?"

"Look at it this way, imagine if someone other than Christians had the actual cross of Jesus. What would Christians be willing to do to get their hands on it?"

"I see your point."

"For the Israelites, it is a tangible reminder that though they suffer, God delivers them, that though they are as a 13 year old against a giant, they are the people of the promise. For the Nephilim it is a talisman of perseverance and survival. Their martyr is Goliath, it's kind of like keeping the bullet that struck you but didn't kill you. For Islam, it is an ancient and holy relic of one of God's great prophets from the time before the Qur'an and the key to holding power in the Holy Land" He paused in his discourse and peered out into the darkened sky.

"What about the Christians?"

"I don't know."

"What do you mean you don't know?"

"I mean I really don't know. I have a theory, but that's as close as I've gotten to understanding the connection."

"And that theory would be?"

"That Christianity has been keeping this secret longer than any other group. From about the time a certain child was born 2000 years ago."

"So that's the secret? That's the thing that the 12 have been protecting and hiding for two millennia, the stone that killed Goliath?"

"That's only part of the story. Each of the 12 holds a different piece of the puzzle."

"What puzzle?"

"I don't know. I asked Alex that very question one time and all he said was, 'There are some things that cannot yet be told and some that must never be told.'"

A flight attendant approached and offered them warmed cashews and a beverage along with a dinner menu. He then turned to the passenger seated nearest them, an elderly man who had fallen asleep right after takeoff. His apparent hearing problem was causing a bit of a disruption as the very patient cabin steward worked with him. In Laura's experience, men of his age with hearing problems were often irascible, but this gentleman had a cherubic face and eyes that twinkled when she caught them. Though he spoke loudly, he was extremely polite and obviously a cultured individual. Robert was not as charmed by the man and rolled his eyes. Laura on the other hand displayed a genuine look of warmth and tenderness toward him.

"Anyway..." Robert said with a hint of impatient disgust, "this obviously has something to do with Walter. If they'd wanted Alex dead I'm quite sure he wouldn't have made it to Rome. The 12 are untouchable, so my best guess is that they need Alex and the Pope to help them prevent World War III."

"When you say 'untouchable' what exactly do you mean by that?"

"The groups that pursue the stone and the secrets are generally not affiliated with any state or government. The Jewish group for instance is not connected to Israel proper. In fact, they're an ancient family of what can best be described as the 'Jewish Mob' and are thought to have been the ones in power that had Jesus turned over to the Romans for execution. But, as with most things in our world, the lines of affiliation and allegiance are often blurred by money and blood."

Their dinner arrived and the same routine from before played out with the elderly man. The flight attendant had to speak abnormally loud to get the man's attention for the meal service. Once settled, Laura gave him a reassuring smile and lifted her cup in a silent gesture obviously indicating her sentiment of "Bon appétit." The man returned a smile, raised his cup and gently nodded in gratitude.

Robert continued from where he'd left off. "All of these groups have thousands of years and untold amounts of wealth invested in courting and protecting the 12. Everyone has their own version of an Armageddon scenario and each believes it ends with their victory and God's blessings. If any one of these groups makes a move against one or any of the 12, the other groups see it as an act of war. The assumption is that the one group is making a move toward an advantage."

"Well surely these 'groups' as you call them have some idea of the secrets held by the 12 or they wouldn't have invested so much time and money."

"Indeed. The speculation has always centered on immortality or world dominance. That was certainly Hitler's belief."

"Hitler?"

"Oh yeah. In fact, that was one of the aspects Alex would talk to me openly about. It seems the Nephilim were instrumental in funding and supporting the Nazi Wehrmacht."

Something about this caused Laura to grow quiet and distant in thought. She watched as the elderly man pushed his food around disappointingly. Without shifting her gaze from the man across the aisle she spoke to Robert, "So the Nephilim were behind the Holocaust?"

"Well, yeah." He said this as if he'd not ever really considered it like that before. He'd mostly always thought of it as a push for world domination starting with Europe.

"Robert, you realize the Pope as a young man was a member of the Nazi youth."

His eyes narrowed at this revelation. "No. I did not realize that."

"And that as a young soldier during World War I, Adolf Hitler worked in the Pope's hometown and is thought to have befriended the family."

Robert stopped eating and was staring blankly at his plate. "If that's true, then..."

"Then we don't have much time. They're not going there to smooth things over, they're going to kill the Pope and they need Alexander to get to him."

Amidst the intensity of their conversation they'd failed to realize the elderly man was struggling to rise from his seat. He was in such a hurry that he disturbed his tray enough to send his china and silverware to the floor. Given his body language, the man was evidently trying to make it to the restroom. With great agility, Laura was already on the floor picking up the scattered meal as she said, "These things are tough to navigate when you're in a hurry."

"Yes they are. Thank you, thank you so much dear." and he was off to the lavatory.

Laura remained on the floor long enough for the gentleman to get by and for the flight attendant to take over the cleaning duties then stood and got out of the way. Robert sat silently until he was certain he wouldn't be heard, "Did you notice anything peculiar just now?"

She withheld any guesses and waited for his observation.

"When the flight attendant spoke to that man twice earlier he practically had to shout at him and had to do so at ear level. When you spoke to him just now, your head was at about shin level, and your voice was directed toward the floor."

"Yet he heard me perfectly."

Robert slowly nodded his head in agreement. "He heard you perfectly."

12

Alexander stepped off the plane, briefly onto the tarmac and was then ushered into the rear seat of one of the five armored SUVs parked neatly in a row. Mitri and Asa joined him on either side while Ana took the wheel. Within seconds of closing the vehicle doors, a motorcycle detail of Polizia di Stato, the civil national police of Italy surrounded their motorcade and they were off without so much as a crackle of a radio or the dialing of a phone. With lights flashing and the familiar dual tone sirens so familiar in Europe blaring away, they roared unencumbered through a private gate west of the runways and terminals. At the gate, four of the hulking American made SUVs turned north along with the police escort. Only Alexander's vehicle turned south.

"I don't suppose I could make my one phone call?" His question was of course rhetorical but he did want to get them in dialogue so that he could gain even the smallest bit of information about where they were going and what was waiting on him when they got there. No one took the bait.

"Quando arriveremo?" Asa directed his question to Ana as she drove.

She looked at the GPS, hit a few buttons then responded, *"Meno di dieci minuni."*

His restaurant Italian was rusty at best, but he was fairly certain they would arrive at their destination in about ten minutes. He looked at Asa, "Italian, really? It's not the most clever language to disguise your communications."

"It's no disguise, merely habit." Ana responded from the front of the vehicle. "When we move from country to country we are trained to begin speaking the native language and dialect as much and as soon as possible so that we blend in. When one grows up in our part of the world, hiding in plain sight is often the only way to survive."

"Is that what we're doing now, hiding in plain sight?"

"In a manner of speaking, yes."

"Would you mind explaining that to me?"

"Not here and not now, but soon."

They rode in silence for the remainder of the short journey. During Alex and Ana's banter, Asa made a phone call relaying to someone that they would arrive in approximately ten minutes and it was nearly to the second that they pulled up to a gated and abandoned Marina. The chain link fencing was rusty, in disrepair and the gates were warped. The silver padlock on the chain however looked brand new and opened easily as Mitri turned the key and swung the gates wide. Ana turned the headlights off and drove straight across the darkened parking lot that seemed to have more weeds than asphalt. As they approached the dock Alexander could see a powerboat and hear its engine idling in a low gurgling churn.

Ana pulled parallel to the dock and the boat. They all got out of the SUV and the two men who'd been waiting with the boat began unloading the luggage. Mitri and Asa boarded the vessel while Ana stood watch. Once the boat was loaded, the two men sped off in the vehicle and Ana directed Alexander to board the boat. Asa untied the line from the weathered dock cleat and Mitri gunned the throttle launching them away from the pier and into the Tyrrhenian Sea.

Over the deep groans of the boat engine, the howling wind and the briny spray exploding from the waves Alexander shouted to Ana, "Where are we going? I thought we were going to a safe house." But instead of trying to compete with the mixture of noise, she shook her head and held up her hands in a gesture indicating that he should be patient. He shouted once more, "You're talking with your hands now. You really get into this blending in thing." She ignored him.

Their boat ride took at least three times as long as the ride from the airport and Alexander was starting to feel a little uneasy about his situation. The engine began winding down and the bow rose as they slowed. Without warning of any kind, a series of soft amber lights illuminated the stern of what was obviously an enormous yacht. As their boat planed into idle speed, a ramp lowered from the yacht and Mitri navigated the powerboat into the mother ship as if he'd done it a million times in the dark, on a windy night in heavy chop. As soon as the ramp locked back into place they were once again underway.

A crewman approached the docked boat and placed a custom fitted set of steps over the side. Mitri went first, followed by Ana, Alexander and Asa. They walked along a side deck then entered the saloon at midship. The decor was not as extravagant as he'd anticipated after taking in the immense size of the private vessel. Everything seemed to be directed toward function over form. Seeing the mega-yacht at a marina, one would assume this was some billionaire's extravagant toy but behind the blacked out windows was a craft designed strictly for business, covert business.

Mitri and Asa continued through the room and down an open stairwell. Ana and Alexander remained in the saloon where a pitcher of water and two glasses sat at one end of a long conference table. This was definitely a prearranged meeting.

"The first thing you need to understand is that Walter Trowbridge's death was no accident." The mostly silent and demure Ana from the flight had apparently remained on the plane. Her demeanor struck him as if she'd removed a disguise.

"And?"

"The Pope will be hit day after tomorrow."

"That would truly be insane."

"My father was a good man who became corrupted by his own power, idealism and obsessions. We're going to have to act quickly Alexander, this assassination cannot happen."

He looked at her with more than a little suspicion. This could easily be an attempt to obtain the data that he'd taken from Walter's blood sample. "As I told your father, any chance of retrieving that data was lost when you tried to access my phone."

"We both know that's a lie. You not only scanned and processed the information, you attempted to transmit it to a secure database."

"Attempted?" His pulse quickened and a sinking feeling rolled from his chest to his abdomen.

"Mr. Kilpatrick, you're not the only one with advanced technology. My father set you up. He knew that you would do the work for him then transmit the data and erase the phone. When you transmitted the data he was able to capture it."

Anger was rising within him but not at his adversaries, rather it was with himself. The connection was solid and he hadn't waited for confirmation. "Even if he captured the data as you claim, it's encrypted..."

"It's already been deciphered." She stopped him mid-sentence. "Mr. Kilpatrick I love my father very much but I cannot condone his plans or ideology. I'm operating against him in this matter with the assistance of people who want the same things you want. When I explain the situation I believe you'll understand why and that speed is crucial."

He was willing to listen but being bested by Ephrem on the data transmission had him on high alert for another trap. Making such a blunder was infuriating, he simply did not operate that clumsily. "OK, you have my attention."

"My father has the evidence he needs and an assassination team that has the benefit of months of preparation is already in motion. That I'm afraid is not even our biggest problem."

His curiosity level spiked off the scale at this comment and his facial expression showed it. "Murdering a Pope is not our biggest problem?"

"Trowbridge was supposed to die after we collected the data."

"But Mitri and Asa were there and are they not working with you?"

"Yes they are. Their job was to obtain the data and make it look like Trowbridge had died in the process. Unfortunately my father inserted himself into the operation at the last minute making our task of keeping him alive impossible. We don't want that to happen again."

"Again?"

Ana filled each glass in anticipation of Alexander needing a drink of water after hearing what she had to say. "Trowbridge was the first domino to fall. By the conclusion of this week every one of the 12 is supposed to have been killed with the secrets they hold collected and handed over to the Nephilim."

"Your father is working with the Nephilim?" Ana had predicted correctly, he drank half the glass and then held it at chest level as he stared into the table surface. "I really couldn't believe that the Pope was in league with them even though that was your father's claim. But this..."

"The Pope is not in fact working with the Nephilim but most assuredly *is* working with the Iranians and Israel is the target. The Pope has engaged in a personal crusade for almost his entire life to retake Jerusalem for the Church and to begin a process of reestablishing the Papal States. His deal with the Iranians gives the Palestinians all of Israel with the exceptions of Tiberias, Nazareth, half the Old City and Bethlehem.

Those would become the exclusive domain of the Vatican. The Muslims naturally want the Temple Mount, the Muslim Quarter and the Jewish Quarter."

"Do they honestly believe the nuclear option will accomplish this extraordinarily ill-conceived plan?"

"It's not nuclear weapons they're working on. The Iranians have everyone looking for enrichment facilities but that's a cover, a very effective cover."

"A cover for what?"

"We don't know, but I'm quite sure my father now knows having read the data you transmitted. Whatever it is, I'm afraid his plan is no less insidious."

"What could be worse than a nuclear holocaust?"

"As dreadful as that would be, unleashing an unrestrained Nephilim would be worse."

He considered that for a moment, "True."

"My father has struck a deal with the Nephilim. They get the secrets of the 12 including the stone and Israel gets the Promised Land, all of it. The Nephilim, with that much information and power get the rest of the world. In effect, he believes he is at the spearhead of the end of days."

"He believes he's the Moshiach?"

"As embarrassing as it is to admit, I'm afraid so."

"Goldman. That's one of the more prominent and direct Davidic bloodlines. Because of his surname your father believes he will gather all Jews to Israel and usher in the age of peace? He believes that he is anointed?"

"Ultimately, yes."

"No one in your organization sees the insanity of this?"

"Gush Emunim."

These two words chilled him and nearly caused Alexander to drop the glass he was holding. "They disbanded over 30 years ago."

"Which is precisely what they wanted everyone to believe. They've been quietly and steadily gaining political and religious power for those 30 years, but certainly not disbanded. Under one name or another, they've been around for an extraordinarily long time."

"Well that certainly explains how your Prime Minister can stand on camera in front of a settlement under construction in the West Bank claiming there are no active expansions in the West Bank." He said this sarcastically, but saw that he'd stated a truth as Ana nodded in agreement. She couldn't argue with his observation.

"It's really gone that far?"

"Yes."

"And it's just Mitri, Asa and you trying to stop them?" He was truly hoping there was an entire army somewhere behind them. It would take no less than that and perhaps not even that to stop the inertia of what had begun.

"Alex, when you dropped out of sight it created a vacuum that destabilized the 12. No one had ever just walked away before. We all thought you would resurface eventually, but when it looked like you weren't going to, the fractures caused by your departure began splintering and spreading."

It was the first time she'd called him anything other than 'Mr. Kilpatrick.' Ana definitely knew more than he'd first assumed. "They could've replaced me."

"No Alex, they couldn't just replace you and you know that. You also know that the evidence against the Pope is not the only information my father was after."

He knew the secrets held by Walter had something to do with the Papacy and until Ana told him that Ephrem had the data, he'd not been overly concerned. Things were taking a rapid turn for the worse though and his concern was beginning to magnify exponentially by the minute.

"The destabilization of the 12 was the opening they'd been waiting for and you handed it to them. Mitri, Asa and I are not the only ones but there are certainly more of them than there are of us. That's how it's always been. Matthew and Thomas are in hiding and we're trying to get to the other nine before they do."

"Matthew and Thomas are hiding?"

"Yes, and while they may be your only friends amongst the 12, they are fairly upset with you nonetheless."

He looked at her silently for a good while. Walking away had been easy but he hadn't considered the potential impact on the others especially now that he knew the ultra-radical Gush Emunim had completely infiltrated the power structures of Israel and had cut a deal with their oldest enemies, the Nephilim. Walter had been the first and the rest would go fairly quickly once the Pope was taken out. While the world stood in shock with their faces turned toward Rome, no one would notice any other event for the time it took for the rest of the 12 to fall. Her words were ringing in his ears, '...you handed it to them.'

"What can I do, Ana?"

"Well, first of all, we're going to need you to die."

82

13

Laura and Robert collected their luggage after clearing immigration. "I wonder how they would've reacted back there when they asked the purpose of our visit if we'd told them we were here to save the Pope."

"Well, I'm fairly certain we wouldn't be standing here right now and that your prostate exam would've come early this year."

Robert admired and appreciated anyone who could find humor in difficult circumstances, there seemed to be a link between that trait and the dependability of that person when things went from zero to shit in 1.2 seconds. This mission had the very real possibility of fitting that profile.

"Well, I wouldn't want to have that happen. Besides, I require mood lighting and some Barry White for my prostate exams."

She shook her head and laughed but adjusted her comportment almost immediately. "I guess you noticed that our friend didn't get off the plane."

"I did. Which means that we were picked up by another that was either on the plane or waiting at the gate as we deplaned. You know what to do, right?"

"Right."

Once the elderly passenger returned from the lavatory, they'd stopped talking and began passing notes as surreptitiously as possible. The plan was to separate soon after leaving the airport. With any luck their watchers wouldn't be expecting them to go in different directions. Forcing them to adjust their surveillance tactics might give them just enough of a window for at least one of them to operate unimpeded and unobserved. Robert would contact his counterpart in Rome and Laura would establish a temporary base of operation as a red herring. Because of the technology that was most definitely being employed to watch them, they would rely on good old fashioned spy craft by using dead-drop messages. The first location was prearranged. The message left there would indicate three more locations where messages would be deposited. A number on each of the three messages would indicate which message was the one to follow. This ruse would continue only long enough for Robert to facilitate a secure base of operation with his counterpart. They would then rendezvous at Laura's location and disappear right out from under their noses with the help of the Pope's handler. He was a man Robert knew well and had worked with many times in the past.

At the car rental counter, Laura leased a white Peugeot 208 while Robert went to the restroom. She hastily loaded both sets of their luggage into the hatch then pulled into the passenger pick-up lane and waited just long enough to give the appearance that she was anticipating Robert's arrival. However, when a stream of buses made their timely appearance to pick up the throngs of tourists waiting at the curb, she squealed out of her parking space and threaded the compact three-door coupe through the maze of pedestrians and cabs. Her hasty launch caused no small amount of yelling and gesturing and also managed to get the attention of a *Polizia di Stato* officer who was already on his radio reporting the erratic driving to another officer on his motorcycle at the exit gates.

Once she was just clear of the passenger loading area and around a slight curve though, Laura hit the brakes, recovered from the lurch of the sudden stop then continued at a snail's pace. The car that had gone after her in pursuit did not. It shot out of the darkened ramp like a bullet and it was this vehicle that the officer on the motorcycle stopped. While it didn't match the description given of the offending vehicle, it was clearly the one grossly exceeding the speed limit of the terminal. Laura calmly made her way to the gate and motored onto the E80 toward Rome.

While this little maneuver was playing out, Robert exited the restroom, made his way to the railway station and boarded the Leonardo Express for his 30 minute ride into the city. His training and experience told him that he was not at the moment being tailed. Even so, he would not let his guard down as some people in the trade were like ghosts when it came to following a subject. Either way, once he was clear of the station he would dial a series of numbers into his phone and he would disappear into the protective abilities of Antonin Carafa within minutes of stepping off the train.

Antonin had come on board as the primary handler for the Pope just slightly after Robert had assumed the same role for Alexander. Normally, facilitating avenues of operation and protection for the Pope was one of the least complex of all the 12. The Swiss Guard provided an extraordinary level of around the clock protection and because he was the Pope, private meetings were commonplace. He could meet with anyone, anytime without having to divulge the nature of the meeting. Just as the Pope's role amongst the 12 was unique, so was the role of his handlers. Because of the visibility in the Pope's role as Bishop of Rome, Antonin acted as more of a liaison between the Pontiff and the remaining 11 than anything else. The others could travel freely without so much as a raised eyebrow. On the other hand, moving the Vicar of Christ from place to place was a significant undertaking that made news regardless of his destination.

Robert and he became fast friends during the time they worked together. Antonin was from a large Jewish Italian family with deep roots in Genoa and they had taken Robert in as if he was a long lost cousin from the New World. They lived in a palatial hillside home complete with crenellated battlements overlooking the coastal waters of the Ligurian. More than any other part of the job, he enjoyed his visits there most and the best part of the day was late afternoon. Most of the Carafa family would gather around four o'clock in the indoor courtyard or 'basilica' as they referred to it. At the center of the cobbled pavement was a quatrefoil shaped reflecting pool where the children would play and splash around while their parents looked on from various café tables. Beyond the planters of lush trees, flowers and plants were the arches of a shaded gallery that encompassed three sides of the courtyard. On one side, the teenagers would congregate and on the opposite side, the older men. From the center gallery was always a steady stream of women coming and going with trays of elaborately prepared food. Kosher northern Italian cuisine had to be the best food on the entire planet Robert concluded, and dining in this environment made him feel more at home and more secure than anywhere an only child raised by his father had ever felt in his life.

"I'm in the city." Robert spoke these words into his phone as soon as the other end connected.

"So I hear." Antonin ended the call without another word.

That was definitely not the response he'd anticipated. A half hour later, stepping off of the train into the throngs of people at Roma Termini, he understood why. As sure as he'd been that no one tailed him at the airport, he was now seeing the corral of operatives funneling him into a trap. To his trained eye the signs were obvious. During his years working the rope line for the President he had to see the crowd and individuals simultaneously, the proverbial forest and trees at the same time, never separately. Here in the train station, the symphony of human activity was not in synch. Heads turned in the wrong direction at the wrong time, a full cup of coffee with no steam rising from it, a suit coat hanging unnaturally because it was tailored to accommodate body armor and various holstered firearms, these all worked together in a way that allowed Robert to see their orchestrated movements as they closed in on him.

The options were racing through his mind: create a diversion and make a break, stand and fight, enlist the help of the authorities. None of them seemed to be optimal. He made his way through the crowd watching his watchers as he went. The exit was about 200 feet ahead of him with a mass of people in any direction.

Looking up toward the undulating lines of the wing shaped ceiling, he scanned the second level of shops to determine a possible point of egress.

His reconnaissance was violently interrupted by an enormously loud explosion that sent people running and screaming out of the terminal. Plumes of smoke bellowed through the mall like a heavy fog rolling in at an unnaturally rapid pace. Robert's reflexes set his body in motion toward the explosion but he was lifted off of his feet before he could take a single step.

Someone had him in a bear hug from behind and was pulling him into the enclosed kiosk right beside him. It was a small shop with purses from floor to ceiling. Its glass walls normally provided a 360 degree view of the area but the smoke was too thick and obstructed all lines of sight. The view became impossible though as the retractable security screens slammed closed and automatically bolted into the floor. He was a prisoner now. They'd obviously planned this very carefully, but he wasn't going down without a fight.

His jailer was well trained. Robert threw his butt rearward in the first motion of a full on Judo throw only to have the man shift his mass to the left and simply drop him to the floor. 'Twice in 24 hours I've been on the ground,' he thought to himself. 'This shit's getting old.'

"Ah Robert, you are truly a beautiful sight when you're angry." Antonin burst into robust peals of laughter.

"What the...?"

"Come. We'll eat."

His pursuers were rattling the solid metal rolling doors that had shut them out, but their time was very limited as blaring sirens and rescue workers closed in on them. It wouldn't have mattered anyway. The shopkeeper opened a diamond tread hatch in the floor behind the register revealing a spiral staircase that they took down into the bowels of the train station.

"The bomb?"

"It was theirs but it wasn't a bomb. An artillery simulator with the whistle disabled and smoke grenades. They almost had you, you know?"

"So I gather. How'd you know I'd be next to your little escape hatch?"

"I didn't! But I am the luckiest man in all Italia. Only, don't tell my wife about the secret door into a shop for purses. Then, I am not so lucky." Antonin broke into more laughter and slapped his old friend on the back as Robert was still trying to clear the clouds of disorientation from his mind.

Robert shook his head and snorted a little laugh of disbelief. A dozen or so of the opposition had been within a few seconds of snaring him in a pincer move, a fake bomb had just sent waves of terror through Rome's largest train station, and here they were in a subterranean service tunnel with Antonin laughing like it was the Carnival of Viareggio.

The muffled sounds of commotion above them indicated the full scale effort that would ultimately result in the discovery that it had been some kind of malicious prank. Little did they know it was actually the first in a series of ominous events that would bring an end to the reign of Boniface X.

"Antonin, we don't have a lot of time. I'm fairly certain Simon is being targeted for assassination."

His friend continued at a brisk pace toward a second spiral staircase that he ascended like a 22 year old athlete. Robert followed behind him and reiterated his concern. "Did you hear what I said?"

Antonin paused for a moment then started to open the hatch above his head.

"Antonin!" Robert raised his voice. "James is dead and they've abducted Mathias."

After peering through the hatch, the stocky Italian threw it back and popped out and extended his hand toward Robert who shielded his eyes as he emerged into the bright sunlight of the rail yard.

"And so it begins." He stood back as he said this holding Robert by his shoulders. "So good to see you my friend. So, so good to see you. Let's eat."

14

lexander's expression remained stoic, it was not the first time someone had ever made the suggestion for him to die. He also knew that they hadn't gone to this much trouble to simply kill him and dump his body into the Mediterranean. "You mean you need for it to *appear* as though I were dead?"

"Precisely."

"Then what?"

"Then we get you into the Vatican, you warn the Pope and find out what arrangements he's made with the Iranians."

"That seems like a lot of work for a dead guy."

"Alexander, the Pope leaves for Lebanon tomorrow. He cannot make that trip. They will hit him en route. There are multiple stages to an extremely well laid plan assuring he will never set foot in Beirut. He cannot be assassinated but neither can he make this trip. He's going to have to decide on his own not to go."

"What's in Lebanon?"

It was Ana's turn to stare into space.

"Ana, what's in Lebanon?"

"I don't know."

"Ana?"

Her response came in single word sentences, "I. Don't. Know."

"Then why are you so adamant that he must not land in Lebanon?"

"On November 9, 1938 in parts of Nazi Germany and Austria over 30,000 Jews were rounded up and sent to concentration camps. Synagogues, schools, stores and homes were ransacked. Families were separated. Men, women and children of all ages were herded like animals, beaten and killed."

"Kristallnacht."

The muscles in Ana's jaws rippled as she fought against her emotions. "It was of course only the tip of the full spear that would eventually plunge into the heart of Judaism, *die Endlösung der Judenfrage.*"

"The Final Solution..." Alexander breathed the words out.

"...of the Jewish question." Again, her jaws tightened and she looked as though she wanted to spit the vile taste of those words out of her mouth. "Whatever it is the Pope and the Iranians have conspired to do, it is believed that it will be tantamount to rolling the horror of Kristallnacht, Auschwitz, Treblinka, Sobibor, and Dachau all into one and all in one day."

Alexander considered what she was saying. When most people thought of the Church's Inquisition they did so in terms of the medieval period, but in actuality it lasted well into the 19th century in an official capacity, and some claimed that it continued today through more clandestine practices. When most people thought of the yellow badges Jews were forced to wear and the ghettos they were crammed into, they did so in terms of the Nazi regime, but it was in fact the Popes who had propagated that cause for hundreds of years before Hitler was born, and in some quarters the Church still reeked of anti-Semitism. The only Church publication to receive direct revision and approval by the Secretariat of State of the Holy See, 'Civiltà cattolica' conducted a campaign against Jews for over 100 years that only abated as late as 1965. The approved rhetoric against Jews in that publication was extreme and vile. Alexander had no trouble believing that the anti-Semitism was real, but the logistics of executing such a plan were nearly unimaginable.

"And you believe that this trip is the initiation of that plan?"

"I haven't seen the intelligence reports, but I believe they exist and I believe they are accurate enough to motivate the Gush Emunim to assassinate Pope Boniface X. But you see why he must not die?"

"Because it will not be seen as a radical group acting independently, it will be seen as the Jews killing the Vicar of Christ."

"Precisely." She drank a bit of water while studying Alexander's countenance. His wheels were turning as she allowed him to arrive at the conclusion on his own.

"Oh my God." He stood and began pacing the floor holding his hand at the back of his neck as if he was trying to make sure his head was still attached. "During the Fifth Crusade, Christians allied with Muslims in an attempt to retake Jerusalem but it failed miserably. Frederick II was so mortified by this embarrassment that he authorized the Holy Roman Empire to completely fund the Sixth Crusade. He was not only successful in retaking Jerusalem, but he got Nazareth, several smaller towns, a ten-year truce and ultimately accomplished more than the previous four crusades combined. All of this while commanding an inferior army compared to all of the previous crusades."

"Keep going." Ana was enjoying his immediate grasp of the circumstances.

"And now, a renewed partnership between them 800 years later represents their own version of the final solution, the Tenth Crusade. If, however your father is successful in killing the Pope, all Western support dissolves for Israel. By the time the world understands the implications of what's happened, the Nephilim will be at all-out war with an economically crippled and militarily weakened West."

"And it will be over before it begins."

"Because the depth of penetration by the Nephilim into the power structures of the West is so extensive, North America will shut down overnight. They've been buying up corporations for decades and shipping the jobs to more profitable venues. They control at least two-thirds of the military industrial complex and own roughly half the gold in the world."

"Did you not find it alarming that Germany recalled its 674 tons of gold from the Reserve Bank in New York?"

"I didn't realize they had. I've been a little out of the loop."

"While you've been asleep, the Nephilim have been busy putting the financial mechanisms in place to activate a global depression. Greece's bankruptcy was a controlled explosion."

"The very reason the 12 was formed so long ago was to remain above the influence of wealth and power.'For the love of money is the root of all evil.' We can stop them."

"But if you're all dead..."

"Then the door is wide open."

Once again her words echoed in his soul, "You handed it to them."

"OK, let's get started then."

Right on cue Mitri entered the saloon and stood by. Ana rose from her seat, "Mitri will take you to your stateroom. The clothes you'll need are hanging on the valet stand. Once you've dressed, join me up top and we'll finish the briefing."

He stood and followed Mitri out of the room. Ana took out her phone and dialed. "We're almost finished here."

"You have the information we need?"

"Yes."

"You showed him the footage of Laura being abducted?"

"Yes."

"And his scan indicated he was being truthful?"

"Yes."

"Good. Transmit the location of the stone and establish the live feed. I'll be waiting."

Her father clicked off on the other end and Ana headed up to the top deck. She had in fact not shown Alexander the footage of the Gush Emunim operatives abducting Laura. He would've never cooperated with the remainder of the mission and would've made it his singular purpose to free her. For now, he would have to be in the dark on that point.

Fifteen minutes later, he appeared through the doorway leading out onto the deck of the boat and came around the side of the bar wearing the Nino Corvato suit that had been on the plane.

"I'll say this for you, your taste in clothing is remarkable."

"The clothes do make the man." She hooked her right arm under his left and guided him to the deck rail.

He recognized the eerie mechanical sounds of a silenced nine millimeter ejecting three shell casings behind him as the reality of the crushing pain initiated in his back radiated through the rest of his body. His knees buckled, but Ana managed to keep him upright long enough to heave him over the side of the boat and into the churning wash below. Asa bent down to retrieve the spent brass. Walking back toward the covered area, she cast her eyes up to the camera that had witnessed and transmitted the execution scene back to her father. Her solemn nod indicated the job was complete.

15

"Antonin, I didn't come here alone and I didn't come here to eat."

"Yes, we know. She lost them at Fiumicino but they picked her back up at la Minerve."

"How do you know this and what the hell are we waiting for?" His patience with Antonin's nonchalant attitude had completely evaporated.

A 1980s model Lancia coupe with patches of weathered silver paint showing through the rust sat just outside the fencing of the rail yard. Antonin reached into the wheel well, retrieved a key and unlocked the door. Before getting in he looked across the top of the car, "We're not waiting, my friend."

"Enough with the word games, Antonin." He glared at him for a moment then ducked into the car.

They eased away from the fence line, got onto the Via Marsala then looped around the station and headed toward the Tiber. Theirs would've been considered a slow-speed get away at best, but with the calamity caused by the explosion and ensuing panic anything else would've drawn too much attention. Antonin threaded every alley and side street with the skill of a 10 year old pick-pocket after hitting his mark. They managed to avoid every bit of the snarled traffic as people fled Roma Termini.

"Your concern is understandable, but I assure you she is fine. We are watching her very closely. As for the Pope, well..." He paused with a thoughtful expression. "That has been in the making for a long time. Whether they get to him or not, tomorrow will be a very different day in this world of ours."

"Whether they get him or not?" The exasperation was evident in his tone. "Why don't you start with Laura?"

"They picked her up at la Minerve, the hotel. She was placing a dead drop for you. When she returned to her car it was being towed. Between her jet lag and the element of surprise she never had a chance. They of course were the one's pretending to tow her car away. We had a choice and the best one was snagging you at the station. They still don't know what happened." His satisfaction with a seamless operation brought a smile to his face.

"Who are 'they,' Antonin? Who has her?"

"Our Israeli friends, the Gush Emunim. The same ones who are going after the Pope."

"And you're not stopping them because...?"

"We need them to believe their plan is intact which, is why we snatched you instead of Laura. They needed her so that Alexander would divulge the location of the stone to protect her."

"This is far more than just the location of the stone, isn't it?"

For the first time since their reunion Antonin's disposition was grave. "This my old friend, is what we've been working against for so very long. Whether you realize it or not, we now stand at Tel Megiddo."

"Armageddon? Come on Antonin, you don't believe that any more than I do."

"Of course not, but there are those who believe it is their divine imperative to bring it about. Those opposing forces are preparing for the battle that will plunge humanity into darkness."

Robert considered what Antonin was saying as they pulled into a parking space at Sant'Eustachio, a church founded in the 8th century as a place to treat the poor and sick and named for a man who, not unlike Job, lost his wealth and family but managed to maintain his faith. At the apex of the roof where one would expect a cross to be, was one of the more unusual renditions of a cross he'd ever seen on a place of worship. It was a stag's head with a cross lodged between its antlers.

"Do they serve Jägermeister at Communion? I could get on board with that."

Antonin looked at him with some initial confusion that cleared as soon as Robert looked upward and directed his nod toward the strange homage.

"St. Eustace, patron saint of hunters and difficult situations. You're the Christian here, shouldn't *you* be the one telling me this?"

"Are you kidding me? I fled the church as fast as I could once I left home. We had to memorize the Bible like we were in some Christian version of a Sunday school madrasa, but we sure didn't learn about saints, and especially not ones that might be found on a liquor bottle."

Antonin opened and held the door for Robert. Compared to the massive cathedrals that marked the landscape of Europe, Sant'Eustachio was humble, yet the detail was no less stunning. The Baroque frieze work, gilded columns, polished wood and marble definitely had the effect of transporting one away from the ordinary. If the indigent and infirm that sought respite here believed human agency might have a role in salvation, then surely it must look like this. Hovering in contrast to the ornate beauty above the altar was an oil painting by the 18th century master Francesco Ferdinandi, 'The Martyrdom of Eustace and His Family.' The depiction of the saint and his family being roasted inside of a bronze bull was perhaps commissioned to remind pilgrims of the cost of discipleship. Whatever the reason, it effectively illuminated the framework of violence that had surrounded Christianity from its inception.

As Robert surveyed the cruciform room, Antonin continued through the nave and up to the altar without breaking stride. Robert had to hurry to keep up. Antonin was built like an English bulldog, but his agility and pace was more like that of a hummingbird. On either side of the altar were two more columns. Again, without so much as a pause, Antonin disappeared around the side of one of the columns. Robert was not far behind him, but was not in time to have seen the hidden door open and swallow his friend. He lowered his upper torso for clearance and followed through the portal and down yet another spiral staircase as the door closed silently behind him.

"Well this is new."

"Yes, it is. It's only been here since the late 16th century." Antonin's infectious laughter filled the catacomb-like tunnel they were now traversing. "Clement VII only barely survived the sack of Rome by escaping to the Castel Sant'Angelo through the Passetto di Borgo, a secret corridor that has saved many pontiffs since. But, once Sant'Angelo became a tourist attraction, other tunnels had to be constructed. This one is the closest to the Pantheon and the Hotel Sole which is where they are holding Laura."

Antonin turned into a narrow corridor that ended at a reinforced metal door. He placed his hand up to a barely visible plasma screen on the adjacent wall. There was a brief flash of light from the screen followed by the dull thud of the door locks releasing. A heavenly aroma engulfed them as they entered the room. Robert could barely comprehend what his senses were absorbing. It was as if he'd stepped into one of lower Manhattan's hallowed Italian restaurants. Beneath barrel vaulted ceilings, long family-dining style tables lined each side of the expansive room. Oil lamps flickered and reflected on the various bottles and glasses of wine along each table. Scarcely any of the dozen or so diners looked up from their meals or conversations as the two of them entered. In fact, only two amongst them even seemed to notice their presence at all. At the far end of the table to their left a noticeably fit young couple sat together with what appeared to be an iPad propped up between them. The man waved and stood half-way to make sure Antonin saw where they were sitting.

Robert was still trying to process his surroundings as they took seats on either side of the two. "Robert, this is Jorah and Judith Greco."

"*Piacere.*" His greeting came out in a tone of uncertainty. "Antonin, what is this place?"

"Ever hear of the Jewish Alliance?"

Robert cast his gaze briefly to the right as something about that name did sound familiar. "The resettlement group?"

"Well, not precisely. Prior to WWII, the Alliance was established as an organization promoting the peaceful absorption of Jews into Palestine. But, during WWII, a violent group splintered off and began a campaign of intimidation, murder and terror. In the decades following the war, several similarly disposed underground groups emerged but their funding was spread too thin. So, over the last seven years all of these groups have combined under one umbrella."

This last statement got Robert's attention, "The Gush Emunim?"

"Yes, though outsiders are the only ones that still use that name for them. They are extremely well funded and extraordinarily secretive. We on the other hand are essentially the original Alliance. Our goals are similar but our tactics are very different. The Alliance exists to assist Jews of the Diaspora in times of crisis and work toward a peaceful coexistence between Palestinians and Jews."

Two servers carrying large trays of food approached their table. A bowl of gnocchi and fire roasted vegetables was placed between Robert and Judith while a platter of lamb chops with garlic and rosemary was placed on the opposite side between Antonin and Jorah. All of them began serving their plates except Jorah. He did not take his eyes off the iPad even while being introduced to Robert. Judith looked over at him and still without looking up he said, "Go ahead." At this she picked up her fork and using the side of it cut one of the gnocchi in half.

"Married?"

Judith laughed and for the first time Jorah glanced in Robert's direction, but only for a split second.

"No," she replied "brother and sister. Twins."

"Oh, sorry. I just... But I see now..."

Antonin was laughing as he finished off one lamb chop and began carving into another. "They are our finest surveillance team and I promise you they are telepathic so be careful."

Robert pushed back from the table, stood and walked over to Jorah's side. The young man turned the tablet so he could have a better view. The screen was divided into nine squares, each showing a live video feed. The upper left appeared to be an empty service corridor with a freight elevator in center view. To the right of that was a view of a long interior hallway with two men sitting on either side of a metal door with a 9 inch square glass window at about head height. Each of the remaining squares had views of hallways and doors that seemed to penetrate more deeply into a building. In the center was a video feed of a woman lying on the tiled floor of what appeared to be a storeroom. Her hands were bound behind her back and though it was difficult to tell for certain it appeared that her mouth was covered. His heart was pounding and every muscle was tensed.

"What are we waiting for? Let's go get her."

Neither Jorah nor Judith reacted in the least to his demand. Antonin took another bite of the lamb.

"Where the hell is this? *I'll* go get her!"

Some of the other diners looked over toward their end of the table in response to his raised and agitated voice, but then went back to their own conversations and meals.

"My friend, finish your meal. We already have her."

16

Alexander's senses were reeling but he had presence of mind enough to align his body for a water landing. The dark waters of the Mediterranean Sea violently swallowed him in a deafening rush of water and air bubbles. Though he was reasonably certain he would surface, the downward descent was unnerving. Something seemed to be squeezing his upper thighs and was spreading upward toward his glutes, then to his upper torso and arms. This couldn't be good he thought as he suddenly remembered that he'd been shot. Was this the sensation of being paralyzed? Had one of the three bullets hit his spine? Was he dying?

Right as the dark notions of his potential demise were sinking in, his descent slowed and then reversed almost simultaneously. Whatever was happening to him was unlike anything he'd ever experienced. His ascent was increasing in speed and without any assistance from him. He broke the surface of the water and took in a gasp of air beneath a swath of stars that seemed close enough to touch. Stretching into the distance was the sound of the yacht motoring away from him and he was sitting in a position similar to that of being in a lounge chair. The Nino Corvato suit was obviously no ordinary Nino Corvato. Nothing had seemed unusual about its weight or drape when he'd put it on, but the water had obviously activated a series of flotation panels, and judging by the fact that he was still pulling and pushing air from his lungs, it must've been bullet resistant as well.

He was beginning to organize his thoughts as much as possible. The rapidity of the events had left him somewhat bewildered, but even now he wouldn't have time to continue his analysis. Somewhere behind him was the sound of waves being broken at a high rate of speed, yet absent of the sound of a boat motor. Whatever was making the sound was headed right for him and he had no way of signaling them so he wouldn't be hit. He began a struggle to get himself free from the specially designed suit so he could swim more rapidly and effectively away from the oncoming danger, but it was of no use. The suit had him in what was supposed to be a life saving grasp. Ironic that it was probably going to be the thing that got him killed. Hoping to create any distance at all between them, Alexander began kicking and thrashing away from the oncoming and invisible behemoth. Whatever it was, it was right on top of him. It slowed briefly. Alexander was whipped around to his side then yanked straight up and out of the water. He was airborne for just a moment, and then was hurled back first into the waiting arms of a commando dressed from head to toe in black.

He was preparing for a fight, but the voice in his ear gave him some reassurance that it wouldn't be necessary. "Mr. Kilpatrick, my name is Daniel Jenco and I have orders to deliver you to the Vatican at 0400. Until that time, please let me know what I can do to make you more comfortable."

Even if the man had been lying, it was obvious that any fight he might have put up would've been short lived. The team that had him consisted of five heavily armed and very serious looking commandos. Besides, he obviously would already be dead or have been left for dead if that was the plan. It was becoming obvious that Ana had done a masterful job of convincing her father that he'd been effectively dispatched. But what about the location of the stone? She'd never even bothered to ask for a viable lie to tell Ephrem.

His line of thinking was once again disturbed by yet another unexpected sound. The unmistakable thump of rotor wash was echoing off the water as a twin-engine Chinook helicopter passed overhead and trimmed out of the sky just ahead of them. A flurry of radio chatter began between the commandos.

"Mr. Kilpatrick, here please." Jenco, the operative that caught him after being flung onboard was indicating a forward position on the port side of the craft. He pointed to a commando on the starboard side indicating that he should brace himself in the same way. The whine of the Chinook's engines grew louder. Alexander straightened his left leg out on top of the tubular gunwale and bent his right knee up toward his chest while tucking it under the tube. With his left hand he grabbed a nylon strap and held his face against the inflated rubber. The boat's pilot gunned the silenced outboard motor and they rocketed up into the chopper via a ramp that had been lowered into the water.

Jenco extended his arm down toward Alexander who was still hugging the craft for dear life. He grasped the man's forearm and was helped up off of the boat. The man reached behind him, felt for something inside the coat collar and squeezed. The tension of the flotation panels released. He performed the same procedure on the trousers then helped Alexander out of the coat. Another of the team put a reflective rescue blanket over his shoulders and ushered him toward a seat in the cabin. A medic knelt in front of him and began asking a series of routine questions beginning with, "Are you OK?" Honestly, he didn't know. He'd been shot three times in the back, hurled off the back of a boat into the sea, thought he was going to possibly drown or just be left to die, nearly run over by a virtually silent boat, snatched up out of the water, smuggled onto the boat that nearly hit him, then ramped up into a helicopter hovering just a few feet off the water's surface. "OK" was not a term he would use to describe his current state of mind.

After a thorough going over by the medic, Jenco returned dragging an oversized dry bag. He rolled the heavy rubberized collar of the bag down and unzipped its top flap. Inside was another set of clothing that he'd seen hanging in his cabin on the plane. Obviously Mitri or Asa had shoved this bag overboard shortly before Ana had done the same to him. "Sir, we're going to need you to change into these."

"Let me guess, you're going to throw me out of this chopper and a parachute is going to deploy from the back pockets of the trousers."

Jenco smiled but was obviously too focused on his task for a back and forth repartee. "No sir, but I'm thinking you'll at least want to show up in dry clothing for your meeting."

Alexander had to steady himself as the Chinook made a sharp bank to the east for the journey inland. He took the clothing from Jenco and began the process of peeling off his suit. Once fully dressed he peered over into the dry bag. There was a hard sided polymer case inside that he was reaching for when Jenco returned and put his hand on his shoulder. He handed Alexander a headset. "These will help."

He fitted the set onto his head, "Much better, thanks."

Jenco reached into the bag, pulled out the polymer case and opened it on the seat between them. "Your new phone." Alexander powered it up and began scrolling through the screens. Jenco pointed to a solitary and blank icon badge on the last page. "You'll need to press and hold this one when you're ready for exfiltration. The screen will go black and we'll pick you up wherever that phone is."

In other words, he thought, don't lose this phone. "OK...what else?

He then held out Alexander's .357 which caused him to smile.

"You know, every time I think I've lost that little gun for good it always comes right back. But I don't think I'll be using it for this conversation. I mean, Boniface has a mean left hook but I think I can take him."

Jenco couldn't help chuckling this time and shook his head. "It's not for him, I assure you. But, if for some reason you end up on the outside of the Vatican walls they'll know it's you within 10 to 15 seconds. They have cameras watching every possible angle outside the walls with foolproof recognition software. If that happens get your ass to Castel Sant'Angelo as fast as possible and break the doors down if you have to. Honestly sir, you probably won't make it, but that's your best chance."

"That would also expose Ana wouldn't it?"

There was a momentary flash of emotion on Jenco's face. His eyes narrowed and he bit his inner lip just enough that Alexander could tell. "Yes, sir." He said this through clenched teeth.

He sat for a few seconds contemplating that potential. "Well then, we just won't let that happen, will we?"

"Sir, I've found that Mr. Murphy tends to show up at the worst possible moments."

"True," Alexander opened the cylinder and checked every round. They weren't his. "But Mr. Murphy, his law and I are old acquaintances. I know how to deal with him."

"I wouldn't trust them either, but you can."

He didn't quite understand at first.

"The rounds. I wouldn't want to go into a hairy situation without full confidence in my ammo either. The best I can do is tell you that I loaded them myself. Three are 125 grain FP XTPs and two are 140 grain FTXs. Those are the two with the red points." He handed him a speed-load strip of the same sequence. "Ten rounds is not much to work with, but it's better than nothing."

His confidence returned. They'd obviously been planning this operation for a while. "Thank you, we'll be fine. We've been through worse together."

"It's not the arrow, it's the Indian?"

"Something like that."

"A lot of people respect your abilities, Mr. Kilpatrick."

"Please, call me Alex."

"On the other hand, a lot of people blame you for this mess."

"Are you one of them?"

"They say you went after the Nephilim on your own. That takes balls. Then you got benched in one of China's toughest prisons, and lived. It takes a hard man to endure that." Jenco was looking at him as if he was making his final judgment based on the merger of all the talk and of having finally met him. "No, I'm not one of them. This shit was going down sooner or later. Our friend down there has wanted to wipe my people off the face of the earth since he was a teenager. Hell, who knows, Alex? Your timeout may have flushed them all out of the shadows giving us the best opportunity we're going to have to protect ourselves."

"Any theories on how he's going to do it?" It was killing Alexander that he'd had it in the palm of his hand and let it slip right through his fingers. One glance at the phone after retrieving the data would've likely revealed what he needed to know.

"Not really. All we know for sure is that the crazy Persian and he are definitely cooking something up."

The radio chatter started up once again. The rapid fire Italian had him a little lost but he could tell they were getting close.

Jenco pulled out a map of Vatican City. "Listen. It's going to be a touch and go so you'll need to be ready to hit it running. He's expecting you and is supposed to meet you alone in the French Garden, here." He pointed to an area just off the heliport. "The Swiss Guard will keep their distance but they'll have you zeroed the entire time. I'm sure you already knew that. After your meeting, you're to go to the Villa Pia, here."

"The Academy of Sciences."

"Right." Jenco's expression grew stern. "Do not let them take you anywhere else. If they try, insist that you go to the Villa Pia first. If they try to force you, make a break for it and we'll do the best we can."

Outside, Rome's warm amber glow was deceptively hospitable. The landscape of his former life had changed dramatically since his departure from it. There was an uneasy balance before, but now it seemed everything was on the verge of collapse. Had his retreat really been the catalyst for all of this?

"Sir? Alex?"

He was adrift in thought as he stared blankly over the 2500 year old city, Roma Capitale. "Sorry."

"We can't assume that the Alliance has not been compromised. If that's the case…"

"If that's the case, then I will likely die for the second time tonight."

Nothing but the slight sound of a high pitched frequency could be heard through their headsets as they looked at each other. The helicopter banked to the north and circled around.

"OK, let's get you ready. Good luck."

Alexander took off his headset and handed it to Jenco who put it on the seat along with the now empty case. He checked the cylinder one more time and lined it up to fire on the first of the three lighter loads. The gardens were dark and there were no landing lights on at the helipad. Jenco gave a hand signal to one of the commandos standing at the side door as the chopper began a rapid and sharp descent.

Standing at the door he reminded himself of what Jenco had said moments before, "It's not the arrow, it's the Indian."

17

"Antonin, you'd better start talking fast. If anything happens to that girl..."

"Robert, Robert...it's OK. Please."

Everyone in the place was now silent and watching the four of them. Robert was still standing behind Jorah where he'd been looking at Laura on the screen. He looked as if he was about to launch across the corner of the table at the throat of his old friend.

"Please, Robert. I swear to you, she is in no danger. If she were, you would have to push me out of the way to get to her first."

Robert eased his stance and relaxed his shoulders that had been poised for an assault. One by one the others went back to their meals and discussions.

"As I said before, she's being held at Hotel Sole. They made the grab while posing as a towing service." He stood and walked over to Robert's side. He pointed to the screen shot of the two men sitting on either side of the door. "But, this man on the left, he is our man." He then pointed to another screen shot in the lower right hand corner of the screen, "And this man is ours as well. The hotel is completely ours and is teeming with our people. We're the ones that directed them there."

Robert retook his seat. He had absolutely no appetite, but needed to sit down. Antonin sat back down and took a sip of his wine.

"Besides, judging by how they say she laid you out, we may need to protect them from her instead of the other way around." With the tension broken, he erupted into laughter. Robert's face turned red.

"How did they...did you...?" He was flummoxed.

"They were on Trowbridge closer than his own shadow. In his day he was the best, but he was starting to slip and they had him nailed down for at least a year and a half. They knew he was going to see Alex before he knew it himself. They orchestrated it because without Alex they couldn't make this work. They needed him more than any of the others because the biggest bargaining chip with the Nephilim was the location of the stone."

"So how long have you had the Gush Emunim infiltrated?"

"From the time they started regaining power in the underground. We knew this day would come, we knew what their goals were and we were well prepared." He lifted his glass in a salute. "The black ops world of your country is to be admired and respected. We learned well at your feet. But now, we are the best in the world at what we do." He took a generous sip of wine.

"And what of the Gush Emunim? Are they as capable?"

"Capable? Yes. Effective? Ultimately, no." He leaned in toward Robert. "They believe in war and death. They believe they will possess and rule Israel by destroying her enemies. I ask you, when has this ever been effective?" He filled Robert's wine glass from the carafe and continued. "We believe in peaceful coexistence even if it is not a perfect peace. There is an old Yiddish saying, that a bad peace is better than a good war. This has traditionally been the philosophy of the Alliance."

Robert held his wineglass by the stem and rotated it but didn't lift it from the table. "So you stand between those who would destroy you and your own people who would, in the end bring destruction to Israel? That's a good place to get yourself killed."

"And yet, we have stood in this place for two millennia." He finished his wine and refilled the glass. "Robert, have you never wondered about my family?"

"Well, honestly no. I love them and feel like I'm at home and on vacation at the same time when I'm with them, but I've never wondered about anything more than how they put up with you." He was teasing his old friend, but Antonin ignored the good natured ribbing as one who had something more to say.

"Robert, Robert, Robert..." He shook his head, laughed vigorously and patted the table with both hands. "For *over* 2000 years, my family has been here through persecutions, expulsions, the inquisitions of the Renaissance, the Fascists, and the Nazis. On and on they keep going, trying to destroy us, but...here we have stood and here we will stand. For over 2000 years the members of my family have held up the obligations of Simon, *not* the Pope." He spoke the pontifical title as if it was barbed wire in his mouth. "And we have done so with honor and integrity even when there were treacherous and murderous Popes holding that office."

Jorah and Judith looked at each other with concern. "Antonin." Judith had a maternal tone in her voice. "Perhaps this is not the best time for this discussion."

"No!" This time he slapped the table with one hand causing the dinnerware to rattle and clink. "Robert is *mio fratello*. I would die for him and I know without a blink of my eye he would die for me. No matter what happens tonight, we are at war. The best we can expect is for Mathias to slow Simon's plan. We have grown sleepy watching and waiting for our enemies to attack us from the front. We build fences and impose sanctions. We demand for inspectors to be allowed to oversee nuclear operations in their lands. We encroach on the land we say is theirs and then call it

115

ours because we are arrogant. We force them into ghettos that we call 'territories' and we antagonize and humiliate them. *We* have become what we hate."

Robert remained silent as did the rest of the room. Even the noises from the kitchen had completely stopped. Antonin took a deep breath as he surveyed the room.

"We have become what we hate and we have gotten into bed with our oldest enemy, the Nephilim. Our next oldest enemies have joined together to destroy us. I ask you, I ask you all...how do you think this ends?" Antonin stood from his seat. "How do you think this ends? The 20th Century was the bloodiest of human history. 230 million died to genocide alone. Yet, what is coming is far worse. And who stands between them?"

No one dared to speak. Robert had never seen his friend like this. Antonin was always jovial and rarely finished even one glass of wine, but these were not the intoxicated ramblings of an old man who feels he is no longer heard or useful. This had the feel of an old soldier on the eve of a great battle lamenting what the young soldiers could not yet comprehend.

"We stand between them. And no one else." He put both of his hands on the table as he leaned toward Robert. "What does your Christian Bible say about peacemakers?"

The question took him by surprise and he felt as though he was seven years old again being called on during Bible drills. "Peacemakers?" He had to think for a moment. "Oh, blessed. They are blessed."

"Yes my friend, but what is the rest of that Beatitude of Jesus of Nazareth?"

He took another couple of seconds and it dawned on him as it never had before, "Blessed are the peacemakers for they shall be called sons of God."

"Jesus of Nazareth, the heir of David was not calling for a new religion, he was rousing those who had fallen into a complacent slumber. He was asking the sons of

God, the Bene Elohim to wake up and once again stand between those who would destroy each other."

Antonin definitely had Robert's attention with this last revelation. Alex had spoken to him of the Bene Elohim once before but it was in a different context, or so he thought.

"For 2000 years the 12 and the Bene Elohim have been the ones standing between those who would destroy each other and the world. We fell asleep 70 years ago and you see what happened then. Now, we've fallen asleep again. Mathias tried to tell us but we wouldn't listen, so he went against them on his own. He was the only one who saw the storm clouds gathering, and what did we do? We hid him in a prison for his own protection. What a laugh our enemies must have had at our expense. We locked away the only one willing to see and speak the truth." Antonin sat down with a sad expression. He looked down at the table, at his plate of bones. "If they had killed him we would have listened *then*. That is how we have always treated our prophets, we laugh at them, deride them and kill them. Then, we decide they must have been right all along."

"Antonin..." Jorah had a panicked urgency in his voice.

"I am finished." He took a small sip of wine.

Without another word, Jorah bolted from the table and burst through the door on the opposite side from where Antonin and Robert had entered. Judith looked down at the iPad. *"Merda!"*

"What?" Antonin demanded.

"It's Laura. She's gone."

18

Alexander hit the pad and ran out from under the rotors that were already lifting the massive aircraft back up into the darkened predawn sky. They'd outfitted him with a pair of New Balance tactical boots that eased his landing and that actually felt pretty good as he jogged toward the French Garden. The khaki pants and light blue shirt wouldn't have been his attire of choice, but they also appeared to be designed with maneuverability in mind. The final piece of gear was a lightweight black vest that he sincerely hoped was made of the same bullet proof material as the suit. However, once he got a look at the rendezvous point, he was fairly certain it wouldn't have mattered what he was wearing. The garden was a terrace on a gentle slope surrounded by thick evergreens. In the middle was a geometrically perfect layout of manicured boxwoods with a fountain at each end of the rectangular plateau. His approach led to a pea gravel walkway that extended the distance of the garden with various entrances to other labyrinth-like pathways. A figure, presumably the Pope, stood in the shadows amongst a copse of cedar trees at the far end of the garden. Meeting him there would put them on the downward side of the slope and there was no telling how many Swiss Guard would be tucked into the lower branches of the trees around them. If they wanted him, they had him.

"Simon."

"Mathias."

It was about as cold a greeting without actually referring to the diminished quality of each other's heritage as one could imagine.

"You've been playing a deadly game with deadly people and the Israelis have what they need to prove it." Simon didn't seem to register what he was saying or perhaps didn't care. "But I don't think it's something that will ever go to court."

"Where is the stone, Mathias?"

It was his turn to ignore what was being said. It appeared this was going to be an exercise in talking past one another. "I'm telling you, your life expectancy once you set foot outside of these walls is about seven seconds."

"Then I would ask you, who is truly playing deadly games with deadly people? Did you come here to threaten me?"

"I came here to tell you that these people are willing to go to any length to stop you and though it wouldn't exactly break my heart if it happened, the assassination of the Pope by a group of Jewish terrorists would destabilize everything we are supposed to protect. I came here to stop you from setting the world on fire."

Simon's grin seemed sinister as it spread across his wrinkled and mottled face like an opening doorway to Abaddon. "You've been gone for a long time, Mathias. Things change. In our world there is more transition in one day than the rest of the oblivious world experiences in a year. You chose to rejoin the oblivious world. You should return there."

"I was quite happy doing just that until James dropped back into my life and then got himself killed."

Simon tried to cover his momentary surprise but Alexander, even in the darkness, had seen the look on his face.

"Technically, having been shot in the back three times and dumped into the Tyrrhenian, I'm somewhat dead too."

Simon looked concerned. "And whom do I have to thank for bringing Lazarus back?"

"In light of your plans, I think you know I can't tell you that. I can definitively tell you though, they *will* get to you. You have a trip arranged to Lebanon, but you'll never make it to Beirut. If their covert means fail they are willing to take you out in a far more demonstrative manner. When the world cries out, they will share the information that Walter carried in his veins."

"You have deciphered it for them." Simon's face darkened as hatred seemed to ooze from his weathered pores. A thousand curses roiled just behind his quivering lips. "You fool." The words curled out of his mouth in a way that reminded Alexander of the wisps of smoke from burning coals. The stench of hatred and death emanated from this man certainly as much or more than any of the other ruinous Popes of the 15th and 16th centuries.

"No matter." The old man's countenance relaxed. "You have come out of your retirement far too late to be of any use to them. The information is of minimal consequence now as well and whether I live or die will not matter."

Alexander knew this was a lie. It may not matter to the execution of his plans whether he lives or dies at this point, but if there had ever been a coward in this office it was the withered man before him. Cowards were never willing to die for a cause.

"It matters to them and I have every confidence that if you don't heed my advice you will become a most unworthy martyr between now and your trip."

Simon appeared to be lost in thought as he again ignored Alexander's words. "You say you came here to stop me from setting the world on fire. The fire was set long ago, Mathias. We are merely picking up where the faithful before us left off."

Somewhere to the southwest of where they stood an explosion ruptured Rome's early morning peace. Instinctively, Alexander went into a low crouch while Simon remained stationary. The trees around them expelled the agents that he'd known were there all along.

"You son of a bitch!" He said this mid-stride as he cleared a low stone partition and tucked into a roll down the slope behind them.

Simon called after him, "The world is on fire, Mathias! It burns the unwashed and illuminates the righteous!"

There was a phalanx of operatives waiting on him as he sprang up from his down-hill roll. He'd already anticipated their countermeasure as he jogged through this position on his way up to the garden and considered how they might come at him. They were trying to funnel him toward the underside of a rock footbridge; it was definitely the path of least resistance and looked like an inviting escape route. He obliged them for the first few yards of his flight and heading directly toward the little tunnel, but just as he reached the opening he ran himself down into a crouch and then uncoiled his legs like a couple of leaf-springs. He launched upward toward the embankment where the Pope and he had been standing. He scrambled up the rocky terrain interspersed with junipers and small boulders then popped up outside of their pincer formation. The sound of an angry bee moving at hypersonic speeds zipped just a little too close to his head. It had been a silenced shot from a sniper and very much unlike the monstrous blast from the small sized Smith & Wesson he'd drawn from his front right pocket. Alexander sent two rounds down on either side of the bridge that in turn sent his pursuers scrambling for cover.

He was counting on the fact that they would underestimate him and that four extremely loud gunshots on the Vatican grounds would cause mass confusion amongst the 900 residents of Vatican City. Sirens were already blaring through the city as first responders raced to the scene of the helicopter crash in Rome's largest public park. Alexander estimated that he had to cover about 150 yards to the Villa Pia. He didn't know what or who would be there, but he really hoped they had a jet-pack. Short of that, he didn't know how he was getting out of there alive. For the moment, he would continue running in an erratic pattern toward the goal line. They wouldn't take the chance of sending an uncontrolled spray of gunfire down range and he was taking full advantage of the difficulty to hit a randomly shifting target. He only had one shot remaining and no time to reload. Could he be fortunate enough to make the distance without running headlong into one of them?

His answer came all too quickly as he approached the walled courtyard of the Villa. Two gunmen taking cover behind two large urns atop the wall encircling the piazza had him in their sights. One round and two tangos was not the equation he'd hoped to experience in the home stretch. The closest cover was a tall thin palm just under 10 yards to his right. Time seemed to slow for Alexander. He raised his revolver taking aim at the sniper to his far left and ran toward the one almost directly in front of him. If he could take out the one on the left while causing the one ahead to adjust his line of fire downward, he might have just enough time to move along the base of the wall and reload on the other side of the enormous columned pavilion just around the curve.

Alexander fired and missed. Shards of stone sprayed outward from the urn. The gunman that had been taking cover there spun back and to his left then tumbled forward and over the meter high wall. He landed in a motionless heap.

His bewilderment would have to wait. He continued his dash into the wall, hugged up to it as much as possible and turned toward the pavilion. The second sniper moved to the other side of the urn, lead Alexander's position just enough, slid his finger from the trigger guard to the trigger, drew in a slow breath and began squeezing. It was too late. His head snapped forward and he crumpled onto the stone piazza. The errant round he'd posthumously fired caromed off the Academy building that sat 20 yards away.

He dumped the four spent casings and one live round, pulled the speed strip out of his left pocket and reloaded. The corner of the pavilion was just ahead and he ran wide of it in the event there was an unfriendly waiting for him. Sprays of dirt began erupting around him as silenced rounds plowed up the earth. He cut in toward the back side of the pavilion, tucked into a roll then slammed himself into a flattened position against the wall and for the moment was out of the line of fire. There was not much time before the tactical team would be on top of him. If he could cut through the pavilion and onto the piazza he might have a chance to grab the downed man's rifle. Alexander's adrenaline was surging and he was processing his surroundings in the minutest detail. All of his senses were hyper alert, but nothing could've prepared him for what he saw when he vaulted himself up onto the cold marble floor of the pavilion. There with her hand extended to help him up was Ana Goldman. Moreover, the sight that momentarily froze him in his tracks was that of a tall woman with a 6.5 Grendel on an AR15 platform methodically picking off shooters as they ran toward her position.

Laura turned toward Ana who gave a single nod. She then flipped the fire selector to three round bursts and laid down covering fire as she crossed behind each of the columns to reach Alexander and Ana on the opposite side.

"Hey."

"Hey?"

19

A panel in the marble wainscoting was open at knee height. Laura took a knee and held her weapon at the low ready while scanning for movement. Ana pushed herself feet first through the door followed by Alexander and finally Laura. Inside they were standing on a platform that put the hidden door at head height. Ana closed and locked the panel into place. They could hear the scramble of feet and muffled voices resonating through the pavilion.

"They think we've made a run for the academy building." Ana said this while walking nonchalantly down the corridor steps.

"How do you know that?" Alexander was still out of breath and noticing for the first time that his hands were scraped and bleeding.

Ana held up her hand in a gesture asking him to give her a few moments of silence. She then pulled her hair back so he could see the earpiece that was allowing her to hear their pursuers every transmitted word. They stopped in front of a steel door at the bottom of the steps.

"I didn't realize the Swiss Guard was so clumsy with their communications."

She held her hand up more emphatically this time and listened for a few more seconds before responding. "They're not Swiss Guard."

After scanning her handprint into the adjacent security screen, Ana held the door open for them. Once inside with the door sealed, Ana was no longer able to receive data transmissions so she removed the earpiece. "*Spada di San Pietro* or simply '*Spada*' for short."

"Help me out here."

"The Sword of St. Peter."

He shook his head and shrugged his shoulders.

"Think of them as Boniface's own Delta Force. You're lucky to be alive."

"Yeah well, the day is young." Laura pulled him over to her. Ana continued down the corridor and disappeared around a curve.

They embraced and locked into a long deep kiss. He tried to keep his bloody hands from touching her and pulled back a little. "My hands...I'm sorry..."

She pulled him back into her arms and forced his hands around and onto her back. Her entire torso began to shake with an emotional energy that moved gradually into her throat and then forced streams of tears. She put her head on his shoulder and allowed her full weight to collapse onto him. The mixture of thoughts and feelings was overwhelming. It was the first time since being in his lap after the morning swim that she'd felt secure. That was both comforting and frightening. She'd never depended on anyone for much of anything, certainly not emotional security. Yet here she was, half way around the world rescuing the love of her life only to dissolve into his arms in a teary mess.

He lifted her up slightly and pulled back enough to see her face. "Hey..." His voice was soft and reassuring. He wiped a tear from her cheek. "God, I love you."

This declaration sent another flood of emotion coursing through her and she held him even tighter. They held each other in silence for several minutes. "Yeah, well

I would think so. This is the second monumental mess I've pulled you out of Mr. Kilpatrick."

They both laughed and Laura noticed for the first time that he'd also been crying. "I guess I didn't realize you had such a propensity for, how did Robert put it? Thinking you could 'take on Hell and half of Georgia' all by yourself."

"So I take it you've met my long dormant handler."

"Let's just say it was an introduction we'll both remember for a long time."

He looked at her with a quizzical look, "Dropped in on you unannounced did he? Poor guy. Is he out of the hospital yet?"

"I think his pride was more wounded than anything else."

Alexander chuckled a bit, "I sent a distress call to him but never imagined the two of you would connect or that you'd *both* end up here."

Laura shook her head as they turned to start their walk back to the tunnel beneath Sant'Eustachio. "For a person of your intellect you sure are oblivious sometimes."

"What's that supposed to mean?"

"What did you think he was going to do, come charging in the second he got the call? For all he knew it could've been a trap. He did what I would've done. He did some recon, got as much intel as he could, then got himself to you as quickly as he possibly could. Which let me tell you, has not been easy. They've been on top of us since Walter made his visit."

"I *told* you."

The withering look she gave him was a clear indication that this was not an 'I told you so' moment. He wisely backed off of the history lesson he was dying to give and chose to

127

listen to how she'd come to this point instead. Ana had filled her in on most of the details of his journey, so there was not much filling in he needed to do. By the time they got back to the dining facility Alexander had fallen into a kind of stunned silence. Between what he'd learned from Ephrem and Ana, the blatant attempt on his life on the Vatican grounds and what Laura was now telling him, WWIII had indeed already begun.

Ana was waiting on them at the door and let them in without a word. "Ana." Alexander wanted to talk to her about Jenco and the helicopter but she disappeared down a side corridor as soon as the door swung open.

He looked at Laura, "They were..."

"Oh, I know. They were going to be married."

"No."

"Yes."

"Boniface knew whomever was dropping me off would be his enemy and he was prepared for them. None of us could have seen that coming. I mean, what Pope has and uses a rocket propelled grenade to take down a helicopter in the middle of Rome? He's an evil man, Laura. I should've unseated him years ago."

"No one blames you for this, except perhaps you. Don't do that to yourself."

Alexander dropped his head as they stood just inside the doorway. "Jenco was a hell of a guy. You could tell." He contemplated the look on the young commando's face as they discussed Ana. "You should go to her."

"No, not now. She's working against her own father and the man her father is trying to kill is the man who just blew her fiancé and several of her closest friends out of the sky. She's about three seconds from carpet bombing the Vatican and no one would blame her. Give her some space."

They walked over to the table where Jorah, Judith, Antonin and Robert were talking in subdued tones. Antonin especially was uncharacteristically somber. He rose from his chair at their approach and managed a smile while embracing Alexander. "It is good to see you, Mathias."

"And you my friend. How long?"

"Too long, far too long. And this one..." He looked with admiration at Laura. "This one. I am happy to have her on our side. We had at least a dozen cameras on her."

"Try two dozen." Jorah interjected.

"We had our own people surrounding her to keep her safe while the Gush Emunim thought they had her. We look away for one second and like a spirit," Antonin snapped his fingers "she was gone."

She had neglected to relay this part of the story to Alexander and she seemed rather embarrassed as Antonin spoke of her abilities like a proud father.

"By the time we got there she was through the door, had knocked their guy cold and was holding our guy that she thought was *their* guy at gunpoint with her hands still bound in front of her. I think if we had not shown up when we did the video would have shown a grown man losing his bladder control." Shades of the jovial Antonin were beginning to shine through as he beamed a mischievous smile. "I think we should have Laura teach at our academy. Our people could learn a thing from her, or more."

"Some things can't be taught." Robert said this with conviction and a touch of humility having been on the receiving end of her defensive skills. He then stood and uncharacteristically threw his arms around Alexander. "You stubborn son of a bitch, if you'd called me right away we could probably be on a beach somewhere right now."

"You know I hate the beach."

Robert shook his head and laughed a little, but Antonin was already shifting gears now that the greetings had been exchanged. "OK, we need to clear out of here, get Ana and put everything together."

"After we get Laura on the next plane out of here." Alexander said this knowing how she would take it but at the moment didn't really care.

"I have asked her to serve as field director on this."

"*Field director!* Absolutely not!" His anger made him seem about twice his usual size. Every head in the room turned toward them.

"I've already said yes."

"Well now you'll just have to say no."

Robert leaned over to Antonin, "I told you not to tell him this here."

"I am Italian, you think this the first time I have seen a hot temper. If we told him in the safe room he would win out. This way, between here and there, he has time to cool down. We will not bring it up again until after we have put all of the pieces together. He will see it is the only way to stop this from becoming another holocaust and that Laura is the only choice for field director."

"If anything happens to her, he'll hold you responsible and I'm telling you, I've seen him fuck up some Nephilim pretty damn bad."

"Robert, it will never come to that. Besides this, she may be the most capable operator I have ever seen, and I have seen the best."

Robert looked over at Alexander and Laura who were still debating the issue with no small amount of intensity, then back to Antonin. "I hope for all of our sakes you're right."

Before Antonin could respond further, Ana came through the door at a rapid clip. She passed through several of them without a word and took the iPad from in front of Jorah who was still brooding over losing sight of Laura several hours earlier. She closed his screen and pulled up the ANSA news feed, Italy's leading wire service. The Vatican reporter was simultaneously translating the Pope's Latin into Italian as he spoke at what was normally a fairly routine press meeting within the Apostolic Palace. As the only reporter present who seemed capable of making the immediate translation, she was providing a live transmission of the stunning revelation that he would resign with an effective date in three weeks.

There was more, but they had heard all they needed to hear. Laura turned to Alexander, "What does this mean?"

"Six hundred years ago, a Pope resigned to prevent a war of epic proportion. This one has just resigned to start one."

20

"Our timeline was limited before, now it is critical. This was more than a protective maneuver, this was a signal for his conspirators to initiate their plans. We can only hope that Mathias' visit to him this morning has caused them to move more quickly than they would have otherwise and in their haste will make a mistake." Without another word Antonin spun on his heels and blew through the door and into a maze of tunnels. The others followed.

The hallways were variously textured with wooden beams in some places, stone walls and bricks in others. After walking for some time it began occurring to Robert, Alexander and Laura that the design was intentionally confusing. The seemingly random patterns of the walls and structures were actually replicated every few hundred yards regardless of how many turns or optional tunnels they took. One series of beams, bricks and tiles looked exactly like the previous series of beams, bricks and tiles. Even discolorations and the little fissures running through some of the materials were repeated elements. Getting turned around down here would be incredibly easy to do, and that of course was the point.

Without warning Antonin came to an abrupt stop. Jorah, Judith and Ana were the only ones that didn't seem to be surprised by the sudden halt. He put his hand into a depression in one of the beams and a set of hidden bolts disengaged allowing him to push into a narrow door that until that moment had looked like a wall of subway tiles. Alexander's consternation from earlier was temporarily dissipated by this act and there was a gleam in his eye as he leaned over to Laura, "I love secret doors and hidden rooms, don't you?"

Unfortunately for him, he was reaching up with his left arm feeling the wall at the very moment he chose to tease her about the safe room in their house. This exposed his ribs which she took full advantage of by giving him a quick shot to them with the knuckles of her right hand.

"Damn!" He flinched and rubbed his side.

Everyone turned back to them but only for a half-second, and then entered the room without them.

"Watch it chief, you're on thin ice."

He took her into his arms, "You don't have to do this, Laura. *We* don't have to do this."

She looked at him sympathetically knowing it wasn't his own skin he was trying to save.

"We can make a difference though."

"Not really, Laura. We can perhaps make a difference this time, but ultimately it will just be another fight another day and when that fire is almost out someone will be setting another one somewhere else. It never ends."

"What do you think I did for the CIA and the NRO, Alexander? I wasn't exactly an archivist. I know this landscape better than most and all that I've learned over the last 72 hours tells me that our worlds are not only similar but there's quite a lot of intersection."

He shrugged his shoulders slightly "I never said there wasn't."

"President Noles ran his campaign on promises to pull all of our troops home and shut down the terrorist detention centers through due process. Remember?"

He nodded, "I know..."

"And what happened? He had his first national security briefing and his entire worldview was turned upside down. Over the course of one meeting he went from being a politician wrangling for funding on the Senate floor to the one man on earth standing between a legion of those bent on destruction and the rest of the free world. His hair turned white in about three days. I don't think Moses' hair turned white because he saw God, I think it turned white because he saw truth."

"Someone's been reading her Bible."

"No, but I've been thinking non-stop about all you've told me and how much more relevant it is to history and reality once we read beyond the literal context. Maybe Moses is a metaphor representing the wisdom that stands between truth and lies, between some divine reality we call 'God,' the people of that promise and the malevolent forces that would destroy them."

He looked at her with a mixture of delight and surprise. "My goodness, Mrs. Wells, I didn't even know you cared."

She rolled her eyes. "Don't do that. Don't minimize this or make a joke out of it. I spent *years* fighting this war from a purely secular standpoint because that was my reality. But I now see, and see clearly that I couldn't possibly have ever prevailed on that battlefield."

"And why is that?"

"Because that's not where the real war is being waged. Those were skirmishes on the perimeter. That's why I was so ready and able to walk away from it, it was hollow. Robert helped me see this."

"Robert?"

"Yes, Robert. You know, we're not all as dense or disinterested as you assume."

"Hey..."

"It's true Alexander. You walked away because you assumed the rest of the world couldn't possibly comprehend, much less appreciate the cost and sacrifices of your world. You walked away because if you couldn't single-handedly take down and expose the Nephilim and their network then no one could and you gave up."

"No, I just stopped caring."

"Nope." She cut him of short. "No sir. You gave up the fight, but you never stopped caring. It's in every book and poem you write and it's even in most of the sermons you preached before I met you."

He looked at her skeptically.

"They're online, bonehead. I've read almost every word you've ever written and it makes me love you that much more. You care alright. You care more than most. You care about the Palestinians displaced from their homeland, placed into what we used to call ghettos and forced to subsist at the basest of levels. You care about the Jews who have been discriminated against, hunted and slaughtered for generations. You care about entire groups of people you've never met, but because they are hungry, alone, persecuted and fed a steady diet of despair you want to give them something more to believe in than a book or piece of land."

"Laura, even if I care, I'm telling you it's the never ending nightmare. Plus, more times than I care to remember the only reason I was not killed was because I'm considered an untouchable, one of the 12. That won't even stop them from killing me now though. In fact, the plan is to kill us all before the end of the week."

"Then what do you have to lose?"

"You! I could lose *you*, Laura."

"They never stopped hunting you, and they won't stop. You knew that then and you know that now. If you really thought you could escape this world you wouldn't have built that room underneath our cabin and you wouldn't have established an offshore account in my name."

His surprise was evident but he didn't even ask. She just smiled and gave him a tender kiss. "I love you, and anyone who wants to hurt you is going to have to go through me."

"You know, there's got to be a way of saying that, that doesn't just totally emasculate me."

She patted his face then burst into barely stifled laughter, "No, there's really not."

He pulled her into him and held her tightly. "Three billion women in the world and I had to fall in love with a badass."

She reached across his back as they embraced and gave him a sharp pinch on the back of the arm.

"Ow, dammit!" She did it again."OW! Stop!"

"Hey, you two." Robert stuck his head out into the hallway. "We'll be happy to move the meeting out there but there are big leather chairs in here."

Alexander and Laura walked toward the door that Robert was holding open for them. She stopped him just before he entered, "Hey."

He turned back toward her and she could see the physical and emotional exhaustion that was smothering him. "I do love you, you know. And you've been making a difference in this fight for a long time. You may not feel like it at the moment, but everyone in that room believes they can stop this disaster from happening because of you."

"Laura..." His disbelief was evident.

"Listen. It doesn't matter how many successes or failures you've logged or how many mistakes you've made. People follow you because you're willing to make mistakes and fail in an all out attempt to succeed while fighting for the right thing. Walter could've gone to any other of the 12 but he came to you even though he knew you might drop him where he stood. Antonin knew that he could trust you not to fold on him with the Pope which is why he was willing to risk the lives of one of his top commando teams to deliver you into the heart of Vatican City. And it worked. Your enemies are terrified of you and they're frantically trying to adjust to your sudden reappearance."

He looked at her thoughtfully but without a word and then turned to enter the safe room where Antonin was busy reviewing several documents with an air of frustration. The room was large and softly lit from the recessed lighting that shone from both floor and ceiling. A bank of monitors covered most of the far wall and a long conference table was in the center of the room with an array of communication devices at each place where, sure enough there were big rolling leather chairs. Robert took a seat at the table, but before Alexander could pull out a chair for Laura, Judith came through a door that had gone unnoticed by them until that moment. She made a direct line for Laura.

"There's a message for you."

"For me?"

"It came in through a back channel at the US embassy. Probably the strangest back channel communication I've ever seen, a janitor with a stick drive."

This obviously intensified Laura's interest. "Where is it?"

You'll have to come with me.

"What did he say?"

"That it's from your angel."

21

Laura took the stick drive and inserted it into the USB port on Ana's computer keyboard. A series of numbers began scrolling vertically on the screen. She keyed in a series of letters, symbols and numbers that eventually caused the scrolling to stop. She then counted from the top series of numbers down to the seventeenth and keyed those same numbers into an empty field. Another series of numbers scrolled onto the screen.

"I need to make a secure call."

"That's no problem."

"Using my phone."

Judith thought for a couple of seconds. "Ah, of course!" She held out her hand for Laura's phone, "I haven't even used this myself it's so new. It's a connection that if detected appears to be transmitting from the Trevi Fountain, but of course who's going to look for a data signal coming from a 300 year old monument?"

Laura didn't say it aloud but thought, 'You'd be surprised.' and handed her the phone. The connection was instantaneous and Judith returned it to Laura. She keyed in a series of numbers and waited for a dial tone then a connection.

"I have a laptop for you."

"Seriously?" She knew Michael was serious but her surprise was such that she didn't know what else to say.

"I was concerned after we spoke so I did some nosing around. We clipped the laptop about three hours ago. When we picked up the feed on the chopper crash at Villa Borghese they sent a car for me. I told them before I left for the day in no uncertain terms; if the Pope even sneezed they'd better call me."

She would've asked but already knew the answer. Michael had been keeping tabs on her since she called. That was the kind of angel she could understand and appreciate, one that helped in remarkable ways without even being asked.

"How did you know to keep an eye on the Pope?"

There was an unnatural pause on the other end. This was unusual for Michael who always seemed to know what people were going to say or ask before they knew themselves. When he eventually replied she could tell he was mentally processing something else. "The religious affiliation cross reference you asked for coupled with the tickets to Rome."

"What is it Michael?"

There was yet another pause. "Laura, less than 48 hours ago you called me with one of the more eccentric search criteria you've ever dropped on me. So then I did a little digging and found out about the bed and breakfast explosion. Dug a little further and guess what? There were some very interesting satellites watching some very uninteresting patches of the North Carolina mountains. I couldn't get everything, but I got enough to see something was very wrong. I put some assets in play to get the laptop but other than that I'm totally black on this."

She was not sure what to think. Going black on an operation without orders from way up the chain was a surefire way to end a career. Personal crusades were severely frowned upon.

"Michael..."

"Let me worry about that." He knew precisely what she was thinking. "I'm not sure how long I can stay black on this anyway. There's a conspicuous absence of chatter regarding that chopper crash and it has our folks scouring every bit of human and digital intel they can ferret out. As you know it's not always what you hear, it's sometimes what you *don't* hear. But before this goes any further, you're going to have to help me with something."

"Of course."

"Laura, there's not much I haven't seen in terms of data encryption and there's never been anything that I looked at and thought I couldn't eventually crack, until now. What is this?"

"What are you talking about?"

"The data on this laptop, it's beyond anything I've ever seen. In fact, I'm not even sure what I'm seeing."

"Can you transmit it to me?"

"Honestly, I don't know and you know how I loathe to admit that."

"Will you talk to Alexander about this?"

"I assumed that would be the case. That's who came running out of the B&B just before it exploded isn't it? It's also who they picked up and put in the van after the explosion."

"Give me five and I'll call you back."

She ended the call and turned to Judith, "Will you ask Alexander to join us without making it obvious that we've got a new development in here? I don't want to take anyone down a rabbit trail until I'm sure there's something to this."

Judith simply nodded her head in the affirmative and entered the safe room. Within seconds she was back with Alexander in tow.

"Before we left I had an old friend dig up some data for me that would help me track you down. That friend has been shadowing me and keeping an eye on my six since then. Right after the Willow exploded, you dropped a laptop that presumably belonged to Walter. He went after it and got it. He's been committed to my preservation for a long time and though he doesn't know what's on it, he's certain we'll want to know."

"This friend of yours, does he work for your old employer?"

"Yes." She said this with a hint in her voice that she knew what was coming next.

"Laura..."

"I know, but he's operating totally black on this and has already been incredibly helpful."

"The reason we don't work with government agencies is that they've historically been heavily infiltrated and influenced by the Nephilim. I'm sorry, but I have to insist, we'll get the laptop then sever all communication with this person." His expression was uncharacteristically stoic. Whether it was the CIA, the National Reconnaissance Office, MI6, Mossad or any other secretive government agency around the globe, operations in the past had been horribly compromised as a direct result of involving them. Her expression was one of bewildered consternation. This truly might have been the first time Alexander had insisted on anything with her. She was used to trusting Michael with her life and now she was being told to lock him out.

"I'm serious, Laura. You're going to have to trust me on this, all of war is deception and the combatants of this realm have thousands of years of practiced deception under their belts."

144

"You don't have to quote Sun Tzu to convince me. It's been increasingly evident over the past 72 hours that this is a completely new ballgame for me, but you're asking me to cut someone out of my life that has *saved* my life on numerous occasions."

"Out, Laura...completely out, or this ends right now."

Their eyes locked into the steady gaze of silent sentinels equally matched in strength, stealth and cunning. A wave of anger surged through her. Judith couldn't decide if she should call for help or just duck for cover as the proverbial paradox of the immovable object and irresistible force were obviously about to collide. Her concerns were astonishingly and quickly dispelled though as Laura's entire countenance suddenly shifted.

"Alright. I understand." She said this with complete resignation and the understanding that, though still difficult to comprehend, this was his world and he knew the pitfalls and blind alleys better than most. She made the connection to Michael and handed the phone to Alexander.

"Can this data be transmitted securely without degradation?"

Alexander didn't answer Michael's question. Instead he rattled off a set of instructions that set up the transfer and simultaneously wiped all data from the laptop. The download was nearly instantaneous and Michael saw that the laptop was now basically dead. "OK, you should have it. Could I speak to Laura?"

Alexander ended the call and instead of giving the phone back to Laura handed it to Judith. "Can you reassign this phone's protocol to a pedestrian number then destroy it?"

"Yes."

"Alexander?" Laura was feeling off balance in light of his sudden authoritative manner.

"And get a clean one for her."

"Alexander." Her tone was increasingly impatient as he sat down at Judith's laptop and connected his own phone.

Without looking up from what he was doing he responded to her, "Yes?"

"I think we need to talk."

"You better believe it."

"What do you mean?"

"I mean, if you're going to be Field Director on this then I'm taking Operation Command. That's the deal. You will work directly through me and no one else. If you think you can't follow my orders without hesitation then we'll have to choose another path." Though he didn't let it show, from the moment he'd started questioning her CIA connection to Michael and his insistence that she sever ties with him, he felt as though he was going to throw up. He'd never challenged her like this, but with her life on the line he was not willing to do it gingerly.

She studied this new facet of his personality and she admired, respected and loved what she was seeing. Though a smile was trying its best to escape from her, she maintained a mission oriented demeanor so that he would know she was taking this seriously.

"Deal."

With that, Judith left the room and reentered the safe room where she approached Antonin, leaned in and whispered the news into his ear.

"Perfect!" He patted the conference table with both hands and laughed his gregarious laugh. "Perfect! Those bastards will not know what hit them with these two at the helm."

Laura entered the room and took an empty chair next to Robert. "So what's next?"

"I don't know for sure, but judging by Antonin's reaction to whatever Judith just whispered into his ear, I'd say we're waiting to hear from your boy."

"He's deciphering the data from Walter's laptop. Should be right in."

Several minutes passed as each member of the group reviewed the information in the packets on the table in front of them. It was a rundown of the events of the past few days. Robert filled in some of the blanks for Laura that required historical knowledge of previous engagements with these groups. They were coming to the end of the files about the time Alexander walked into the room. He appeared to be somewhat stunned and looked only at Laura as he entered. With tears welling in his eyes and a lump in his throat he took a seat beside her.

22

"They've got a plan in place to distribute a weaponized strain of Hemorrhagic Dengue Fever." The room gave its full attention to Alexander. "Cardinal José María Morazán of Honduras has overseen the development of the strain in a secret laboratory in the mountains outside of San Pedro Sula. Given the age of this information, they're either in the final stages or have completed the process."

"Morazán?" Antonin's expression intensified at the mention of this name. "The Vatican liaison to the International Monetary Fund and World Bank? He is a raging anti-Semite and extraordinarily outspoken about it. Some say he likely will be the next Pope."

No one commented on this analysis of Morazán, but it had an obvious effect. Knowing glances were exchanged around the room. A man with that much global clout and with so much to lose politically if he was indeed a viable candidate for the Papacy would not be involved with the manufacture of biological weapons unless in the endgame those considerations were of no consequence.

"There's no known vaccine or treatment for Dengue Fever." Laura interjected across the momentary silence. She sat back in her chair and folded her arms across her chest. "It makes Malaria seem like the sniffles. A weaponized version of the hemorrhagic strain..." Her voice trailed off as she contemplated the implications.

"It would be catastrophic." Alexander finished her thought. "However Boniface, humanitarian that he is, has apparently developed a vaccine and treatment in cooperation with the Iranians. His funding, their facilities and it all looks like a legitimately funded health services laboratory. Of course I don't think they intend to distribute the vaccine very widely."

"How do they intend to disperse the virus? Detection devices could surely be set up to recognize it in air or water. We need to get on this." Robert was visibly shaken by the news.

"I'm afraid it's a bit more complicated than that. If it was distributed via aerosol or in the water supply then yes, we could detect it, but that's not the plan at all." Alexander took a breath before telling them because he almost couldn't believe what he was going to say, "Apparently they're going to use Mosquitoes."

"*Mosquitoes?*"

"According to Trowbridge's data, they've devised an entomological warfare system. Arthropods are the natural carriers of the disease as it is, so if they've developed an efficient means of distributing infected mosquitoes we could be looking at a pandemic within a very brief period of time."

Ana looked stricken at the prospect but was unfamiliar with the disease. "What exactly are the symptoms and effects?"

"Six to ten days after being infected, the victim experiences an intense headache and fever. Within 24 hours of the onset of fever, blood vessels begin to hemorrhage, shock sets in and they die. That is with the standard strain of Hemorrhagic Dengue, I can only imagine what they've come up with in the weaponized version." He looked to Judith, "Can I access these monitors with my phone?"

"Absolutely." She was half way to him while responding in the affirmative and took the device from him once there.

After hitting a few keys on her tablet the monitors came to life. After a few more keystrokes his phone was connected. An enormous photo of Laura in waders fly fishing on the White river flickered to life on each of the oversized monitors. It was his home screen and he worked quickly to access the data so that a series of targets scrolling onto the screens would replace the images. Tel Aviv, Jerusalem and Manhattan were most prominent among them. A dark silence blanketed the room and without a word he scrolled to the next screen where the names and locations of the laboratories in el Zapotal, and Tehran.

"We're going to be spread thin. We'll need a team in el Zapotal as well as a team in Tehran, that is if we're not too late. If our intel shows they're already on the move, we'll need teams in the target locations which will spread us thinner still. We have to assume the Gush Emunim is several steps ahead of us and now know they've been infiltrated." The pain on Ana's face was evident at this remark but she said nothing as Alexander continued. "I need a complete understanding of our assets before I can continue."

Jorah, Judith and Ana all looked to Antonin with a look of confusion as Alexander transitioned from giving a briefing to giving orders. Antonin addressed their questions before they asked. "Alexander will be Operations Commander for this and Laura will be Field Director. I will consult with him, but all Alliance communications and directives that would normally flow through me will instead flow through him. If I disagree with him on anything, you will never know it. This is his operation and we will follow his lead." He studied each of their faces to make sure they'd registered what he was telling them which, as he'd expected, they had.

Alexander took this as his cue to resume his organizational structuring. "Judith, we need keyhole satellites on those facilities, and drones overhead as soon as possible. Also we'll want any available images from the past two weeks. Accurate intel and assessment is crucial and we've got a nearly impossible time table."

Jorah, who had been mostly silent throughout the entire meeting, spoke up, "Already on it." He said this without looking up from his iPad that he was using to re-task satellites. "The drones are in the air from some of our assets in Guatemala and we should have live images available in the next half hour."

"Laura, I need Ana and you to put your teams together then meet with me after I've had time to review the images." Alexander then turned to Antonin. "Who do I talk to about logistics: transportation, safe houses, equipment?"

"Robert and I are at your disposal."

"Perfect. We'll keep this as our command center for the first phase of the operation then move accordingly for the second. Let's get going."

Everyone except Robert, Antonin and Alexander cleared the room to go make their preparations.

"Robert, could Antonin and I have the room for a few minutes?"

The look on his old friend's face conveyed a momentary sense of hurt at being shut out, but he understood and gave a nod as he turned to follow the others.

Alexander waited until the door was completely closed before he spoke. "How long have you known?"

"Walter knew this day was coming. He understood these things better than anyone. Every 500 years there is a significant upheaval that takes decades or more to work itself out if it ever does, he saw this almost prophetically."

"How long, Antonin?" His patience was in short supply at the moment and Antonin understood.

"Around the time you were sent to Tilanqiao he came to see me. Without any prior knowledge of our activities he described with great precision the rise of the Gush Emunim, the Alliance's infiltration and even Simon's complicity with the Iranians.

He possessed an innate ability to see all of the players, hear all of the news and of course what they were *not* saying and then pull the true story together with alarming accuracy. It was then that he told me of his research confirming Laura's heritage. Sending her to affect your release was the initiation of her recruitment. Of course, your falling in love with her and running away was not part of his plan." Antonin couldn't keep himself from smiling at this observation.

"How did he even know to look? There have only been three daughters and there are so many myths, legends and misinformation about them it's difficult to know fact from fiction. How could he possibly have put this together with any certainty?"

"Correction my friend, there has only been three daughters we *know* of. How many have come and gone without our knowledge? If it hadn't been for Walter, we wouldn't know about Laura. As for certainty it is all in the genetics. According to Walter, it was simply a matter of compiling the genetic material for testing."

"Compiling genetic material?" Alexander looked at Antonin as if he was off his beam. "The last daughter was executed by the French for heresy in the 15th century, and the two before her were...well, I don't have to tell you."

"Alexander, I realize you do not want this to be true but I think you know that it is. When Walter came to you he had just come from Honduras with the evidence against Simon but more importantly he was bringing you the proof of Laura's identity."

"I should've killed him when I had the chance."

"Alexander!" Antonin's voice was sharp in its rebuke. "What would that have accomplished? We owe Walter a great debt, he very well may have stopped WWIII and he gave his life to do it. No one will ever know his name or that he died to stop a global holocaust, but *we* will know and we are the ones who will finish the work he began." He studied Alexander for a few seconds in silence, then asked, "What happened between you two?"

Alexander ignored the question and looked instead at the monitors that were now locked back into the picture of Laura from his home screen. She was the most beautiful person he'd ever known. Beautiful in every way. He had hoped to settle in with her and live a peaceful life away from these horrors. The current circumstance was the nightmare that seemed to dog him on the periphery of his consciousness during those precious few years of calm. Now, it was once again his reality. Rather than protecting her from his world, she was being thrust into it head first.

It was as if Antonin could read his thoughts. "My friend, we do not often have the luxury of choosing our fate, more often it chooses us. Some were born to stand between the great lies of this world and those they seek to consume. Try as you may, you cannot run from your heritage. The great lies and those who preach them will seek you out to destroy you because you are all that stands between the innocents of the world and them."

"They know who she is now." He didn't take his eyes off the monitors as he said this.

"Who?"

"The Nephilim. They know who she is now and they will do everything they can to destroy her first. And I am the one who gave them the proof. I transmitted that data without even checking to see if it went through or if it was intercepted, which of course it was."

Antonin smiled and tried to smother a laugh that burst out anyway.

"What the hell's the matter with you?"

"I am sorry. I really am."

"What's so damn funny?"

"Ohhhhhhhh, my dear Alexander." He put his arm around his shoulders. "My dear arrogant Mathias. They've known who you were for a long time. They haven't gotten to you have they? And let me tell you, she is far more capable that *you* are." He laughed heartily as Alexander shook his head in disgust. "They only *think* they know who she is. They were scared of you, yes." His voice lowered into a powerful whisper, "But they will be *terrified* of her."

He knew Antonin was right and perhaps he was right about being chosen by fate. He was not a big believer in fate, but who was to say? Who would willingly choose the role as a Daughter of Enoch? Yet, at crucial moments in history they had emerged and turned back the tides of catastrophe. Alexander continued staring at her smiling face and the rushing waters of the White river frozen in time. He considered all he knew of Enoch and of his lineage. Supposedly the great-great-great-great grandson of Adam and the great-grandfather of Noah, Enoch's presence could be detected throughout the whole of Jewish, Muslim and Christian scriptures. Some belief systems within the three Abrahamic faiths claim that Enoch is an immortal and lives today, but perhaps even more enigmatic than that are the texts identifying a lineage of daughters. In writings attributed to him, Enoch proclaims that his daughters' greatest advantage is that the sons of men will underestimate them and that they will destroy the pillars of lies upon which empires are constructed.

The door opened behind Alexander. It was Laura and Ana. She looked at the monitors that had her likeness plastered across them. "Would you *please* take those down?"

He took out his phone and killed the connection.

"We've got a preliminary allocation of teams." She took a seat but rather than joining her, Antonin said something in rapid fire Italian to Ana and they exited the room. Laura watched them go then looked back at Alexander. "What just happened?"

"We need to talk."

23

Laura sat in silent disbelief as he finished telling her what he'd learned about her heritage from Walter's data. Even though her head was swimming at these revelations, the recent and mysterious events were beginning to make more sense to her. She was still a long way from actually believing that she had some kind of ancestral link to this newly discovered world, but was nonetheless convinced that she'd been pulled into the most compelling and deadly conflict of her life.

She pinched the bridge of her nose while staring down at the conference table, "So, what? I'm one of the 12 now?"

"No, it's a bit more complex than that and I'm afraid there's just not a lot more I can even tell you." She looked at him with irritation as if he was holding information back from her. "I'm not holding anything back, it's that we just don't know."

"Then how can we be sure he was even right about me being a so called Daughter of Enoch?"

"Honestly, Laura we can't, at least not right now. Though if anyone had the ability to have done the research and come up with accurate results that would've been double then triple checked, it would've been Walter. I grew to dislike him and eventually hate him, but I always respected his abilities and intellect."

She stood from the table and began pacing and thinking. "Is this even relevant to our current mission?"

"It's actually more relevant that you can imagine." He then stood, pushed his chair under the table and leaned back against it. Laura stopped pacing and looked at him. "The first of the daughters that we know of was Deborah, the 12th century BCE prophet, warrior and judge. The next was Mary Magdalene..."

"Mary *Magdalene*?" She interrupted him with extraordinary exasperation. "This is ridiculous. Wasn't she a prostitute?"

Alexander shook his head, "No...she was *not* a prostitute." He detested this misogynist characterization of Mary that had absolutely no factual basis. "She was not married to or even in love with Jesus of Nazareth. She was a powerful woman of means who was financing and leading an underground insurrection against the ancestors of the very people we're fighting against today."

"The Nephilim?"

"Indirectly, yes. But back then it was the Herodians who held the seats of power in an uncomfortable alliance with Rome. They were essentially the Jewish Mafia and they had all of Judea in a death grip."

She leaned back against the edge of the table. "I can't process this right now."

"I understand, but you need to know that you just became the Nephilim's prime target and it is completely my fault."

"*Your* fault?"

He bit his lower lip and drew a deep breath that filled his chest. His guilt was immense. "When I transmitted the data I was careless. Ephrem intercepted it which means the Nephilim also now have it."

"I don't quite understand why I would be their prime target though. I only learned of their existence a few days ago."

He pushed off of the chair he was leaning against and stepped in front of her. "It's not what you know right now that concerns them, it's what you will eventually learn."

"Enough with the mystery, just say it."

"Each of the 12 has always held only one piece of the puzzle. That was the intention from the beginning. It is believed that if any one person possessed the combination of knowledge and artifacts, the allure of that kind of power would be irresistible. They would have the ability to bring the world to its knees."

"Alexander..." Her skeptical tone indicated that she clearly heard what he was telling her as something more attuned to a fairytale.

"Look, it's not as mystical as it sounds. What is it that you've always heard? 'Knowledge is power.' This is the standard bearer for that adage. The secrets we protect have been desperately sought for generations and as I've been telling you from the beginning, they will do anything to get them."

He could tell he was having only a minimal impact on her sensibilities, so without a word he went to the door and stuck his head out into the corridor. Antonin was standing patiently alone.

"I need an absolutely secure room."

Antonin's eyebrows raised in curiosity followed by his mischievous grin. He then pushed past Alexander into the room, keyed in a few strokes on a keyboard at the head of the table. The room had seemed quiet before, but it absolutely deadened when he did this.

"All yours."

With this he turned on his heels and exited leaving Alexander and Laura to themselves.

Alexander pulled a chair out for her and waited until she was seated before taking his seat. "One of the world's oldest religions, one that has influenced all three Abrahamic faiths, is Zoroastrianism. The exact origins are not known by those outside of its closest ranks but we know that it originated with a prophet referred to as 'Zarathustra' or 'Zoroaster' who lived in what is now modern day Iran."

"I'm familiar with them. Since September 11 we've all become experts on the religious history of Iran, Iraq, and Syria. You get the point."

"Here's one bit they may have missed at the NRO briefings. The Magi or the 'three wise men' as they are often mistakenly called, were actually Zoroastrian priests and there were 12 of them, not three."

Laura's mind began racing through her biblical knowledge but this was doing nothing to quell the emotions welling up within her. There were times when a truth was known not by its factual presentation but rather by the sheer energy and weight of it.

"The number three grew from the mention of the gifts of gold, frankincense and myrrh in Matthew's Gospel account. In actuality there was only one gift that they bore. It was a gift that Herod wanted desperately."

Though she couldn't imagine why, it was almost as if the core of her being was running from what Alexander was telling her. Part of her wanted him to stop.

"The one artifact that made the true heir of David the true king of Israel had been in their possession for one thousand years. It passed from David to Solomon on his deathbed and then from Solomon into the protection of the Zoroastrians. Without it, ten of the twelve tribes of Israel refused to accept Solomon's son Rehoboam as king and Israel split into two kingdoms. By the time Herod the Great came to power the kingship was a completely politicized position obtained through treachery and alliances between powers. He was not even really Jewish."

"Herod?"

"Right. He practiced Judaism, but only did so out of political expedience. He was in actuality an Edomite and was not considered truly Jewish by observant and nationalist Jews. To make it worse in the eyes of those over whom he ruled, he was elected by the Roman Senate as King of the Jews and secured his position by executing his rival. They only recognized him as king under extreme duress and Herod knew it. They would never accept him as the true king. By the time the Zoroastrian priests arrived in search of the true heir of David, Herod was a paranoid and poisoned old man who had killed all of his political rivals including members of his own family and wife. Once he determined what it was they had in their possession, he ordered all of the young male children in the vicinity of Bethlehem to be murdered. The Massacre of the Innocents."

"The Stone of David."

Alexander silently nodded his affirmation.

"Israel was never meant to be what it became. Israel was established as a light to all nations, a beacon of truths amidst a generation of lies, but power corrupts and Herod was more corrupt and vacuous than any that had come before. The true heir of David would not lead a great army or nation; he would lead as a light of peace and truth to all nations. He came and spoke with the authority of the one foretold by Zarathustra and Isaiah. He spoke of the things that made Israel who they truly were instead of what the secular monarchies had made them."

Laura's abdomen was stretched tight with anxiety as she contemplated the implications of what he was telling her. She suddenly realized she'd been holding her breath.

"There's always been speculation about what Jesus of Nazareth was doing between the ages of 12 and 30, but there is a group of people who have always known. The Zoroastrians have always known because they are the ones with whom he spent those years, learning and growing amongst the most ancient priestly class."

"Why are you telling me this?" Her disposition was tinged with fear. The implications were staggering. "Are you even *allowed* to tell me these things?"

Alexander smiled. "Laura, it won't be long until you know more than I've ever known. Just as Deborah, Mary Magdalene and Joan of Arc, you will be entrusted with *all* of the secrets. You are now at the epicenter of history. It's not *me* that they will follow into battle. It is you."

She could do nothing but stand in stunned silence, but it was time to get the operation in motion. Alexander stuck his head once more out into the hall, "Let's gather the troops."

Antonin was about to head straight to the dining facility to round everyone up but stopped and turned back to Alexander. "How are you?"

He didn't have the words. Tears were burgeoning just beneath the surface and he gritted his teeth as he stepped the rest of the way into the hall without answering.

Antonin adjusted to the more pertinent question, "How is *she?*"

"She's still trying to comprehend it all but is more focused on this mission than anything else."

"She is more remarkable than the rest of us even know, is she not?"

Alexander peered back through the open door where Laura was poring over images of an isolated warehouse east of el Zapotal del Norte in Honduras. "She is the finest person I've ever known, Antonin. Absolutely the finest."

24

"The most vexing enemy we have at the moment is time. We're looking at some serious flight hours assuming you can provide us with a C-17 and a mid-air refuel. Commercial is of course out of the question." Laura was looking over the 11 person team roster Ana and she had put together and estimating that they would have at least 800 pounds of gear.

"What would you say if I told you I could have you on the ground in Honduras in less than two hours?" Antonin looked at Alexander, grinned and then looked back to Laura for her reaction.

"I would hire you as my permanent travel agent." Her quip belied the sincerity of her tone. "What've you got?"

"A ZEHST jet. It cruises at Mach 4 above the atmosphere."

"Zest?"

"Zero Emission High Speed Transport. It uses biofuels with water vapor as its only byproduct. Once you are 20 miles up, they kick the ramjets in and you can be sipping a cold Salva Vida within the hour." Antonin was clearly proud of this particular technology. "Europeans have always built the fastest toys."

"Alright then, since time is no longer against us, or at least not as much of a factor, let's take a look at gear."

Mitri took this as his cue. "I've drawn 10 H&K MP7s with suppressors and reflex sites. We're all qualified on them and comfortable." He did a double check with Laura and Ana as he said this. They both gave him reassuring nods. "Asa will be with the perimeter team and will provide cover with a DTA SRS-A1 .308 compact sniper rifle. He's exceptionally accurate with that weapon, which is surprising for someone who can't even figure out which end of a fork to use." A few of the other team members chuckled as Asa ceremoniously presented his middle finger to Mitri. It was obviously an inside joke and Alexander was happy to see this level of banter between them. It meant they'd worked together before and trusted and cared enough about each other to be mildly abusive with one another.

Mitri continued with his briefing and listed the various specialty items each member would carry. These included insertion tools and the necessary chemicals to destroy the virus and the lab equipment. Drones would take out the remaining structure of the facility once the ground force confirmed all traces of the HDF virus had been eradicated. Ana then took over with one of the more unusual equipment descriptors.

"Once we're airborne, we'll change into the interactive camouflage and cloaking units."

Laura had already received a briefing from Ana on this technology, and given the fabric Alexander had shown her in their safe room, she couldn't wait to see this particular fabric in person. One of the team members, a fireplug of a guy named Seth Montalto, stepped out of the anteroom wearing one of the suits. It was a form fitting, black body suit with an integrated helmet. Without being instructed to do so, Montalto reached with his right hand to his left arm and depressed a pressure switch that caused the entire suit to take on the precise coloration and lighting of his surroundings. His image seemed to melt into the wall behind him with only the darkened visor and soles of his shoes visible.

"For those that have used this suit before you'll be glad to know the single omni-directional camera has been replaced by two, one each on the underside rim of the neck guard."

After deactivating the suit, Montalto indicated two bumps the size of LED nodes on either side of the helmet.

"They can still be damaged or obscured but are far less vulnerable than the first-generation cameras. Also, given the relatively brief time of insertion, power reductions shouldn't be an issue. These have been upgraded for extended use with the tradeoff being a slightly reduced bullet resistance."

"How *reduced?*" Mitri asked with trepidation.

"I'll give you the stats if you really want them, but essentially it only marginally increased the effective distance of most high velocity sniper rounds. They're still completely effective in close-quarters combat situations."

"In other words, keep that fuel drum sized ass of yours down and you won't have anything to worry about." The room erupted in hearty laughter as Asa took the opportunity to return Mitri's earlier gibe. Both Laura and Alexander knew this level of verbal sparring would increase right up until the moment they jumped into the mountains just north of San Pedro Sula. It was their way of affirming the bond they shared. It was an unspoken message that said, 'I will torment you all I want, but I will die before I allow our enemy to bring harm to you.'

"OK, guys...we'll depart from Sant'Eustachio in 15. Gear checks on the tarmac and wheels up at 2400 Zulu. Digital sand tables are loaded onto your hand-helds and will be linked to the HUD in your helmets once you lock them in. Check those *before* you jump, please. No more surprises for farmer's daughters, Monty?" The room burst into laughter once again as Montalto shook his head and squeezed his broad frame back through the door to the anteroom without a word.

"Farmer's daughters?" Laura was feeling nostalgic toward the back and forth between this group of dedicated brothers and sisters and was hungry for more.

Ana leaned closer to her as the others were dispersing. These stories were normally kept within 'the family' and she didn't want to upset that code even though she was fairly certain no one would mind. Laura and Alexander were quickly becoming part of their family. "Actually I'm pretty sure it was the farmer's wife that he walked in on having a pre-dawn tryst. He hadn't checked his handheld connection before jumping and by the time he hit the ground the data was inexplicably scrambled and pixilated. The barn he was *supposed* to enter was one we'd secured as a rendezvous point for exfiltration. The identical one he *chose* to enter was 20 clicks away and was occupied at the time by a farmer's wife and her friend getting their morning exercise in the hay. He had the camo-suit activated but managed to startle the couple which set off a chain of events that began with barking dogs and ended with shotgun blasts. No one got hurt but we're pretty sure the affair ended that night and Monty now triple checks his HUD connection and carries a compass and map."

Laura smiled, "Yeah, he's not living that one down anytime soon."

"Oh no...never."

"On the other hand, I bet that farmer would give him a commendation if he knew where to send it."

Montalto exited the anteroom and breezed past them with the suit now hanging over his arm. Ana grinned for the first time since the Chinook had gone down. Alexander observed the smiles between them as he approached but didn't dare ask. Smiles before an operation indicated confidence and he wasn't going to mess with that.

"15 minutes...see you up there." Ana followed the rest of the group out the door leaving the two of them alone once more.

The door closed and they looked into each other's eyes. "What a difference a day makes, huh?"

"I hate this, Laura. You know that."

"I know."

"It's not that I think you're incapable of doing this, in fact quite the opposite."

She grabbed him around the waist and pulled him into her. "Hush."

"I just..."

"I said, hush." She kissed him with a passion that surprised him.

She pulled slowly back from his lips then pushed her face in toward his cheek, brushing her nose and lips along his jaw line until she reached his ear. "My god, I love you."

He made a half-hearted protest, "Oh, so you can talk but I can't?"

She whispered a gentle "mmm-hmm" into his ear then nuzzled and kissed his neck. Her soft manner shifted suddenly into a more aggressive embrace. She pushed upward on either side of his torso and around to his back with her hands. She pulled her hands down from his shoulders to his waist where she dislodged his shirt and then ran her hands up and under. His calf muscles tightened instinctively as she dug her fingers into the muscles of his lower back.

"Laura...you're killing me."

She looked into his eyes and held his gaze in a way that caused the room to fade into nothingness. If it was possible for a lifetime of experiences to be forged into one moment in time, Alexander thought surely this was it. Without prior consciousness, their souls had begun knitting together to form an inviolable fabric of love, trust and mutuality. The confirmation for both of them was within this moment.

167

Poets had tried and failed every time to adequately describe such beauty and now Laura understood why. Some truths are too profound for words.

Alexander placed his mouth above her ear and drew in a breath of her intoxicating scent, "I don't know how else to say this but I've never known anything to be more deeply true in my life; I have loved you forever."

Laura pulled him into her as closely as she could. Words were no longer necessary.

25

After a relatively quiet take off, the ZEHST plane climbed rapidly into the Stratosphere where just as Antonin had said they would, the pilots engaged the rocket engines that propelled them to a scorching 3000 miles per hour. Though the aerodynamics resembled those of the Concorde, that was where the similarities ended; the ZEHST was designed to fly twice as high and more than double the top speed of the now decommissioned hyper-sonic jet. A commercial version was slated for production within 40 years, but for certain organizations with the right connections and extraordinary levels of funding they were already available in tactical configurations.

The perimeter team sat on one side of the fuselage while the infiltration team sat on the other. Ana would oversee the perimeter team that consisted of Asa, Montalto and three other skilled operatives: Di Nola, Pane and Russo. Asa was the trigger man on the DTA sniper rifle and Montalto was his spotter. In addition to their MP7s, Di Nola and Pane would each carry MK48 Mod 1 belt-fed machine guns that fired 750 rounds per minute. Finally there was Russo, who besides his standard gear would be jumping in with a MK47 40mm grenade launcher. All together it was a 90 pound complement of highly destructive automatic weaponry. No one would ever accuse Russo of failing to carry his part of the load on an operation, especially since he could put any number of various high-explosive and pre-fragmented air-exploding grenades pretty much wherever he wanted at an automatic rate of fire. When the tangos started swarming it was often his personal version of shock and awe that turned them back.

The infiltration team was to be overseen by Laura. Their equipment was designed for rapid movement and portability. Their firepower was fairly consistent across the team with only a couple exceptions. Laura carried the MP7 and her trusted HK45. Mitri was the breach man and carried an Armsel Striker commonly referred to as the 'Street Sweeper.' This was a 20 inch 12 gauge shotgun with a revolving cylinder that would fire 12 shells as fast as one could pull the trigger. It stood by itself as a weapon of overwhelming force when it came to clearing a room which, just happened to be Mitri's forte.

The remaining members of the infiltration team included Mazza, an unusually tall and lanky Italian Jew who rarely spoke an unnecessary word, which had earned him the moniker "Quiet Man." He never complained about the nickname though. He absolutely relished the irony of being a demolition expert with such a designation. Moreover he also happened to be a huge John Wayne fan and couldn't think of a better character to be named after. He would be responsible for mixing and employing the explosive chemicals that would destroy the HDF virus and its production elements. He would also be the last one out of the area upon exfiltration to make sure the drones finished off the warehouse.

Finally there was Garo and Barrone, two of the best shooters in the business. They were cousins from Tuscany who had started hunting at the ages of seven and eight respectively. While most of their buddies were off playing Football, Garo and Barrone preferred to devise and practice trick shots such as hitting two different targets by splitting one bullet on the edge of an axe, or striking matches by barely grazing the white phosphorus tip from various distances. By the time they were teenagers they were so well known that hunting reserves would invite them to entertain guests with hours of spectacular feats of marksmanship. It was at just such an event that Antonin Carafa had encountered the two young men and had kept tabs on them until they were at an appropriately recruitable age. The affable duo matched perfectly with Antonin's gregarious style and ways of doing things. Even during times of limited or blacked out communications, it seemed they always instinctively knew the moves and adjustments Antonin would want them to make.

The Command and Control team was no less impressive. Alexander would be calling the shots based on feedback from Laura and Ana as well as from the drone imagery that was already being fed live to the Operation Center below the streets of Rome. The advanced systems they were employing through the drone instruments meant that he could see every good guy and bad guy and predict with relative certainty what each of them was going to do next. He would also be able to see what each team member was seeing via the same feed but collected through individual visor cameras and microphones. With all of the available data combined with consultation from Antonin and Robert, this would likely be a devastatingly successful mission. Unlike the rest of them, Alexander had no formal military or special ops training. His expertise came from years of battling fiercely determined, intelligent and powerful enemies. It didn't hurt that he was one of the most brilliantly deceptive tacticians any of his friends or foes had ever encountered. This was not however a cultivated skill, it was rather a talent with which he was born and it all came down to incredible powers of perception and intuition about people. "Get into your enemy's head, convince them that you're two steps behind them," he'd repeatedly said to Robert over the years they'd worked together, "then show up three steps ahead of them."

The monitors showed that the warehouse was not heavily fortified or guarded. Disguising such an operation in the rural industrial areas on the outskirts of San Pedro Sula was not difficult. Creating too evident of a defensive footprint would draw the attention of a paranoid government that had gained its power by means a coup just a few years prior. The most obvious choice was the one Boniface had adopted, hide in plain sight. All one truly had to do was make reasonably regular payments or donations to various law enforcement agencies to be assured of the freedom and anonymity to conduct business there, legal or otherwise.

"Are you getting these images?"

The team was suited up and going through all of their systems checks as they streaked across the curvature of the earth high above the Atlantic. Laura accessed the glowing thermal images being transmitted from the drones above the warehouse and was seeing them on her heads-up display. There were a half-dozen sentries posted and patrolling the exterior of the building. The touch of a pressure switch changed the image to reveal the warehouse interior. There were what appeared to be two guards at each entrance for a total of eight, a skeleton crew of lab workers and a solitary individual sitting at a desk. All told it was what one might expect at a medium security facility in the middle of the night.

"Affirmative. Looks like they're not expecting company."

"Don't buy into that. It's the enemy you *can't* see that will get you every time."

"Alexander..."

"I'm just saying, everyone's obviously going to be watching this building very closely."

"We can be relatively certain Ephrem has deployed assets here or is close to doing so. He has the same intel we have and he has the advantage of a day's head start."

"Yeah, well I think you're currently soaring above the planet in our equalizer."

"True, but that just means we might be knocking on the door and saying 'Trick or Treat' at the same time."

"And you know what to do if that happens."

"Affirmative."

The pilot's voice interjected over their private conversation. "30 minutes till our descent to 20 Angel." This was their intended jump altitude, 20,000 feet, and it was time to start making final equipment checks. The verbal sparring was over; it would be all business from now till mission completion.

"How long's it been since you've made a HALO jump?"

She knew what he was going through and as tempting as it was, she wasn't going to chastise him for worrying. Sending his wife across the ocean at 3000 miles per hour to jump out of a plane four miles above the earth, free fall for 16,000 feet, deploy her chute at 4000 feet and then run into a building full of highly virulent strains of a deadly virus being protected by people who would attempt to kill her on sight was probably not the easiest thing he'd ever done.

"It's going to be fine, Alexander...really. I've done this more times than I can count and these are some of the best operators I've ever seen. Plus you'll see everything I see. In. Out. Over."

"And yet, not one aspect of this operation has been rehearsed."

"That's just how these things go sometimes and you know it. How many times have you had to make it up as you go along?"

He was a wreck inside and he didn't answer. Instead, he decided to put all of those emotions aside. If he was going to be of use to her, he needed to treat this as any other operation. "It's time to start the supplemental oxygen at 100 percent, then cut it back to normal at the 1-minute warning, maintaining that level through canopy deployment."

He couldn't see the smile on her face as she heard his obvious shift from overly concerned husband to Operations Commander. She appreciated his confidence in her more than he knew. "Roger that, C2."

Alexander hadn't heard that designation for 'Command and Control' in several years and he'd sure never heard her use it. This was the part of a mission most operators disliked most, the moments right before insertion. No matter how much intel had been gathered, the expertise of the team, or the force majeure, one simply could not perfectly account for the number of variables and opportunities for things to go wrong. This however was where he excelled. Simon or Ephrem Goldman might be an equal match for him in terms of strategy but tactically, now that he'd shaken the dust off from his five year hiatus, they were at a distinct disadvantage. With Jorah and Judith running surveillance, Robert and Antonin providing oversight on the perimeter and building interior, Alexander would be able to absorb the situation in its totality and move his operators as a Grandmaster moves his chess pieces.

"20 minutes." The pilot gave the update that meant it was time to go dark until they were on the ground. The team would continue checking their equipment and intel updates as they were fed into the integrated devices of their suits. Except for vital signs, C2 would now be out of communication with the operators. Alexander stared at the data screen that registered Laura's blood pressure, heart rate, blood oxygen level, rate of respiration and neuro-imagery. There was only so much compartmentalization he could do when it came to her. For the next half-hour he would sit in silence staring at those numbers and logarithmic graphs that represented so much more to him than mere statistics. He ran through every scenario he could possibly imagine and some that most people couldn't. By the conclusion of the day, his status amongst the Alliance operators would go from mythical to legendary.

26

The ZEHST plane made a surprisingly smooth transition from the upper reaches of the Stratosphere as they descended 16 miles to their designated jump altitude. Ana stood from her seat and gave the signal to her team to stand. Asa, Montalto, Di Nola, Pane and Russo lined up in single file and began checking each other's rigging. On the other side of the fuselage, Laura, Mitri, Mazza, Garo and Barrone did the same. There were two exit doors aft of the cabin, one on either side. With the cabin now depressurized and the ZEHST having slowed to around 200 knots, Laura activated the automated hydraulic door openers. A rush of air filled the space as the portals revealed the murky darkness of the night sky. The longitude and latitude digits scrolled rapidly on their display screens as they waited for the series on which they would lock: 15° 35.5076 N 88° 01.2521 W. The drop zone was in the northeast quadrant of an irregularly shaped octagonal perimeter defined by security fencing and tree lines. In the center of the octagon was the warehouse, a large corrugated metal building with three roadways leading from the west, north and east sides of the building to the outer fence line. The main entrance was on the east side of the building and was lined on either side with the same type of security fencing that surrounded the property. To the south of the building was a dense stand of trees, foliage and two manmade lagoons. The DZ they'd chosen offered less natural cover, but had the advantage of being the least accessible to defensive forces and gave them the most direct access to the least guarded area of the property.

They entered Honduran airspace along the eastern shoreline of the country commonly referred to as "The Mosquito Coast." From there, they made a direct flight over sparsely populated stretches of mountainous terrain until dropping down to 20 Angel just north of el Zapotal and west of their target. The plane made a sharp bank to the southeast. The longitude and latitude digits locked into place and Laura hit the button turning the jump light from red to green. In mere seconds the entire team was out of the plane, into the air and in relatively close proximity as they plummeted toward the earth. Even within the cocoon like environment of the specialized suits the wind noise was similar to that of a Category 5 hurricane. Adventurers and daredevils had the luxury of contemplating the sensations and vistas offered during such free falls, but every member of this team had each of their assignments singularly on their minds during the 90 second drop to chute deployment altitude.

"Orion 1 check." Laura's voice streamed over the secure link which elicited a series of responses from the rest of the insertion team: "Orion 2 check, Orion 3 check, Orion 4 check, Orion 5 check."

Ana then followed suit with "Aquilas 1 check" and received a similar response from the perimeter team.

At just under a mile above the ground, the entire team deployed their navigable canopies bringing them to an abrupt mid-air halt then a resumption of descent at a severely decreased rate of speed. The perimeter team dropped just inside the fencing while the insertion team dropped as close to the building as possible. Ana and Russo hit the ground and took a centerline position on a knoll where they furiously deployed the grenade launcher, tripod and computer fire control. Di Nola and Pane replicated his actions 20 meters on either side of him establishing lanes of fire that would cover the entire area of operation. Asa and Montalto dropped onto a hillside 400 meters to the northeast from which they would cover and communicate the possibility of external defensive forces moving in on them.

As planned, Laura, Mitri, Massa, Garo and Barrone dropped within the protective fields of fire at the northeast corner of the building. All eleven team members had activated their cloaking camouflage after canopy deployment which rendered them almost completely invisible as they took up their positions. The nature of the fabric also rendered their thermal signatures almost totally undetectable. Night vision was even more useless against the futuristic garments registering only subtle blurs of sporadic and unidentifiable motion.

They approached the steel service door in silence. According to their heads up displays, there were two guards just inside the entrance. Laura withdrew a small pistol-like device and opened a cup shaped bowl around a probe where a barrel would ordinarily be. She placed it over the deadbolt lock facing and pulled the trigger. The inaudible sonic waves began agitating and holding the locking pins in relation to the necessary series to turn the lock. When she was ready, she gave a quick "tsk-tsk" into her mike that let Mitri know it was time to breach.

The group back at C2 was watching this precision choreography with rapt attention. Judith and Jorah were making constant adjustments on their keyboards as they monitored every aspect of surveillance. Robert and Antonin watched in silence poised to begin relaying pertinent information to their respective teams.

"What the *fuck?*" Alexander broke the silence with an exclamation that reverberated throughout the command center and into the earpieces of the team.

The Greco twins had seen the same thing at the same time. Alexander's verbal reflex was just quicker to respond to the complete disappearance of every tango's thermal image.

"Orion 1 we just went dark on tangos, over."

"C2 we show same. Continuing breach with night-vision, over."

"Affirmative."

Laura pulled back and took a knee with a direct line of sight on the door. Garo, who'd been right behind her at the door with his arm between her torso and the doorframe and his grip on the handle, jerked backwards and planted himself up against the wall as Mitri dropped the Street Sweeper's barrel in front of him and rushed the entrance. Barrone followed close behind scanning the upper reaches of the room with his MP7. Mazza and Laura filed in behind them breaking left and right with Garo bringing up the rear.

"Clear!" Mitri continued scanning the room as he crossed the barren concrete floor. There was a second-story balcony that framed the upper level and a single I-beam joist that spanned the ceiling with a manually operated block and tackle.

"Orion 1, what's going on? Every damn tango has disappeared."

"Affirmative, C2. The two tangos that appeared just inside the northeast entrance are in fact not here."

"Stay sharp, Orion." Alexander was experiencing a new sensation. When it was his neck on the line, these kinds of occurrences had a calming effect and sharpened his focus. With *her* neck on the line, he was somewhere between furious and explosive.

"Jorah, what in the goddam *HELL* is going on down there?"

Robert and Antonin whipped their heads towards him in unison then looked at Jorah who was not taking his eyes off of the monitor while making keystrokes at a feverish rate. "Working on it."

Realizing it was not an issue with their technology, Alexander took it down a notch. "Judith, broaden the circumference on those drones. I don't care if an iguana wiggles its tail, you throw everything you've got at it."

She'd already put everything in place to carry out the order before he gave it. As soon as he spoke the words, she made one keystroke that sent the instructions to the three drones circling the area that in turn began spiraling in outward concentric circles scanning every inch of the terrain as it went. Every single member of their team was accounted for, but every other human image that had been there before had completely vanished.

"Aquila 1, I want you to bring it in and reverse the fields of fire. Aquila 3 and 4 get to the warehouse and get on top. If they're coming, it'll be from the rear."

"Roger that." Ana had just finished creating an exit in the fencing for the exfiltration and was scrutinizing any and everything in her area. "Let's move, Aquila."

The insertion team was stacked on the door to the next room. It was the largest room in the structure. This is where the lab equipment and stores of virus would be found. They followed the exact same entry procedure from before with the exception that Garo spun back toward the cleared room as he entered the second. He would have to trust that they would have his back as he covered theirs. The room was about 30,000 square feet and completely dark. Their tactical lights and night vision visors showed that there was an opaque heavy-mil plastic wall that hung like a drape from the third story ceiling to the floor. There were three others just like it that together formed a square interior room.

Alexander took all of this in as he watched through Laura's visor-cam. "Orion 1, you picking up anything at all?"

"Negative, C2. None of the tangos that showed before are here, inside or out."

"Put Mazza on the rear door and put Garo on the northeast corner of that cleanroom exterior, Barrone on the southwest corner. Mitri will enter from Barrone's side and you'll enter from Garo's." Alexander was putting the two best shooters in place to cover the two alleys off the plastic walled clean room. Mazza would keep watch on the room they'd entered through while Laura and Mitri passed through the curtain.

"Roger that, C2."

Everyone got into place with complete efficiency of motion.

"On you, Orion."

Without hesitation Laura gave the order, "Go."

Mitri pushed into the divide where the walls met. Laura did the same on her side. As soon as they stepped into the interior, motion sensors activated overhead lighting causing their night vision to immediately power off and their cloaked suits to take on the coloration and suddenly brightened hues of the room. They were both sweeping and scanning the room, Mitri with his Street Sweeper and Laura with the MP7. Except for what appeared to be a dark liquid in the center of the floor, the room was empty. Right as they were looking upward toward the ceiling, they both saw a solitary drop of liquid fall into the amorphous puddle on the floor.

Everyone at C2 saw the same thing that Laura and Mitri saw and at the same time. There was a collective gasp. Suspended in mid-air two and a half stories above them in full Eucharistic vestments was Cardinal José María Morazán.

27

"I s that...?" Laura began asking the question even though she already knew the answer.

"Why, yes it is." Everyone in the room, both inside and outside of the plastic, jerked their heads from side to side as they scanned their respective areas for the source of Ephrem Goldman's voice that echoed throughout the metal structure.

The Aquila team tensed up at the sound of his voice coming through their earpieces but none more so than Ana. A similar response had occurred at C2 with Alexander being the most tense amongst them. He was about to give the order to evacuate but she beat him to it.

"Let's move."

"Oh, but I would be so very disappointed, Mrs. Wells. I've not had the pleasure of making your acquaintance and I was so looking forward to it." Ephrem said this with a timbre of antagonism.

"Move, Orion. Now." Alexander reinforced her order.

"I'm assuming that Mathias is speaking into your ear about now. Giving orders from the great beyond are we, Alexander?" Ephrem waited for some kind of response but Alexander was not going to play into his hands. He might've been guessing or he might've had confirmation but he was not going to be the one to confirm it for him. "Come now, we're all playing with the same deck of cards in this little game of ours. Mitri, Asa and Ana are all here, it's just difficult to tell with those nifty suits of yours.

With this, Ana broke from her position and entered the warehouse through the door they had just breached. "No need for concern though, this is a business arrangement." Ephrem continued, "You have something I want and I definitely have something *you* want."

"Ask him what he wants." Ana said this as she was still crossing the floor of the first room.

"And what do we have that you want?" Laura was still scanning the room as she spoke. "You obviously have the virus in your possession; this place has been cleaned out."

"Oh we have the virus, but that's what *you* want now isn't it?"

Ana passed by Mazza who was still covering the entrance to the larger room, then edged her way into the clean room while disengaging the cloaking unit as she entered.

"Well I don't know for sure, but I believe that's my progeny entering the room now."

Ana removed her helmet. Her thick black hair was pulled back into a bun and her bangs were plastered to her forehead with perspiration. Her eyes were narrowed like those of a hawk searching for her quarry.

"Where are you? You're behaving as a coward." She looked up and saw the grotesque sight of Morazán hanging in the air. He was suspended from the center I-beam by a chain that seemed to be hooked into his upper back. His feet were pointed downward but at odd angles as if his legs were frozen mid-struggle. "And you've murdered a Cardinal"

"No!" The ferocity of anger in his tone was unmistakable. Seeing his daughter after her betrayal had obviously consumed him with rage. "No, Ana...I have simply carried out a sentence against one of Israel's most vile enemies, a traitor to his so called religion of peace and a conspirator in a plan to destroy our people...*your* people."

Keeping her right hand on her sub-machine gun, she released her left hand from the fore grip and slapped at the right side of her exposed neck where she'd felt a slight prick. Before she got her gloved hand back onto her weapon, the realization of what had just happened cascaded across her with dread.

"Get your helmet on!" Laura also realized what had happened. She looked from Ana back up to the deceased Morazán. The skin of his hands had ruptured as had that of his face. Dislodged by the flow of blood, his mitre was askew. The blood that had not been absorbed by the thick silk chasuble was dripping down into the growing puddle.

"Oh I'm afraid you're far too late for that." The ice in Ephrem's voice poured through the speakers as another mosquito pierced her exposed skin, then another.

Ana put her helmet on anyway. "Come out and face me you coward!"

"Ironic, isn't it? That only the female mosquito bites." His reference to her collaboration with the Alliance was both clear and chilling. "There is only one coward in this family and it is she who has bedded with our enemies."

"You would murder your own daughter?" Laura's instincts were telling her that this was only the beginning of a larger plan that he had in store for them. She needed him to give something away, to say anything that might provide insight into that plan.

"Oh, not at all Daughter of Enoch..." All but Laura, Alexander and Antonin were taken aback at this enigmatic reference. "If she dies, it will be at the hands and will of your husband. There is more than enough vaccine for her very close by, and the price for knowledge of its location is very easily rendered."

"Tell him where it is, Alexander." Laura barely had the words out of her mouth when Ana interjected.

"No! Tell him nothing! Let his insane quest die here and now."

The terse dialogue was interrupted by Jorah's voice through their earpieces, "Tangos dropping in on you. Counting a dozen in an arc from 0°N to 90°E and a half-dozen dropping in at 320°W."

Pane, who had shifted along with his machine gun to the north side of the building facing back into their own drop zone began folding up his bipod and gathering his ammo.

"Pane, set up on the northwest corner of the building in the tree line on the western side of the road." Alexander gave the order Pane had anticipated receiving.

The shooters extraordinaire Garo and Barrone had already broken away from the corners of the clean room and were nearly to the northeast exit by the time Alexander gave his order for them to take up positions in the tree line on the eastern side of the road.

The next sound anyone heard was the rapid succession 'chunk-chunk-chunk' of Russo's grenade launcher followed by three concussive explosions as the pre-fragmented grenades exploded in midair sending shrapnel flying in every direction 500 meters beyond the perimeter fence. This was punctuated by Pane and Di Nola's machine gun bursts whose tracer rounds were lighting up the surrounding area with streaks of flying terror. Of the dozen tangos attacking from the northeast, those that failed to take cover quickly enough were being immediately folded over by the silenced .308 rounds that Asa was sending directly to them at 3000 feet per second.

"You've now got twelve more coming in at 135°S. They're going to be dropping inside the perimeter and they just dropped a box." Jorah was referring to the

184

package that had landed just prior to the commandos. It came in under its own chute rather than being tethered to one of the jumpers so it was obviously a serious piece of equipment.

"Judith, as soon as they get within proximity, Light'em up." Alexander barely had to give the order as she'd already painted the target with a laser from one of her drones and had a Hydra-70 rocket poised to take out whatever they'd just put on the ground. She watched and waited as three of the tangos approached the box. The pad of her index finger pressed lightly against the trigger control on the joystick. Her screen sizzled with a brief amount of digital snow, and then went black.

The aerial explosion caused the team to tense up, but not a single one of them took their focus away from the targets they were engaging.

"They've got drones in the air." Jorah's statement nearly went without saying as that had been the general assumption when one of their own was taken out. "Two more dropping into visual range."

Judith had already pulled the trigger by the time Jorah got the last two words out of his mouth. The tango drone that had its sights set on the northeast corner of the building where Russo, Di Nola and Pane were positioned suddenly exploded. Judith wasn't showing it, but Jorah knew very well just how pissed off she was at the moment.

"Another dozen tangos coming in at 230°W." Jorah's news was most unwelcome.

Mitri swept Ana up and into a fireman's carry as it was obvious she was already weakening from the virus that was blazing through her system. Laura pulled the plastic curtain aside to let them through as Ephrem's voice boomed overhead, "Just tell me where the stone is and we can all go home tonight."

"The exfil point is 400 meters outside the DZ. We'll do a stack and run up the tree line of the northern roadway. We've weakened their forces most there." Laura was orchestrating their exit strategy when Alexander interrupted.

"Belay those orders. Pull it in to the warehouse. Everyone!"

Every member of the team was well trained and didn't hesitate to reverse on a field command when C2 gave a directive, but that didn't stop every single one of them from considering that they'd just been ordered to their death.

"What are you doing? Ana's dying, we're pinned down from every direction, our only choice is punching through their softest point and making a run for the exfil location. Going into the warehouse is exactly what they *want* us to do." Laura had switched to a closed communication with Alexander to make her protest even as she followed his order.

Instead of responding through the closed channel, Alexander made his one remark through the open channel so that everyone could hear it, "It's not the arrow, it's the Indian."

Laura didn't understand the basis of the reference, but every other team member did, especially the weakened and feverish Ana. Daniel Jenco was speaking to his friends and fiancé through Alexander. It had been the last thing he said as Alexander went to confront Simon. He'd learned from some of the others that this was his way of reminding them that it was never about the warrior in the fight, but about the fight in the warrior. They'd heard him say it before every operation. Alexander revived it for them at very moment their mission confidence was waning. It had its intended effect. A surge of strength and confidence swept through the group as they reversed the order of their stack and run back toward the warehouse.

Just as Barrone cleared the trees, the northern end of the roadway erupted in an explosion that sent shards of timber, asphalt and metal flying in every direction. A Frisbee sized hunk from a concrete barrier caught him on the left thigh. The protective qualities of his suit prevented it from severing his leg, but he was fairly certain his femur was broken as he splayed forward carried by the momentum of the impact. Garo had instinctively done a tuck and roll as soon as he'd heard the

186

explosion and once the mixture of shrapnel had passed safely by he looked back for Barrone.

"Eli!" He saw his cousin's body sprawled out on the ground and had no idea of his condition.

Barrone was conscious but in a large amount of pain that was made obvious by his strained reply, "Probably going to need a little help here."

Garo switched his HUD to Barrone's vitals. His blood pressure and heart rate were up as was respiration. However, neural activity was base line calm. "You're too damned stupid to be scared."

"Yeah, yeah. Just come help me up, asshole." Garo's relief was immeasurable but he would never let Barrone know it. Of course, he already knew.

Within a few more seconds everyone had gathered in the smaller of the two warehouse rooms just inside the northeast door. The din of automatic weapons fire continued outside as did the explosions from the rockets Judith was raining down on the tangos. They were all obviously waiting to hear something from Laura or C2 on their next move but in the extremely brief lull of communications a most unexpected sound came from the corner of the room. A metal floor hatch slammed open on the concrete floor. Everyone whipped their weapons toward the noise and focused on the lone figure emerging from underneath the warehouse. No one was more shocked than Laura to see who it was.

28

"**M**ichael?" Her mind was racing. She hadn't laid eyes on him in at least three years but it was definitely him. His sudden presence was jarring to her senses. Adding to her confusion was the fact that though he was essentially a clairvoyant analyst, Michael Stallworth was absolutely *not* a field operative. He was 50 years old, had the mental acuity of a man half his age and the soul of one twice his age. He was a gentleman and a scholar, but he nonetheless lacked the mettle necessary to survive much less thrive in the heat of a battle. There had also been Alexander's warning regarding his potential corruption that was now pulsing in tandem with a natural relief to see her long time lifeguard. It was creating a tornadic swirl of emotion within her.

"Follow him." was all Alexander said as the corrugated metal walls of the building began pealing open under the heavy fire it was now sustaining. "Mitri and Ana first."

The team formed a tight 360° around the opening in the floor and sent the ailing and unconscious Ana down first immediately followed by Mitri, Barrone and Garo. Even over the clamor and confusion of the firefight, Ephrem's manic screams could be heard.

"Take it down! Take the damned building down, you incompetent fools!"

Judith had already taken out the two remaining drones and was repositioning on what they now knew was a launch platform for TOW missiles. Asa and Montalto

189

prevented the tangos from unpacking the weapons system from the top of the warehouse up until the order was given to pull it in. With their suppressing fire now absent the tripod and computer fire control were being rapidly assembled. It wouldn't take long to have the first missile ready to fire.

Laura was covering everyone else as they slipped down into the earth. Bullets zipped and screamed throughout the room as they pierced the thin metal walls and ricocheted off the support beams. Though she was in a low crouch against a wall and behind one of the beams with the MP7 trained on the open door, an errant bullet caught her right arm. She was protected by the suit but it still felt like being hit with a sledgehammer. She dropped completely flat as she gritted her teeth letting out an involuntary and pain stricken growl.

"Please come through that door you son of a..."

"Get moving, Laura." Alexander was watching the TOW missile assembly on his live satellite feed but had heard her take the round through his headset. He'd also heard the near and rare curse she was about to utter regarding the culprit.

Everyone made it into the tunnel and Laura followed with both her arm and her pride throbbing. She reached up, slammed the door closed and turned the reinforced locking mechanism. The rest of the team was scrambling down the corridor and through a rusty metal doorway. Compared to the secret subterranean passages they'd been traversing back in Rome, this was a rat hole. It was an earthen tunnel with rotting timbers and the occasional sheet of plywood holding it open. The floor was a muddy path punctuated with pools of water ranging from one inch to three feet deep. They were all slogging and thrashing along, with their progress slowed by the gumbo like surface. They were humping it out of there as quickly as possible.

"Abort and follow! Abort and follow, you cretinous leeches!" Ephrem's screeching commands went unheeded as the warehouse erupted in a powerful explosion. They had unleashed the TOW and were preparing to follow on with a second. "NOOOOO! They're in a tunnel! They're in a tunnel, goddammit!"

The tango field commander ignored the crazed man's orders and gave his own. "Neighborhood's about to get crowded; let's pull it in guys."

As the second TOW took the remainder of the building down, three Blackhawk helicopters crested the next ridge over and they were coming in hot. They hit the clearing just to the west of the warehouse perimeter and were loaded and gone within half a minute.

The team made it clear of the underside of the building in their escape, however under the force of the explosions the tunnel collapsed and pushed an engorgement of mud, rocks and splintered support beams rolling toward them. Laura narrowly escaped being engulfed by the mass before it stopped but was now struggling to free herself from the shin-deep muck beneath her. The pockets of air under her boots were creating a suction that was preventing her from pulling her legs upward. Mazza and Pane turned back to help liberate her from the vice-like grip. Michael ordered Mitri to lay Ana down in the most shallow water he could find.

"And get that suit off of her." Mitri found a spot with only a couple of inches of water and did as he was told. Her visage was shocking to him at first. Her eyes were completely blood shot, her nose was bleeding and her entire face was streaked with red as her vascular system had already begun hemorrhaging. Her vital statistics being monitored back at C2 indicated dropping blood pressure, an increased heart rate and a body temperature of 105.2° Fahrenheit. Mitri continued releasing the various pressure closures that kept the suit fastened to her body. Underneath, every bit of her skin that was not concealed by the composite material body suit showed the same red streaks that had the very look of death about them. Her respiration was shallow with a rasping gurgle as blood pooled in the back of her mouth.

Michael knelt beside her and dropped the small olive drab day pack off of his back. His LED headlamp cast an artificial blueish-white glow that gave the surrounding soil a pallor of grey. "Take these and cut away the midriff." He handed a pair of EMT scissors to Mitri who removed his gloves and pinched a portion of her body suit between the thumb and forefinger of his left hand and began cutting with his left.

"I sure hope there aren't any of those mosquitoes down here." He continued cutting away the material while watching the backs of his hands for the demonic little insects.

"Those weren't mosquitoes and no, there aren't any down here." Michael was preparing an IV bag by injecting what Mitri assumed was the vaccine for this virus into it. He then held the dromedary bag aloft and instructed Mitri to keep it there. He then snapped a four inch square piece of material onto the end of the tubing where a needle would ordinarily be found. He peeled the facing off of it, activated a small plunger on the back of it and slapped it onto Ana's exposed abdomen just below her rib cage. He held his hand there for several seconds.

"Active transdermal patch." Michael could see the question on Mitri's his face that he obviously wasn't going to ask. At the time, the only thing that mattered was saving his friend's life and this stranger with an IV seemed to know what he was doing. "It uses ultrasonic waves to disrupt the skin and deliver the fluids. Her vascular system wouldn't be able to handle a standard IV right now."

"Is she in pain?"

"Very likely, and it will get worse. It's sometimes called 'break-bone fever.' Unfortunately pain medication tends to exacerbate the hemorrhaging."

The rest of the team was standing by watching with apprehension as Michael worked on Ana. Mazza, Pane and Laura now out of the mire, approached from the collapsed end of the tunnel. A cacophony of voices was faintly echoing from the opposite direction. Asa, Montalto and Di Nola instinctively took up defensive positions along each side of the corridor.

"They're with me." Michael said this as he stood and called into the darkened tunnel, *"Aquí abajo."*

The voices grew excitedly louder as a soft glow of light began erasing the darkness out in front of them. Seconds later a group of four locals carrying an assortment of equipment approached and went straight to work unfurling an emergency litter for Ana. They placed a plasticized pad covered with a light fleece that had a radiator like pattern snaking across every inch of its surface. They lifted Ana onto the stretcher then folded the other half of the pad over her. One of the men had a rather heavy looking apparatus on his back that he turned toward one of his compatriots. The man opened a compartment on the side and uncoiled a half-inch tube that he then connected to the pad.

"This will help bring her fever down. It's a cooling blanket." He gave some quick instructions to the four Hondurans who then lifted Ana and began walking down the tunnel. "It's a pretty good hike and the tunnel gets pretty narrow in places." Looking at Barrone who at the moment was being supported by Garo and Pane he continued, "We can send a litter back for you."

"I'll be fine."

"The rest of you go ahead, we'll catch up." Garo said this as he shifted his weight to adjust for the slippery mud beneath his feet.

"Alright then. It's a direct route from here to the safe house with no alternate tunnels. If you change your mind about the litter, just radio ahead. The signal strength between here and the safe house should be clear."

Laura took off her helmet and joined Michael, "Let's walk and talk."

They fell in behind the stretcher while the others kept a distance and rotated out in helping Barrone navigate the serpentine cavern on his broken leg.

Michael didn't wait for Laura to inquire, "When Alexander realized the potential layers of deceit surrounding this facility and operation he got in touch with me. Honestly, Laura I don't know how he did it."

"Did what?"

"Well, he got me on a secure line in my office that only three people besides me are even aware exists: the commander of the Joint Special Operations Command, the National Reconnaissance Office director and the CIA director. Then, he told me to get out of the building, to go to an address he provided and under no circumstances was I to take any of my electronic devices with me."

The tunnel narrowed down to the point that it forced them into single-file with Michael allowing Laura to go first. She cut through the pass and they continued on this way for several yards.

"I got to the location and was whisked away in a van that took me to a private airfield where I was put on board a Citation X and flown down here. I was midair before I heard another word from him. He told me my office had just been ransacked as well as my house and that he'd been waiting to see if that would happen before contacting me. I asked him the obvious question of what he would've done if it hadn't. He didn't respond."

Laura picked up her pace as the suspense of his explanation built. The tunnel gradually widened so that they could walk side by side once again.

"Once we landed, a black Hummer rolled right up to the plane and we headed out of the city toward el Zapotal. Even if he hadn't told me where we were going I would've known as soon as we landed. I even knew where we were going as we drove out to Zapotal, I knew we were going to Maria Delgado's house."

"Maria Delgado?"

"That's where this tunnel leads. That warehouse was a CIA black site about 18 years ago. It was my first assignment. I made all of the arrangements for the transport of operatives going to and from the site. The funding couldn't be handled directly so I set up an operating account through the Corps of Engineers. We gave Maria

Delgado temporary housing and tore her dwelling down. It was a cinder block hut with no windows, electricity or plumbing. We built a new house with reinforced walls, windows, a sturdy roof, and indoor plumbing. We also ran electricity out to the village and she was the first to be connected. By the time we completed the house and tunnel, American journalists had filed Freedom of Information Act requests related to the Contra war and the interrogation program being conducted at the black site. It was promptly shut down and Maria moved into her new home which quickly made her the *gran dama de Zapotal.*"

"How did he know about it?"

"I have no idea. Your husband knows way more than he should about a lot of things."

"But why would they ransack *your* office? Do you think the CIA knows about this operation now?"

"Laura, that group that just descended on you like a swarm of hornets...that *was* the CIA."

29

The Hondurans carrying Ana arrived at a steep underground staircase. The surrounding walls were lined with wooden shelves lined with canisters of dried beans, preserved meat, vegetables and several flats of fresh eggs. Onions hung from the ceiling in nylon hosiery with knots tied between each bulb. This had apparently become Maria Delgado's root cellar.

The man on the leading left corner of the stretcher used his elbow to push a round Bakelite doorbell button. The signal traveled up the twisting wires and into the house above where Maria Delgado's daughter saw the lights flicker on then off. She went to a pantry with a multi-colored drape hanging over its entrance. She bent down, pulled a cotton rug out and unlatched the hidden door. The four men struggled up the stairs but managed to keep Ana relatively still as they clambered upward. Michael and Laura followed not far behind as did the rest of the team with the exception of Barrone, Garo and Pane. They were still moving at a slower pace.

Vivian Delgado rattled off instructions to the four men that Laura could now see were actually young men ranging from their mid-teen years to early twenties. They took Ana to a back room where there was a handmade lumber cot with a mattress and pillow made up for her. As they passed by Maria's room she called out to them but they continued about their task uninterrupted. Instead, Vivian went to the door of her room where only the sound of an oscillating pedestal fan could be heard circulating the tropical air.

"¿Bien, mamá?"

"Sí." Her fragile voice could barely be heard above the fan.

"El Sr. Miguel está aquí." Michael and Laura walked up just as she was letting her mother know he was there.

"She knows you?"

His attention was divided between her question and listening intently for Maria Delgado's response. It had been a little over two years since he'd been to see her and he had no idea of her health or condition.

"You've been here before?"

"I'm sorry. Yes, since we've had a higher concentration of field agents here than anywhere else in the world for the last ten years, I've made it a point to get by and see her when I was in country. The downside to building this house for her was that we also made her a target for thieves. The first couple of years after we pulled out were the worst."

Laura had seen this all too often. Local assets would be recruited to assist in various ways only to be abandoned once the mission was complete. Depending on the political or economic climate of their country, those individuals often became the subjects of harassment, beatings, kidnapping, thievery and even murder.

It took a few more moments for Maria Delgado to respond, but when she did it took Vivian by surprise as the diminutive octogenarian pulled back the threadbare sheet covering her door. In her youth she'd been less than five feet tall, but the forces of life, time and gravity had drawn her closer to the ground with each passing day. Her silver hair was pulled back into a tight bun and even though her weathered, tobacco-leaf brown face showed the years of a hard life in an industrial suburb of the world's most dangerous city, her large brown eyes retained the same hopeful gleam they'd had nearly twenty years prior.

"*Mamá*!" Vivian was already trying to usher her back toward the bed, but Maria's bare feet, flattened and widened by a lifetime of going shoeless, held their ground. Her smile, though missing more than a few teeth, was worthy of the red carpet on Oscar night and to Michael was twice as valuable.

He stretched his arms toward her as he stooped down for a big hug, "Maria Delgado!"

"Miguel, Miguel, Miguel!" Her tiny countenance was filled with laughter and joy at his presence.

A group of small children that had been playing outside in the early morning sun on their arrival came running into the house but stopped short at the pass through as if there'd been an invisible barrier. They piled together at the doorway and studied the group of strangely attired Gringos with intense curiosity. As Michael exchanged a nearly indistinguishable provincial Spanish dialogue with Maria, Laura turned her attention to the children. The moment she smiled at them they broke through the invisible barrier and rushed her. Most of them wrapped their arms around her legs and those that couldn't squeeze into the group hug latched onto her hands. A chorus of still more indistinguishable Spanish erupted around her. She struggled to keep her MP7 out of their reach but they seemed completely unfazed by the presence of so many deadly weapons.

Vivian turned her attention away from trying to herd Maria back to bed and began shooing the kids out of the house. Laura tried to indicate that it was no problem but was secretly relieved that they were off of her. Any other time she might not have felt that way, but with Ana's life in the balance and a flood of unanswered questions, the faster they could get out of there, the better. By the time she turned back toward Michael and Maria he had gently walked her back to her bed and was now sitting beside her speaking in softened and serious tones.

Their conversation didn't take too much longer as Michael leaned in for a parting hug. He stood, gave Maria Delgado a kiss on her forehead and came back through the bedroom door.

"She was asleep when I came in last night and I now wish I'd woken her. Eighty-seven years old and she's still the best source of information in Central America."

"Something tells me I'm not going to like what she had to say."

They walked together back into the kitchen where the rest of the team was gathered. Barrone, Garo and Pane had arrived and Di Nola was examining the broken leg in preparation for a splint.

"Let's step outside."

Laura took in their surroundings. It was little wonder to her that Maria Delgado had been targeted by thieves and extortionists. Most of the other homes were little more than stick-built shanties with the occasional concrete dwelling between. Emaciated livestock roamed the dirt streets freely making the sight of shoeless kids all the more poignant. The aromas were a strange mixture of a pleasing citrusy wood being burned in adobe stoves and that of raw sewage cooking in the morning heat. High above and all around them though were some of the most lush and beautiful mountains she'd ever seen.

"First time in Honduras?"

She was still captivated by the conflicting admixture of sights, smells and sounds. "Yes."

"It's a landscape of beauty and horror."

"That seems to be my new normal."

Michael made a sharp transition from their philosophical observations to that of his conversation with Maria. "We can't stay here, we can't go back to your original exfiltration point and we *sure* can't go into San Pedro Sula."

"Then I hope you have a tunnel that will take us to Rome?"

"According to Maria, the CIA hit the warehouse three days ago?"

"*Three* days?"

"They cleaned everything out and apparently staged it for your arrival."

"Our satellites and drones indicated a defense complement but when we breached the building, there was no one home."

"Computer controlled thermal generators. It's a new technology about the size of a hockey puck that when activated fools thermal imaging equipment into 'seeing' the heat signature of whatever shape the programmer desires."

"What is the CIA's interest in this?"

"Until now I didn't know they had one at all. I do know that some time ago we developed a weaponized strain of HDF but couldn't come up with a vaccine or treatment so the project was abandoned. Whoever was running that little operation back there was successful in creating both, according to Alexander."

"The Vatican."

Michael gave her a confused look. "The Vatican?"

"Well, in collaboration with the Iranians, yes."

He stared silently into the hills for a moment. A bird with a high pitched clarion call signaled her warning as she took sudden flight from a nearby tree. Michael pulled Laura by the arm back into the house and closed the door just as a shiny Ford F-250 with a contingent of national police came roaring past stirring up clouds of dust as they went.

"They're out looking for strays from last night's raid."

"Strays?"

"Yeah, it doesn't matter to them who they get as long as they get somebody. The current president here loathes the CIA presence but has to tolerate them. He was a victim of Battalion 316 and their agency trainers back when the black site was operational. He was tortured for a month up at that warehouse only to be released and find that his entire family had been murdered or sold into slavery, depending on their gender. He ignores them out of financial expediency based on funding from the U.S., that is until they pull something like they did this morning. Then, if he can prove it was them, he has some extraordinarily powerful leverage. Which is also why we can't go into San Pedro. Everyone's looking for someone who sticks out."

"Well, we certainly do that. So what's the plan?"

"Alexander said that if we ended up here to hold tight until we heard from him."

"Do you have the meds you need for Ana's treatment?"

Michael's expression was one that clearly indicated he had no idea how to say what he had to say. "Laura, I don't have what we need at all. I gave her fluids and an anti-viral that will slow the progress of the fever and hemorrhaging but the only effective treatment available is in the possession of the Vatican or Iranians if what you say is true."

The others overheard Michael say this. Mitri approached him with urgency, "You don't have the antidote for this?"

"I'm afraid I don't."

"How long can she go without it?"

"I don't know. If it's the same strain or similar to the one we developed then my best guess would be less than twelve hours."

"Then let's get the hell out of here! Where's our new extraction point?"

"Mitri, we're working on that. OK?"

The barrel chested warrior had lost one of his best friends when Daniel Jenco's helicopter went down. Now Ana, that same best friend's fiancée, was on the precipice of death and he was not going to let her go without staging an all out fight to save her.

"No, it's not OK. You get on the horn with C2 and tell them I'll haul her out of here on my back and hijack the first plane I see if I have to, but I'm getting her out of here. And by that I mean sooner than later."

Laura's handheld began buzzing in its arm pouch. Now that the helmet was disconnected she would have to answer manually. She pulled it from the enclosure and saw that it was C2 and began giving a situation report.

"We're holed up in a village house near the compound." She was careful not to give too much detail. "Ana is stable for now. Barrone's leg is broken pretty badly."

"Laura..." It was Robert's voice on the other end instead of Alexander's. "Laura, Ephrem has Alexander again."

30

The line was silent for an exaggerated stretch of time. "Laura, did you hear me?"

"That's not funny, Robert." Her heart sank into her gut as everyone in the room got quiet.

Robert's voice was as mixed as his own emotions. He was attempting to maintain his mission bearing but was finding it difficult to do as he had to tell Laura this latest development. "I'm sorry, Laura but it's no joke. As soon as he knew your team was safely in the tunnel he left exfil instructions for us then bolted out of here without so much as a word. We were all focused on getting your extraction lined up except for Judith who was keeping one eye trained on the monitors that showed the perimeter around Sant'Eustachio. About a minute after he shot out of here she put the images up on the large monitors and got our attention. It was Alexander running through an alley toward the Pantheon. When he hit the Villa della Rotonda two Nephilim stepped out in front of him and a third came up behind him. They were enormous." Robert's voice cracked as he struggled to maintain his composure. He'd seen them before but it had been a long time. Aside from the occasional professional athlete, the Nephilim stayed largely out of sight. Watching helplessly as they descended on his friend was not easy. Each of them was over seven feet tall and as broad and thick as the sedans passing by on the street.

"Robert, what happened?"

"Well, he folded the one on the left like he wasn't even there, but the other two were on him before he could make another move. The one behind him went low and bulldogged him while the other caught him in the forehead with an elbow." Robert took a deep breath to keep his nerves in check. "He took a damn hard hit and was evidently unconscious as they threw him in the van. It happened so fast, most pedestrians didn't even notice."

"Go after him! Did you go after him?"

"We are watching every inch of the streets, train stations and airports in and around Rome." Antonin had obviously been listening in on the conversation and was trying to reassure Laura that they would find him. "But the van they used was disguised to look like a Best Tours of Rome van. There must be one hundred more just like it within a five kilometer radius."

She had been bewildered when Walter Trowbridge showed up at their cabin. She was perturbed when Alexander started describing his former, secret life to her. The fear she'd felt when the Willow Bed & Breakfast exploded and the angst when she determined he'd been abducted was nearly unbearable. The current circumstances however ignited a roiling firestorm at the core of her being. They'd flown half way across the globe in an hour and a half only to find that her former employers had already invaded their old warehouse, stolen the virus containers and equipment that they'd gone there to confiscate from Boniface and the Iranians and laid a trap for them. Ana was lying in the next room dying and Mitri was on the verge of becoming a raging bull in an effort to get her out of there. And now Alexander had gotten himself abducted once again by the grossly malevolent Ephrem Goldman who, now twice thwarted, would certainly go to any extreme to get what he wanted out of him. The walls were closing in on her, Boniface and the Iranians on one side, the Gush Emunim and Nephilim on the other and she was determined not to get crushed in the middle.

"You listen to me and you listen closely. I don't care who's watching. I don't care if you land that ZEHST jet on top of this whole village. The situation here *and* there is about to deteriorate rapidly and none of the elements responsible for this crisis can be dealt with from here. You can bet that within 24 hours the Gush Emunim will release this virus in the Palestinian territories and God only knows where else. The only potential vaccine and treatment for what I can tell you first hand is a terrifyingly invasive and destructive virus is sitting in a warehouse in Tehran; and we need that yesterday. Whatever timetable he gave you, accelerate it to immediate."

Robert and Antonin looked at each other, then over to Jorah and Judith. Without saying a word, their expressions clearly acknowledged and conveyed complete agreement.

"There's a flurry of activity in and around San Pedro. If anyone at Langley suddenly remembers the tunnel, you won't be safe there anyway." Robert was keying coordinates into a digital data package that he would transmit as he spoke. "You should be getting some coordinates now."

Laura reached for her helmet and put it on while clicking her handheld back into its sleeve compartment. The coordinates and a digital sand table of the landing zone flickered onto her heads up display.

"Three miles north of your location is the village Delicious del Norte." A pulsing red marker beacon indicated the location of the village on her display. "On the very eastern edge of the village is a little church up on a plateau. The valley between that plateau and the next ridge over is your LZ. We were going to pull you out after nightfall but we've gone ahead and scrambled a stealth-modified Blackhawk out of Bananera just north of Morales in Guatemala." Jorah had actually already set this into motion the moment he saw they were all in agreement on making the extraction imminent.

"The best route would be the terrain northeast of the roadway but it's next to impossible without the ATVs from the original exfil point." Laura was taking Ana's and Barrone's conditions into consideration. Hauling the two of them across the rolling hills for three miles would be next to impossible without the all-terrain vehicles that had been prearranged by Antonin for the initial extraction plan.

"And the roadway between Zapotal and Delicious del Norte will be jammed with national police."

They were all considering the difficult options when a most unexpected little voice piped up from hallway door. *"Tienes que irte pronto y necesita llamar Socio. Llame al Socio."*

Her rural dialect was such that even those in the group that spoke the language fluently could not understand her. However, having understood her perfectly, Michael strode across the room laughing and embracing her warmly when he got to her. *"Eres hermosa, Maria Delgado!"*

Laura understood *his* Spanish perfectly, "You are beautiful, Maria Delgado...OK, so tell us why that is."

"She just said we need to get out of here soon and that we need to call Socio." He laughed a deep laugh at this stroke of brilliance.

No one in the room understood and Mitri's patience was wearing thin. "Who's Socio?"

"He's a bus driver." Michael turned back toward the group with the phone already up to his ear. "But not just *any* bus driver. He drives for Brigade Tours out of San Pedro. Their only clients are American mission workers."

It was obvious no one was any further enlightened as to why that was significant. "Mission groups get a free pass down here on just about everything. They bring millions into the economy every year and basically keep Honduras as a political priority for the US government. No administration in its right mind would cut off the single largest facilitator of faith-based mission groups in the Western Hemisphere, and no Honduran administration in its right mind would harass them while they're here. In fact, a few years ago there was an organized shakedown going on through customs. The agents would suggest certain 'fees' for bringing in medical and relief supplies. Once the 'fees' reached exorbitant levels, the mission teams began complaining. The issue was resolved in one day and hasn't been a problem since." He didn't elaborate, but he didn't have to. Honduran justice was often swift, severe and for the most part went unreported.

Laura understood the importance of what Michael was conveying. Essentially they would be hitching a ride on their own rolling Switzerland. "How soon can he get here?"

Michael held his hand up to indicate that the connection had been made. He then handed the phone to Maria Delgado. Only the scantest of conversations took place before she was giving the device back to him.

"Gracias, mi querido."

The petite hickory stick of a woman simply smiled, gave a polite nod to the room and returned to her bed. Her days rarely contained this much interaction and activity and it had drained what little energy she possessed.

"He should be here within the hour."

"Did you get that?" Laura continued her conversation with Robert.

"Affirmative. Looks like about a half hour ride from where you are to Delicious del Norte. If the bus arrives in an hour we'll have a tee time in 90 minutes. Believe it or not, that works out perfectly with the Blackhawk in route."

Antonin, though he had no reason for it, was feeling a measure of guilt for letting Alexander fall back into the hands of the enemy. It was not a conscious process, but he began assuming the protective posture left vacant by Alexander's absence. "Laura, you have got to be certain your cloaking suits are activated and that Ana is concealed on the floor of the bus, there still may be a search at a checkpoint. If things get hot you have only one choice. None of you will make it out of Honduras alive if they discover and capture you."

"Roger that, C2." Her ability to remain polite was very close to being taxed beyond the limit. She appreciated his concern and the reminder about the cloaking suits was warranted. However, reminding her that she might need to order the deaths of the relatively innocent members of the national police was not necessary.

"And you know if it looks like they are getting suspicious, it would be better to engage them while you still have the element of surprise."

Because of the helmet she was wearing, Michael couldn't see the expression on her face, but he didn't have to, he'd seen it often enough when someone thought she might benefit from some hand-holding on mission specifics.

"Antonin," her voice cut through the satellite link like a fresh scalpel. "I don't care *who* it is, if they get between that LZ and my team they will have just drawn their final breath on this mortal plain. Orion 1 out."

Antonin swallowed hard, signed off and then looked around the room. Jorah, Judith and Robert all averted their eyes as he looked to them to see if they had registered the verbal ass-kicking he was sure he'd just sustained. Robert especially had to tuck his face down toward his right shoulder to hide his smile. His abs were getting a great workout as they quivered to keep his laugh suppressed.

"Remarkable." He said this aloud, but to no one in particular. "No wonder he fell in love with her."

31

Alexander began regaining consciousness and made an attempt to lift himself off of the van floor. His head felt like it had been cracked completely open and the associated pain was causing a dizziness that prevented him from being able to remain steady on his hands and knees. His arms gave out first, sending him down onto his elbows. His stomach lurched and he vomited, a good sign that he was concussed. Not wanting to fall into his own breakfast, he tried to force himself to roll over onto his left side rather than to his right. However, as soon as he began the struggle to do so, an anvil sized fist crushed into his ribs. The pain was blindingly severe and he landed head first into the mess he'd hoped to avoid. Ephrem would want him alive, but this was definitely going to be a rough ride. Every living Nephilim knew who he was and would've given anything to have been the one locked in the back of a van with him for just a few minutes.

His massive jailer was on his knees but still managed to consume the majority of the cargo space with his upper torso. He reached as quickly as he could for his pocket and the .357, but the giant was having none of it. With one hammer blow delivered with his palm, the behemoth snapped Alexander's right arm causing him to scream out in pain.

A divider panel slid downward and opened up a view of the cab. One of the Gush Emunim operatives was driving the van and spoke something in Danish to the Nephilim. It must've been something along the lines of telling him to ease off the beating. He looked at the back of the driver's head as though he wanted to twist it off, then looked back down at Alexander as if he wanted to crush his skull beneath his foot. With a grunt of disgust he reached down and in one motion, violently slid Alexander's entire body into the lower portion of the metal divider as one last act of aggression. He then rocked back onto his calves glowering at Alexander.

The head trauma he'd endured was causing him to feel groggy, but he didn't want to pass out if he could prevent it. He began counting seconds off in his head. Hopefully this would keep his mind active enough to stay awake and at the same time provide an estimation of their location based on how long they would be driving. Though he'd lost all sense of direction during the assault, by the time the van came to a stop, he'd counted off roughly 1600 seconds. Based on that length of time and the sounds of jet engines he was fairly certain they were back at Fiumicino airport.

The next sound he observed was that of an automatic gate sliding along being pulled by a chain drive mechanism. The van began rolling once more, but this time it was for only a few minutes. The metallic popping of a hydraulically operated aluminum door being lifted informed him that they were about to pull into a private hangar. His insight was soon born out as the rollup door of the box van opened to reveal Ephrem Goldman's plane being prepared for flight as well as two more gargantuan men standing on either side of the vehicle.

One of the two Nephilim standing outside of the van grabbed his legs and pulled him out into a grip so tight that Alexander thought his head was going to explode. He could feel the grittiness of his broken ribs rubbing together and the pain from his right arm spread throughout his body like fingers of lightning. The other of the two began strapping his arms to his sides from the shoulders down to his wrists with duct tape. He finished off with two laps around his neck and mouth. The giant from the van unfolded himself from the cargo space and gave Alexander a solid shove from behind that sent him sprawling helplessly across the smooth concrete floor. The two that had applied the duct tape restraints then picked him up and rather than walking him up the steps into the plane, heaved him head first through the hatch where four Gush Emunim operatives then dragged him to the center of the cabin floor. The largest of the Nephilim tossed the roll of tape into the plane and one of the operatives bound his legs from calf to ankle. They then disappeared into the recesses of the plane without saying a word.

It was somewhere around an hour before he heard anything other than the clamor of external flight preparations, but at least it had been an hour devoid of abuse. The next sounds in the cabin were those of the two pilots entering and seemingly ignoring him. They came and went with barely a word between them over the next half hour before finally settling into the cockpit. Not long afterward, Ephrem Goldman stepped aboard. Alexander couldn't see his face, but could tell it was him by the gate of his stride and the peppery scent of his cologne. He expected some form of taunt or disdainful greeting from Ephrem, but instead the determined zealot glided by him as if he weren't even there.

As the pushback tractor connected itself to the landing gear to pull them out onto the tarmac, Alexander had a thought he'd not had in all his years as one of the twelve. Maybe this was really it. He'd typically stayed ahead of people like Ephrem Goldman and the Nephilim by doing the unexpected. If the obvious choice had been to go right, he would go left. He would think of the dozens of ways his enemy might respond or react and then do the one thing that they would never have anticipated. It had worked beautifully for years, but perhaps his gutsy and often reckless tactics had finally caught up with him.

The melodic tone of perfectly tuned jet engines began whirring to life. The nose of the plane bounced slightly as the pushback disconnected. Slowly, they began rolling around the side of the hangar and toward the network of runways. It seemed for now at least, they were going to ignore him.

One thing he'd never done was to underestimate or take his enemies for granted. The Nephilim had not always employed the most effective tactics but they were at least astute enough to engender partnerships with wealthy and powerful people of extraordinary intellect who were always hungry for more wealth and more power. For Alexander, engaging the Nephilim had never been too difficult. Engaging them in physical battle had even become somewhat thrilling for him. If one hit them fast enough and hard enough, he discovered, they would crumble fairly easily. They weren't accustomed to taking hits and all one had to do was find a weak spot. On the other hand, if one of them ever got you in his grasp, he'd crush you like a bug if he wanted. Alexander's entire body was a throbbing reminder of that particular truth.

It had been five years since he'd done battle with them though. He recognized that he'd gotten a little slower since that time and it was becoming clearer that he now also lacked the passion with which he used to fight. The stakes were the same and probably a little higher than usual at the moment, but the carnage that his life had become before meeting Laura had taken a good bit of the fight out of him. Up to a point, he'd been jetting around the globe playing the world's most dangerous game in which he'd felt relatively invincible. It was exhilarating to be in on some of the world's biggest secrets, to know what governments or private global conglomerates were going to do sometimes before they themselves knew and to throw a wrench in the works that would frustrate the most nefarious of their plans. However, the personal price he'd paid, as is often the case with many warriors, had been too high. It had cost him his family and ultimately led to the most painful experience of his life. That's when he'd lost all desire to play by the rules and committed to waging his own war on the Nephilim. He was so engulfed in rage in those days, he'd also made an oath to personally end the life of Walter Trowbridge.

The plane came to a rolling stop at the end of the runway. The engines escalated gradually from a whir to a roar as the pilots powered up to propel them into the air. Each slight bounce along the runway racked his body with a pain that seemed dull compared to reliving some of the memories from the year before he was thrown into a Chinese prison. Whatever torturous methods Ephrem had in store for him in an attempt to get the location of the stone, he was certain he'd already felt pain that was equal or greater.

He wasn't certain, but his intuition was telling him that they were headed east and would eventually land in Tel Aviv. The CIA had very likely already delivered the virus stores into the hands of the Gush Emunim. A release in the Palestinian territories, Syria, Iran and Egypt was almost certainly on their immediate to do list. A Dengue Fever outbreak would seem like a naturally occurring crisis. By the time anyone figured out what was truly happening, millions would have died and the US and Israel would be able to publicly condemn the act as one of a rogue militant group. However, because of the connection to Boniface and the Vatican, the Iranians would know very well what had actually happened and would hit back with extraordinary force and violence. In fact, Alexander was quite sure that they were already preparing to do so in the wake of having lost the virus to the Gush Emunim. Such a flagrant attack could not go unchecked by Israel and the U.S., which of course would've been the intent on their part from the beginning. The Gush Emunim was doing the work for them by drawing the Iranians into a fight. This would inevitably lead to the involvement of the Arab League and bring about the full force of World War III. The Nephilim would use the opportunity to feed the global imbalance by lending enough of their support to weakened militaries to perpetuate the war. This tactic had proven highly effective during the Second World War as they divided their support variously between the Axis and Allies. Alexander knew that they'd been waiting for all of the elements to line up for such an opportunity and the lessons learned over the intervening years would shift the balance in their favor no matter who ended up with Jerusalem as their prize.

As keen as his powers of concentration were, his thoughts were interrupted by the increased cabin pressure. As they climbed to cruising altitude it was providing him with new horizons of pain in his head and side. Taking a deep breath, Alexander relied on his extraordinary abilities to compartmentalize pain and separate it from his consciousness. He knew that he had just one shot this time. The sling was loaded and his timing and aim would have to be perfect. Then again, it might just be time for another stone.

32

Michael learned many years prior that Honduran time was not the same as time anywhere else on earth. A noon meeting could actually mean a two o'clock meeting, and 'in an hour' might actually be in an hour, or it might mean not at all. He was pleasantly surprised to see Socio rolling up in the Brigade Tours bus within the anticipated timeframe. Maria Delgado's son-in-law swung the gate wide so the bus could enter their little fenced in compound. The team was ready for a rapid loading. Asa and Montalto activated their suits and stood guard on either end of the bus. As he stepped off the bus, Socio saw the two of them virtually disappear right before his eyes. He made the sign of the cross just inches above his forehead and chest then backed wide-eyed back into the bus.

Once the perimeter was determined to be clear, the remainder of the team activated their suits. Garo assisted Barrone out of the house and the short distance to the bus. Di Nola, Pane, Russo and Mazza handled the stretcher and the fever stricken Ana while Mitri provided cover as he moved along behind them. Not wanting to see any more than he already had, Socio kept his head locked over his left shoulder and his eyes on the gate while silently muttering the Lord's Prayer.

After gently laying Ana down in the center aisle of the bus, each team member took alternating seats on either side of her and facing each other. They then leaned forward, interlocked arms and placed their helmet covered heads ear to ear. With the suits activated this made it virtually impossible to see Ana who because of her raging fever was not wearing one of the suits and was instead still wrapped in the cooling blanket. Once everyone was in place, Asa boarded the bus by the rear door and Montalto boarded through the front where they took up firing positions. Laura followed and took the front seat next to Socio who even amidst the commotion still had not moved his head or gaze an inch.

Michael, the only other one of them without the benefit of a cloaking suit remained in the house for just a few minutes longer. He stepped into Maria's bedroom, kissed her on the forehead and slipped a small roll of twenty dollar bills into her little hand. On more than one occasion she'd acted as his own little angel and he was fairly certain, one way or another, this would be the last time that they would see each other.

"Adiós mi angelito."

"No es adiós, Miguel. Hasta luego." She also knew it was the last time, but saying goodbye seemed too final for her. The gift of community with the few people who visited from outside the brutality of her existence was an indescribably beautiful one. Seeing them part was always painful but knowing there were people on the outside that cared about something other than taking advantage of her people was the hope to which she clung. After the Gringo agents pulled out so many years ago, it had been Michael who'd kept tabs on her and made sure she was safe. When one of the larger gangs in Honduras took up residence in Zapotal and began terrorizing and exploiting the residents, there was an almost immediate evacuation of them within just a few weeks. One day they were setting up drug processing facilities, gambling dens and whorehouses and then only a few weeks later, they were just gone. She'd never asked him, but she always felt it was her Miguel. There had been some inquiries made back up the chain to Langley but those got lost in the shuffle, especially since the end result was an unprecedented truce between the two most violent rival gangs in San Pedro Sula.

As a rule, Michael was not demonstratively emotional, but this farewell was particularly poignant. His career with the agency had begun here in Zapotal during the black-site days and apparently was now ending here with as unlikely a set of circumstances as he could've imagined. Maria Delgado had been there in the beginning and like a ruddy old cedar, she had survived rooted in this one spot while the world devoured itself all around her. He turned to leave before she could see the solitary tear fall from his cheek.

He took the seat right behind Socio and patted him on the shoulder indicating it was time to go. With any luck, they wouldn't get stopped along the way, but if they did, the story would be that Michael was scouting Delicious del Norte as a potential site for a year-round medical clinic to be sponsored by a group of non-denominational churches in the States. Hopefully, they wouldn't look too closely. The suits were yet another feat of micro-fabric engineering but if anyone took more than just a casual glance, it would be obvious that something was amiss. Socio on the other hand, didn't even want a casual glance as Maria's son-in-law once again opened the gate and held traffic for them while they pulled out onto the dirt road.

It was only about one hundred yards to the turn for the road to Delicious. Socio made the sharp bend to the right blowing his horn as he went as a warning to those that he wouldn't otherwise be able see until it was too late. Children darted out of the way but remained dangerously close to the bus as it passed. Some of them beat on the sides of the bus as a means of greeting while others chased along behind them laughing and yelling for him to stop and give them a ride. Unfortunately they would be stopping sooner than they'd hoped and it wasn't to take on passengers. Just a few hundred feet beyond the turn, the pickup full of national police that had gone by earlier was now parked on the side of the street where the officers had set up a road block at the widest pass in the road. A shirtless man wearing cut off shorts and sandals was handcuffed and lying face down on the side of the road while the other occupants of his Toyota Tercel were trying to decide where to go now that their friend was being arrested. When the patrol captain saw the bus, he ordered them to move the car off to the side and motioned for Socio to pull forward.

Michael grabbed one of the Brigade Tours ball caps, put it on his head and displayed the most convincing eager missionary face he could muster. A total of eight officers armed with automatic weapons flanked each side of the road ahead while two stood in the bed of the truck giving them a greater vantage point over passing vehicles. Socio eased the bus into the midst of them coming to a stop where the patrol captain stood. He obviously recognized Socio by the upward nod of his head he gave in the way of a greeting. He then looked at Michael who was smiling and giving a polite wave. Everyone else on the team was keeping as still as possible and taking very shallow breaths. Ana, who was in a state of semi-consciousness, turned her head slightly to the left causing a good deal of tension for her comrades hovering above her. This slight motion however seemed not to draw any unwanted attention. Michael slid his window open and in his best booming American accent let out a big *'Hola!'*

The patrol captain looked at him, ignored the greeting then looked back to Socio and waved them through without a word. As they passed, the eyes of every officer scanned every inch of the bus but seemed not to detect anything out of the ordinary. Once clear, Socio let out the air he'd been holding in his lungs causing him to slump somewhat in his seat as he deflated. He then took a big drink out of a liter-sized plastic bottle of water and wiped his forehead with a yellow bandana. Hoping to convey that he'd done a good job, Michael patted Socio once again on the shoulder which caused him to nearly jump out of his seat. Michael tried to hide his laughter.

"Bueno, Socio. Es bueno."

Socio didn't speak a word but instead just kept driving, and doing so at a rate of speed generally faster than he normally would've on the rough and washed out dirt roads of the villages. The ride was jarring to every occupant, especially for those awkwardly huddled around Ana, but no one was complaining. They all wanted as much distance between that patrol and them as possible.

The road they were on became little more than a winding mountain trail that cut between various home based businesses selling produce, beauty products and household wares all of which could be seen hanging from the rafters of lean-to sheds. Turning into Delicious though, the quality of homes seemed to improve if only slightly with more cinder block homes and fewer shanty type businesses. There was also noticeably less litter and garbage strewn about. Laura thought to herself that the difference between the two villages was striking. Even in the impoverished mountains of Honduras there seemed to be neighborhoods and then slightly better neighborhoods.

The road through Delicious was a large sweeping 'S' that wound around toward the center of the village and then to the base of a steep hill. Unlike the dirt road they'd been traveling, the roadway going up the hill was paved with cobblestones and had a sharp dog-leg turn to the right halfway up. Socio gunned the accelerator to gain enough momentum to make the climb. Just as he turned into the curve he laid down on the horn and held it down until arriving at a large solid metal gate painted a flat green color that reminded Laura of older military vehicles.

A door had been crudely cut into the gate and reattached with hinges so that pedestrians could come and go without having to open the entire gate. As the deafening horn reverberated off the metal, Laura saw a beautiful set of deep brown eyes appear in a rectangular peephole slot that had short pieces of rebar welded vertically across it for security. The door opened to reveal a teenage boy looking curiously at Socio. He took his hand off the horn, opened the driver's side window and yelled something that didn't sound very kind to Laura but was nonetheless effective in getting him to open the gate with expedience.

Once the bus cleared the opening, the boy closed and secured the gate. He then ran toward the bus but Socio had hastily parked, jumped out his door and met him half way. Even as Socio argued with him and held his hands up to prevent him from passing, the boy craned his neck around the rotund bus driver trying to get a better look at who the passengers might be. Michael and Laura watched the back and forth between the two until the boy finally relented and left through the pedestrian doorway in the gate. Socio followed him, locked the door and peered through the slot long enough to make sure he was really gone.

They were within the confines of a walled compound that had a small concrete, open air church in the center. Socio parked on the eastern side of the building and as close to the perimeter wall as he could maneuver. The wall was about three feet higher than the top of the bus and was topped with iron spikes and shards of glass to deter trespassers. As everyone got off the bus, Laura went to the rear and, remaining cloaked, climbed up the ladder and onto the roof for a better view of the LZ.

Stretching before her was one of the most beautiful vistas she'd ever seen. It was a lush, deep valley of green surrounded by mountains that soared into the bright morning sky. A flock of what she soon realized were wild Macaws flew out of the forest canopy, caught the rushing winds of the ridge lift and swooped up into the air in a rush of brilliant color. The relatively untouched landscape seemed to whisper something hypnotic and beautiful to her soul. Such beauty in the midst of such violence. Without conscious articulation, Alexander's presence was becoming palpable in this moment. She suddenly realized it had been the contrast of his own landscape that had captivated her. He was the very personification of beauty amidst violence, a deep and tender soul cast into a world of death and destruction.

Her thoughts were interrupted by the sound of a vehicle in the distance. She followed the view around to the north and west where the natural beauty was gradually replaced by the structures, sights and sounds of the little village of Delicious del Norte. Down the hill they'd just driven up and past an enormous cistern Laura's eyes locked onto a chilling sight. It was the Ford F250 of the national police patrol. Just as she saw the teenage boy that had opened the gate for them talking with the patrol captain, he seemed to look right at her. She froze.

33

The process of landing, pulling into a private hangar and deplaning had essentially gone in the precise reverse order of his crude boarding procedure. Ephrem, who had remained out of sight for the entire flight, strode past him once more without acknowledgment. The pilots followed suit while the four Gush Emunim operatives pulled him up and began dragging him to the door. With just slightly more care than the Nephilim had exercised, they took him down the steps and loaded him into another box van.

The pain he was experiencing had become its own entity. Through controlled breathing and the use of some meditative techniques he was able to keep that entity at bay sufficiently to concentrate on the task at hand. His first observation was that they were definitely not at Ben Gurion airport in Tel Aviv. The scarcity of air traffic combined with the size of Ephrem's Gulfstream G650 jet made it a certainty that they were in Haifa. That was the only other runway in Israel that was capable of handling such a large jet and Ben Gurion had rarely been so idle. Haifa would put them closer to Syria than to the Palestinian territories and Alexander assumed this must be their destination, but within twenty minutes he discovered that they were in fact traveling south rather than north.

The van pulled off and into a closed transport weigh station. A hulking black GMC Denali pulled right up to the rear door of the box van as it was rolled up by one of the Gush Emunim. The man in the front passenger seat got out and opened the rear door. Ephrem stepped out into the hot afternoon sun that triggered his photic sneeze reflex. He pulled a handkerchief from the inner breast pocket of his charcoal suit, lightly touched it to his upper lip and then replaced it. The bed of the van was a good three feet off the ground with a welded angle-iron step hanging about half way down. Ephrem popped up into the back unassisted and in two steps. He unbuttoned his suit coat and sat in a rearward facing passenger seat. He remained silent as the door was rolled back down and the van got back underway.

Based on the little bit of terrain he had observed from his position on the floor of the van and the cast and direction of the sunlight, they were about to get onto the Trans-Israel Highway. That clearly meant they were headed for the West Bank. Gaza was a possibility but of the two, the West Bank was a far more attractive target for the release of the virus.

Now fully underway for what would be about a two hour journey, Ephrem reached and flipped a switch on the wall beside him. A set of six trim lights in the ceiling of the cargo space illuminated their surroundings.

"Believe it or not I admire you, Alexander."

It was just the two of them in the cargo area. His arms and legs were still fully bound and except for where his perspiration and saliva had loosened the tape so was his mouth. Perhaps this was the torture they had in store for him, listening to Ephrem for two solid hours.

"Had anyone else played the game by your rules they surely would've been killed by now. Yet...here you are." The cadence of the van rolling over the expansion joints in the highway filled the silence as Ephrem silently studied Alexander. "Very nice maneuvering in Honduras by the way. If not for that little escape plan we would have your wife in our possession right now and something tells me you would be more forthcoming with the information I want."

The mention of Laura and the allusion to torture did not sit well at all with Alexander. From the moment he learned of her connection to the Daughters of Enoch, a flicker of dread and fear had come to life within him. He knew that

Ephrem would stop at nothing to get what he wanted. Anyone willing to kill his own daughter would be capable of anything. Even if Ephrem did not succeed, Laura would be hunted by those just like him for the remainder of her life.

"You're not the only one capable of those kinds of tactics though." Ephrem's expression was almost gleeful. "And Antonin Carafa is not the only one capable of infiltrating an organization."

Alexander could feel his blood pressure spike. If Ephrem wasn't bluffing then this was most unwelcome news. A mole in the alliance could be the undoing of the entire operation. Antonin ran a very tight organization but there was always a possibility of a sleeper agent. Every organization is comprised of people and people can be motivated and manipulated into doing just about anything.

"You're thinking to yourself, 'Where has he gotten to us? At what point in our operation will the walls come tumbling down?'" Ephrem's brilliantly white teeth gleamed in stark contrast to his tanned face. "The possibilities of countermeasures must be exploding through your brain right now, but I assure you it is a waste of time. It is already in motion and you're here, and they're there." It was almost as if he couldn't wait to explain just how masterful his plan was and how futile was Alexander's situation. "By the end of the day, we *will* have her and frankly," he leaned down so that his face was only about two feet from Alexander's, "I can't wait to see how the great Mathias reacts to the sight and sound of his precious Laura being mercilessly tortured. My promise to you though, is that we will stop torturing her precisely one hour after you've told us everything we want to know."

He'd often been told he had the capability of giving a look that could send ice water through another's veins. He was capable of masking the ferocity of his intentions, but at the moment he chose to convey his unmitigated malice with every fiber of his being. Even though he was bound and gagged on the floor of the box van as Ephrem's captive, the villainous little zealot jerked back slightly as though he'd been hit by an invisible fist. He attempted to recover from the momentary shock of fear and doubt that had been delivered. Ephrem gave a weak grin, sat back in the leather captain's chair and pressed his fingertips together forming a small cathedral with his hands.

"This is going to be a *most* enjoyable day."

They continued in silence for about another hour after Ephrem withdrew an iPad from a titanium sided portfolio and worked with absolute focus during that time. For Alexander it was an opportunity to continue planning and devising tactics that would ultimately lead to Laura's safe return. Regardless of everything else he had to accomplish, that was at the top of his list.

Ephrem reached into his coat pocket, pulled out his phone and read what must have been a text message. He then picked up a phone receiver next to his chair and spoke in Hebrew to whom Alexander assumed was the driver. They slowed for about fifteen minutes then resumed their normal speed for another half hour. When they slowed again Alexander could hear the Azan being chanted over the speakers from a nearby mosque. He could also tell that they were winding through a maze of barricades making short distances forward then making sharp turns and repeating the process for at least ten minutes. They then came to a full stop and Alexander heard the driver speaking to someone outside the vehicle. It sounded like pleasantries were being exchanged and was punctuated with laughter. All of this was followed by an unusually loud clanging of what must have been a rather large gate being opened. As they rolled forward, he could tell that they were crossing over a series of traffic control spikes. They were obviously moving through the West Bank Barrier, the highly controversial concrete wall that stretched for over four hundred miles and that in places reached nearly thirty feet into the air. The fact that their vehicle was not searched gave Alexander an uncomfortable feeling.

Ephrem returned his iPad to the portfolio, stood and stretched his legs and back then removed his suit coat and hung it on the back of his seat. There was a series of hard sided copolymer trunks on one side of the cargo area that Ephrem began opening. He took several smaller containers out, closed the trunk lids and put the smaller containers on top.

"Laura and her team are about to be picked up by a stealth-modified Blackhawk helicopter that they and you believe will deliver them to the airport in Bananera. However, the pilots whose services you've enlisted belong to me and will instead deliver them into our hands. The non-essential members of the team will be eliminated and the information extraction will begin. You my friend will have a front row seat to the festivities."

He retook his seat as the vehicle's attitude began angling upward on a steep grade. Alexander struggled in vain to keep from sliding down toward the door.

"Now, as I said we will cease the process of torture precisely sixty minutes after you tell us all that we want to know, so obviously you'll want to cooperate as soon as you feel she can tolerate no more than an hour beyond what you've already allowed her to endure."

The vehicle crested the peak of the hill then began a descent on an equally steep downgrade. Alexander slid back toward the front of the van. At the bottom of the slope they made what felt like a ninety degree turn to the left and then continued at a gentler angle. The acoustics changed dramatically and Alexander was fairly confident that they had pulled into an underground facility. Within only a few minutes they came to a stop. Both the passenger and driver doors of the van opened and closed. The doors of another vehicle opened then closed. That same vehicle cranked, shifted into gear and drove away.

Ephrem reached to the panel of switches and turned on a plasma screen monitor that showed what appeared to be a white porcelain embalming table sitting on a gravel floor. The inconsistent electrical current caused the examination light hanging from the ceiling to shed a ghastly and fluctuating glow onto the bloodstained surface of the table.

"I suspect within the hour you'll be reunited with Laura, albeit digitally." He flipped another switch that activated a series of speakers, the quality of which provided them with every nuanced sound in the as for now empty room that was a world away. Even the minute ticking of the metal roof expanding against its timber rafters in the Central American sun could be heard.

"It's not really the screams of agony that tend to affect the loved ones of torture victims, but the guttural moans and labored whispers begging for death. Wouldn't want you to miss *any* of those."

Alexander strained against his rudimentary but all too effective restraints.

"No need to struggle my dear Mathias. In fact, here..." Ephrem reached down and unwound the tape around Alexander's head as roughly as he could. "Feel free to tell me exactly what you think of me. We'll just consider it foreplay."

Alexander worked his jaw muscles and rolled his aching head forward for the first time in hours. His mouth and throat were parched with thirst but he managed to screech out his pleading message.

"I'll tell you everything you want to know."

34

Laura stood perfectly still and spoke quietly into her mike, "We're going to have company soon."

The patrol captain, seeing nothing out of the ordinary looked back to the boy then spoke into his handheld radio. While he was looking away, Laura took the opportunity to jump down from the top of the bus onto the grassy lawn below. She found Michael still on the bus feeding another dose of medication into Ana's IV line.

"That patrol we passed is on their way up here to check things out. The boy is down there talking to the captain now."

Michael rattled off some rapid fire Spanish to Socio whose countenance melted into one of fear and urgency. He hustled off to the other side of an outbuilding to the south of the property while Laura spoke into her mike again, "Let's wrap it up and move it out, guys."

Mitri took charge of getting Ana off the bus. Asa, Montalto, Mazza and he carried her as gently as they could and got her situated back onto the stretcher. Laura, Pane, Di Nola and Russo set up firing positions at the edge of the church building and on the either side of the bus while Michael led the others to the outbuilding where Socio stood. The big Ford's Diesel engine roared powerfully as it pulled up the hill to the gate.

On the other side of the outbuilding was an outdoor privy with two stalls. Socio directed the team to the first of the two stalls, opened the door and pointed to the back wall. Michael was the first to edge into the narrow doorway. The odor was horrific and he couldn't keep from grimacing as he worked quickly to open the hidden doorway behind the seat. He went through the door and dropped the few feet to the sloping ground below. He motioned for the others to follow.

It was a tight squeeze for all of them. Mitri and Asa went through first and pulled the leading edge of Ana's stretcher through as Montalto and Mazza guided it through the passage. Garo and Barrone got through just as the driver of the patrol vehicle started sounding the horn. Laura, Pane, Di Nola and Russo broke from their positions and sprinted to the outhouse where they met Michael coming back through. One of the officers had gotten out of the truck and was banging loudly on the metal gate with what must have been a nightstick.

"What are you doing? Let's get out of here." Laura tried to usher Michael back through the portal as she said this.

"Can't. If they find Socio up here without me they'll torture him to find out where I went and then kill him. If he comes with us it will only be a matter of minutes before they figure out where we are."

Laura knew he was right but couldn't quite get her mind around leaving him there to face the Cobras. This, she'd learned, was what this particular branch of law enforcement was known as in Honduras. Much like their namesake, an encounter with them usually proved to be deadly.

"We'll be fine. Just go...now."

"Let us know when it's clear. We'll come back for you."

"Laura, go. The chopper is almost here and you can't afford to delay. I'll stall them as long as I can but you make sure the pilots know it's a touch and go. You never know when a rocket propelled grenade will pop up from the back of a pickup truck."

She grasped his shoulder, gave it a squeeze and then stood aside to let him the rest of the way out of the unlikely escape hatch. She guided the last three through and kept a watch on the gate as Socio and Michael constructed a hasty story on their way to greet the patrol. She was on the other side and closing the door when she heard Michael's appalling tourist-Spanish kick back in, "*Hola señor! Cómo estás? Me llamo Richard Lyons.*" She shook her head and smiled. Clearly she'd underestimated his ability to perform the work of a field agent.

They made their way silently down the slope away from the wall and into the open terrain. If anyone happened to be watching they were certainly scratching their head in disbelief. With the cloaking suits activated it seemed the very air itself was rippling around a floating cot with the outline of a human body showing through the cooling blanket. No one who didn't already know of their presence was watching though. In Rome, Jorah, Judith, Antonin and Robert watched the satellite feed with vigilance as they crossed the valley floor and just a few miles away the Blackhawk crew watched their own satellite feed just as vigilantly on their heads up displays.

Once the team reached the designated coordinates, the helicopter made its appearance just over the horizon. Outfitted with Blue Edge rotor blade technology and a noise canceling parabolic wave generator, the angular craft was shockingly silent as it hugged the terrain and swept down toward the landing zone. Laura, Russo and Pane whirled around and knelt with their MP7s trained on the upper edge of the wall in anticipation that the patrol would hear enough of the sound distortion to know something was not quite right. They didn't have to wait long for the reaction as the officers scrambled to the top of the bus to determine the source of the oddly muffled thumping.

It took the first officer just a few seconds to register what he was seeing and only barely hearing. When it finally clicked, he raised his weapon to fire. This was the scenario Laura was hoping to avoid. She really didn't want to engage the local authorities. In terms of this particular operation they really were just doing their job. In the split second before she squeezed her trigger though, a sound something like a chainsaw running at full throttle cranked up behind them. They all hit the ground and flattened out as they recognized the unmistakable and chilling sound of a M134 Minigun blasting four thousand rounds of 7.62x51mm NATO per minute at the top of the wall and bus. Concrete dust spewed into the air as the fury of lead from the six rotating barrels shredded the wall. The officers that had been on top of the bus were obliterated in that same fury. It was an extremely overwhelming display of firepower that Laura found to be totally unnecessary when some covering fire from their small arms would have sufficed. She began screaming into her mike for the pilot to call off the assault.

"Cease fire! Cease fire! We've still got a man on the ground up there! Good God! Cease fire!"

The remnant rain of empty shell casings spilling onto the chopper floor and the hum of the spinning barrels was all that could be heard in the wake of the destruction. Fortunately, Michael and Socio were being questioned inside the church building and had both become virtually one with the tile floor at the first sounds of gunfire. The officer that had been interrogating them had not been as lucky as a ricocheting round caught him in the neck. He was bleeding profusely and Michael went immediately to work on him by ripping his shirt off and into strips of make-shift bandaging.

"*Soy médico.*" He tried to reassure the injured officer with this lie that would hopefully save both of their lives. He was in fact not even close to being a doctor but was fairly well versed in advanced first aid techniques.

The patrol captain came in at a low run around the corner and through the open doorway of the church yelling into his radio as he went. His eyes widened at the scene on the floor. Michael and the injured officer were in a rather large pool of blood. Socio sat close by, every inch of his body in a terrified shake. He pointed to Michael, "*Médico.*"

In his worst possible American accent, Michael asked for a first aid kit, *¿Tiene algún botiquín?*

The captain yelled some instructions to one of the two remaining officers outside who returned with the first aid kit within seconds. Michael needed to seem as frightened as Socio which didn't require too much acting ability. Even though he knew what had just happened, being anywhere in the vicinity of the business end of a minigun was nothing short of horrifying. His hands shook convincingly as he reached for the red nylon bag.

On the other side of the wall, the chopper crew finished loading everyone, retracted the fire breathing gun, secured the door and disappeared over the ridge more quickly than they'd appeared.

"A minigun? Seriously? You didn't have the Sidewinders ready to launch?" Laura was accustomed to doing things surgically and with as little collateral damage as possible. She wondered as she berated them where Alexander had come up with these trigger happy clowns.

"Our orders are to get you out of here alive and that's what we're doing." The curt reply came from the pilot who had the throttle pulled all the way pushing the chopper past its 200 mph threshold.

The rest of the team waited for her response but she kept it to herself for the time being. She would take this up with them once they were on the ground. This washed up Warrant Officer was due for a double dose of attitude adjustment and she was just the one to deliver it, however her primary concern at the moment now that they were in the air was Ana. With Michael stuck back in Delicious, she was now in Mitri's protective care. Her condition seemed to be deteriorating.

Laura removed her helmet and looked at Mitri who was cradling her feverish head in his lap while constantly checking her IV and vitals. "How is she?"

"Hard to tell. This virus is extremely invasive. Whatever this is," he gave the IV bag a slight squeeze "it's keeping her alive for now but we've got to get to the vaccine. How far to Bananera?"

"At the speed he's flying I'd say we're about a half hour out." She pulled her handheld out of her sleeve to double check. It was powered up but the screen was completely blank and none of the functions were responding.

Apparently this malfunction had just occurred and had done so within each of the team members units. Montalto, the most vigilant when it came to malfunctioning digital equipment, already had his helmet off and a Silva Ranger compass concealed in the palm of his hand. He checked his analog wristwatch. Even if they'd been flying south to avoid the airspace over San Pedro Sula, they should be on a westward bearing by now. They were instead heading east.

Without lifting his head, Montalto cut his eyes up at Laura who was already cued into what he was doing. His stoic expression told her everything she needed to know. The rest of the team picked up on their silent communication and steeled themselves in preparation for what was next. Hands eased to weapons and fire selector switches were surreptitiously clicked to single fire mode. They were in close quarters and automatic gunfire would be extremely dangerous. This team of shooters was so well trained and knew each other so well that an identical field of fire scenario was silently constructed in each of their minds.

Ana, on her stretcher, took up most of the cabin floor. The rest of the ten members of their team sat around the perimeter in various stages of folded up discomfort and awkward positions. The four enemy crew members sat with their backs to the cockpit and watched their passengers intently. It seemed everyone in the cabin understood what was about to happen. They all were on high alert and waiting to see who would move first.

234

Laura arched her back pretending to stretch, then pushed her hand down her right thigh and to the back of her calf as if she was relieving the tension in her muscles. However, when she came up, she did so in one powerful motion and launched out of her seat with the speed and force of a cheetah. She led with her fist wrapped around the black-linen micarta handle of a custom made Hammond FE3 tactical knife. Jim Hammond had designed this variation of his much larger combat knife with Laura in mind. She'd field tested several of his blades for him over the years at the agency and this prototype quickly became her favorite. Its heft, balance and fit made it seem like a natural extension of her arm and the grip lent itself to the iron like Isshin-Ryu punch that the operative sitting directly in front of her was about to experience

Even with his senses alerted right before her assault, he was completely stunned as she pounced on him. Her fist, fortified with the knife handle, caught him squarely on the left side of his neck followed by the reverse slash of the razor sharp blade and then her elbow back across his jaw for good measure. This one shot takedown was all the more effective as she disarmed him with her left hand. She then used the weight of the snatched weapon in a rocket-like sideways jab to crush the zygomatic bone just under the eye socket of the next operative over.

The third operative managed to get his weapon up and aimed it directly at Mitri who was kneeling next to Ana. Before he could pull the trigger, Mitri threw his weight toward the back of the cabin, pushed his haunches up off the floor and then kicked full force with both legs knocking the sub-machine gun upward and sending a three round burst overhead.

The operative sitting directly behind the pilot was afforded the most cover behind a half-partition. Only Laura had a direct line on him but she was occupied in a grappling contest with the one Mitri had just kicked. The partially covered operative had his handgun trained on Mitri's head. His finger curled around the trigger but before he could squeeze off a round, a 9mm hollow point round entered just below his temple. The man slumped in his seat and dropped the pistol to the cabin floor. A shocked and grateful Mitri looked toward the back of the cabin to see who had covered and saved him but couldn't tell. Most of the team had been pinned down and unable to move into the fray. Montalto however, flew midair across the cabin and landed his brick sized fist directly into the face of the operative who was giving Laura all the fight she wanted. Her right arm was still weakened from the round she'd taken back in Zapotal so she pulled back and gave Montalto enough room to land three more crushing blows with the rapidity of a jackhammer. He wrapped the man's head up in his arms, grasped his face just under the jaw and torqued his solid chunk of body mass rearward. A disturbing crack and squishing noise made it clear that the man's neck was now broken. Montalto looked at Laura to be sure she was ok. His eyes were wide, his nostrils were flared and he was drawing slow, deep breaths. She grinned appreciatively at the stout fireplug of a guy, "Thanks, man. That was close." He might never live down his misdirectional farm adventure with anyone else on the team, but he'd never catch hell from her.

With all four operatives in the main cabin neutralized, they all looked around for a quick check on each other. Mitri looked up from Ana and toward no one in particular. His eyes were red and swollen with tears. She was gone. But even more poignant for Mitri was the sight of the Sig 9mm compact loosely gripped in her right hand. One round had been fired.

35

Ephrem's expression was an odd mixture of surprise, distrust and victory. "Oh, I'm quite certain you will tell us everything we want to know and I'm even more certain that it will be more truthful than the fabrication you've already constructed for me."

"I'm serious, Ephrem." Alexander's voice was strained but sincere. "I've had it. I can't do this anymore. You've all robbed me of what might have been a real life and I won't do it anymore. If you'll guarantee Laura's safety, you can have everything I know: the location and purpose of the stone, the locations of the other 9, the inner structure of the Alliance. You name it, it's yours. Just let Laura and me walk away. You get what you want, I get what I want."

Ephrem slid a cabinet door to the side and withdrew a device that resembled a modern interpretation of an old Yashica box camera with dual lenses. He powered the little device up and appeared to be synching it to his iPad. He worked silently for a few minutes getting everything set up the way he needed it. Rather than propping Alexander upright, he attached a flexible tripod to the device and positioned it on the floor about a foot away from the top of his head. He viewed the image on his iPad. It was a strikingly clear image of Alexander's Anterior, Dorsal and Parietal Cortices with color gradations indicating various levels of synaptic impulses. Ephrem adjusted the box a couple of times, then returned to his seat. His phone rang just as he sat.

Alexander couldn't hear the voice on the other end and all Ephrem said during the call was "Thank you" before disconnecting. He knew Ephrem was monitoring his brain activity, specifically the areas associated with creating falsehoods. It didn't matter though, he had every intention of keeping his word and telling the truth.

Ephrem focused intently on the iPad. He seemed to almost vibrate with an ecstatic energy as he worked. After several minutes of silence he peered over the top of the tablet. He tried to maintain his normally dignified air but could barely contain his joy as he spoke. The words came out in buffeted breaths as if his wind was trying to get ahead of his speech, "We now have the Palermo stone." He had the appearance of a commander watching the castle walls of his enemy being breached. Alexander had to concede, albeit to himself, this was an unexpected development.

"Let's see, right now you're thinking that like those before me I've gotten my hands on the Palermo stone that's housed in Italy, that I've been duped by the many fake fragments of the *Royal Annals* scattered across the globe. Well guess what my dear Mathias, the Presidential palace in Egypt fell just this morning and our operatives found the stone exactly where Andrew said it would be."

"Andrew?"

Ephrem stood suddenly from his seat and kicked Alexander in the gut. "Did that hurt?"

Alexander was completely winded and felt as though he was going to vomit and probably would have if he'd had anything on his stomach. Ephrem screamed the question at him again, "Did that *hurt?*"

"Yes." He spit the word out of his mouth as it crested on a wave of silent rage. The kick had hurt but the thought of Andrew being killed hurt more. Sylvano Andrianmanelo was one of the few he genuinely liked amongst the twelve. During their precious few encounters they'd developed a bond as kindred spirits often will.

Ephrem observed the image on his iPad as he answered, "Good."

Alexander held his anger in check, "So you've killed Andrew and gotten your hands on the Palermo Stone. It won't do you any good."

"Your years away obviously dulled your senses, Mathias. If I knew the Palermo stone in Italy was a fake and knew enough to pursue the unknown half in Egypt, then certainly I know that the second half exists and I suspect" he consulted his watch "I'll know its location within the hour."

His senses were not dulled in the least but he wanted to know how much Ephrem knew and apparently it was quite a lot. He didn't have to pry further though. The egomaniacal force within the diminutive Jew wanted desperately to demonstrate just how smart he truly was.

"You see, Mathias, in the typical arrogance of Germans the Nazis tried to take over the world by fostering a master race, but we have been silently biding our time for generations. We've always known our time would come. The genesis of the Gush Emunim is rooted in the sands of the Sinai Peninsula and the Exodus. Since that time, the outside world has tried to scatter and destroy my people, but that one element has remained true in its aim. We have always focused on the end game. We have survived by keeping out of sight, collecting information and waiting until it was our time. Well, the time is at hand and I am the living culmination of an eon of hopes, dreams and plans. I am the Moshiac, the one chosen and raised up to deliver my people from the last 2000 years of wilderness. Today, I strike the rock of oppression with the staff of redemption. Every tear that has been shed by every Jew for all time will spring forth from the ground as the waters of justice that will drown our oppressors and quench our burning thirst for freedom. The world has amassed armies against us generation after generation, but today one man emerges from the desert, from the House of Bread and he will have conquered them all. I am that man, Mathias. I have always been that man."

Alexander didn't speak but he didn't have to, the look of resignation on his face told Ephrem everything he wanted to know. He was a bruised, broken and bloody mess lying on the floor of a box van in the depths of an underground parking garage somewhere in what he now knew to be the city of Bethlehem.

"Just let her go. Let her go. Prove to me that she is free and safe and I will make this very easy for you."

Ephrem smiled an almost paternal smile, "Oh Mathias, it will be simple for me regardless of your participation, but surely you understand that as a Daughter of Enoch, we cannot allow her to live."

Alexander instinctively strained against the duct tape that bound him at this remark. Another wave of rage surged through him, but he held his tongue.

"Once Laura is secured to the table we will engage in a fascinating technique of Nociception. This innovative form of torture comes to us from the brilliant scientists of your own country. You should be proud." Ephrem spoke as one intoxicated with power and bloodlust. "By observing thermal, mechanical and chemical changes we can determine her precise thresholds of pain. Once a nociceptor is stimulated we observe the various autonomic responses and can induce the most excruciating pain imaginable or the most exhilarating pleasure. Taken to its extreme, we've observed that a subject can simultaneously experience an orgasm and the sensation of being ripped in half and burned alive. It's the most effective enhanced interrogation technique I've ever seen. Genius actually."

This was a new horizon of torture that Alexander had obviously missed in his absence and gratefully so. The overt inhumanity of warfare in all of its grisly outward display was gradually being replaced by more gruesome and covert displays of violence. The macro was being replaced by the micro.

"Please, Ephrem I will take her and disappear and for good this time. You will never hear from us again. You have my word."

240

"Enough!" Ephrem's volatility was triggered but Alexander couldn't determine exactly why. He'd been looking at his iPad as Alexander pled for Laura's life but that didn't seem likely to be a trigger for this sudden burst of anger.

Ephrem's face burned crimson in contrast to his silver hair. His eyes narrowed as he removed his futuristically styled glasses. He placed the tablet on the counter behind him at sat back down in the leather captain's chair. He rubbed his forehead with his index and middle fingers, pressing in as though he was trying to dislodge some bit of unwelcome reality. His jaw quivered as a precursor to the scream that came from somewhere deep within his soul, *"Goddammit!"* He slammed both fists down on the arms of the chair. His glasses sailed out of his left hand and went skittering across the floor. He stood above Alexander.

"You *will* tell me *everything*!"

Alexander watched him intently as he went to the containers he'd taken out of the larger cases earlier. Ephrem, his hands shaking with rage, struggled to open the lids to each of the three boxes. After a few cumbersome attempts He managed to get them all open and returned to his iPad.

"The chopper has disappeared and Laura with it." He looked as though he wanted to kick Alexander again but pulled up a control panel instead. A faint, high-pitched whisper emanated from the back corner of the van.

"It doesn't matter though. You'll tell me all I need to know regardless." He indicated the space around them, "This van is now filling with Auto-Robotic Arthropods, each with enough Hemorrhagic Dengue Fever to kill a camel."

"Robot Mosquitoes?"

"Yes. Another invention of your sanctimonious government for which I am ever grateful. Boniface and the Iranians were going to release these in all of the significant

Jewish centers of population while hoarding the vaccine and antidote, but his plan was undone from the start. Now it is time to reverse the tide of his blood crusade, and it begins with you."

"Won't they affect you as well?" Alexander's voice broke slightly as he posed the question.

"Unlike you, Mathias I've been inoculated. They will seek out my body heat and sting me, but it will have no effect. As soon as we discovered the location of the production facility in Tehran we sent in a team to obtain their stores of vaccine. And now," he held a syringe aloft "if you want to avoid the violent eruption of your vascular system while experiencing bone crushing pain, I suggest you start telling me everything you know now."

Alexander felt a sharp prick on his cheek followed by another on his neck. Ephrem winced as the artificial life forms were obviously injecting him as well.

"You're going to kill me anyway. Give me this one thing; secure the van so that no one but you hears the words that I will speak. If I'm going to betray the world into your hands I'd like to do so privately."

Ephrem hesitated for a moment as if he was going to grind Alexander's face in defeat but then his countenance shifted. "If nothing else, Mathias you have been a worthy competitor but prophecy is impossible to overcome. The end will be what the end will be no matter who or what gets in the way along the path."

He reached to another control panel and keyed in a code. All external communication shut down and every screen went blank except for the iPad that now displayed the inner workings of Alexander's thoughts. "You have the floor."

Another of the hyper-light metallic drones pierced his skin. "The Stone of David is at the Dome of the Rock in the Bir el-Arweh."

"The Well of Souls, of course. The place beneath the Dome where spirits await the Day of Judgment, how very poetic of you. How fortunate that their wait is nearly over." Ephrem beamed with satisfaction. His eyes darted around as if he wanted to make sure he was the only one consuming this monumental information. "And now, the rest, Mathias. Surrender its secret. Set yourself free and give up the secret of the Stone."

36

In the moments before the Blackhawk disappeared from radar a harrowing sequence of events had taken place. The four operatives in the cabin had been neutralized as had the pilot. This had been the result of one of the stray bullets loosed by the operative Mitri had kicked during the fight. That left the co-pilot as the only remaining opposition. Laura crawled over the center console, leaned across the pilot's lifeless body and unbuckled his four point harness. She unlatched the door.

"What the *fuck* are you doing?" The copilot's protest was cut short as Mitri shoved the barrel of a .45 into his neck.

"Whatever she damn well pleases, asshole."

With that, Laura heaved the pilot out the door and took his place. "Give me your helmet."

Instead of removing his helmet, the co-pilot dropped his right hand to his side, but it was a fatal mistake. Mitri gave him two hammer blows to his carotid just under the jaw line and with his head now strained to the left exposing his neck, Mitri crushed his trachea just below the cricoid cartilage with the butt of his pistol. He removed the helmet and handed it to Laura.

She put the helmet on, checked the systems controls then just as if she'd been raised in the cockpit of a Blackhawk, pulled back and left on the cyclic stick, adjusted the collective, shifted the pedals to a port attitude and throttled it hard. Mitri braced himself against the partition and looked at Laura with an even greater amount of respect.

"You think you got this, Captain?"

"Roger that. Check on everyone else, we'll be at Bananera in no time."

As soon as they leveled out of the turn she opened it up as hot as she could and engaged all of the stealth features. This was definitely not her first time behind the stick of a Blackhawk, but it was the first time for her to be in this generation of one. If she had not been flying out of one storm and into another, she would've enjoyed herself immensely. As it stood, Laura was fairly certain the fight she was leaving was merely a warm up for what lay ahead and they were down two. Barrone's broken leg put him on the bench and Ana's death would take more of a toll than a simple reduction in force. These were pros, but losing a comrade always had a deleterious effect no matter how hard the warrior was. Unlike paid militias, these people were fighting arm in arm in a battle and for a cause most of the world didn't even know about. She thought about Alexander, the man she'd known before Walter Trowbridge and the man after. She considered how he'd walked away. There was a lot more to this and when the dust settled, she was going to find out what that was.

Laura checked over the communications suite and made adjustments to the Have Quick frequencies as well as the safe voice satellite link. She didn't want even a hint of a signal being picked up by the bad guys.

"Orion 1…C2, over."

There was an echo and a brief delay followed by the very excited voice of Antonin Carafa, "Thank the heavens above! Where are you?"

"We're full tilt to the LZ. The chopper crew was working for Goldman so we had a bit of a delay. I need a sitrep on Alexander."

Antonin laughed through his own exasperation, "A bit of a delay?" His laughter continued, "And your Alexander, he is either crazy, brave, stupid or all three."

Robert broke into the conversation, "Like I told you when we first met. It's why I gave him the codename 'John Bell Hood.' He *meant* to get abducted."

"*What?*"

"Headlong into a firestorm taking on Hell and half of Georgia, that's our boy. We've been in contact with Matthew and Thomas; he was working with them on an end-around."

"An end-around?"

"We'll have to go into details later. For now, we've got your jump coordinates. It's east of Jerusalem, it'll be daylight and things could get hairy. The Israeli Defense Force has gone dark on us as has the Prime Minister. We assume that's a bad thing. On the other hand, they can't really afford to get involved against us either."

"When you say east of Jerusalem, just how far east are we talking?"

"You've already guessed it, the West Bank. The good news is that Matthew and Thomas are already on the ground with two teams of their own."

"And the bad news?"

"The Nephilim are on the ground and we have reason to believe Boniface is mad as hell and has his operatives in route."

"Great." Her sarcasm wasn't lost on Robert.

"While you're getting rigged up for the jump, Jorah and Judith will have the new data loaded and transmitted. We'll have some human intel from Matthew and

Thomas but live satellite and drone images may or may not be available. Israel has their airspace buttoned down pretty tight."

"Roger that. Just give me the coordinates and tell me who not to shoot. I'll take care of the rest."

"No Lone Ranger stuff, Laura. I can't handle two of you."

"Fair enough. Speaking of the Lone Ranger, we had to leave Michael Stallworth in Delicious. The CIA is going to want his head on a platter. Think we could get him out of there while his head is still attached?"

After several moments of silence, Antonin chimed in, "We can have a crew headed his way right after you hit Bananera. Does he have communications?"

"I'll transmit his protocol. Assuming the Cobras haven't scooped him up, I'm betting he's sitting at Maria Delgado's house in Zapotal."

"Consider it done, Laura." Antonin's voice then took on a serious tone, "OK, tell me."

She took a deep breath. The cabin was quiet as they rocketed through the air toward the airport at Bananera. Everyone at Command and Control stopped what they were doing in the brief lull of radio communications.

"Two casualties. Barrone sustained a broken femur and is stable," She bit the inside of her lip. It was as bad as telling a parent their child had died. "And Ana didn't make it."

Antonin sat back into his chair, closed his eyes and rested his chin and mouth on his folded hands. For several seconds only the electric hum of the connection could be heard. He breathed a deep sigh but said nothing.

Robert broke the sad tension by keeping them operationally oriented, "Roger that, Orion 1. We'll reconnect after wheels up. C2 out."

"Orion 1 out."

They continued in silence for the remaining 15 minutes of the ride to Bananera. Laura keyed in the secure frequency for the ZEHST jet and gave them a heads up on their ETA. Just as she put the chopper down, the jet came screaming out of the clouds, made a pass and was on the ground by the time they had off-loaded.

They made their way across the tarmac with hardly any interest from those at the airport. Flight control was well paid to look the other way by more than a few organizations and the locals would be more surprised by a day that a paramilitary group didn't do a touch and go there. A ground crew took possession of the Blackhawk and secured it in an Alliance controlled hangar and began prepping it to go after Michael. Within 10 minutes, Laura's team was on their way back into the Stratosphere and on to Jerusalem.

Laura was sitting in the same seat she'd sat in on the way over, forward cabin, port side. She was reviewing the digital sand table through her Heads Up Display of the building and surrounding area where they believed Alexander was being held. Mitri, already fully rigged for the jump, came and sat next to her.

"We grew up together."

Laura removed her helmet and put in on the empty seat between them, Mitri's was tucked under his arm and he sat forward in the seat to accommodate the bulk of his chute. She didn't say anything but leaned toward him and gave him a nod of understanding.

"When I was a boy my mother was killed by a bomb blast as she and her friends were leaving a theater in Tel Aviv. I was an only child and my father never remarried, so even though we were the same age Ana kind of became the sister and female influence in my life. We were each other's first kiss, first dance and were inseparable for most of our school years." He looked away from Laura for a moment.

"She even went along on my first 'real' date. We learned not to do that anymore since we had more fun together than my date and I did." He smiled broadly at what had obviously become a fond memory then looked back at Laura who already had tears welling in her eyes. "Everyone thought we were an item or would be or should be, but it just wasn't that way between us. You know?"

She reached across the empty seat and squeezed his thick forearm. "I know."

"Anyway, we were in the IDF together then we were both recruited into Mossad at the same time. When I got recruited by Antonin into the Alliance she stayed at Mossad for another year then went to work for her father. We didn't see each other for almost two years and then without so much as a word she showed up out of nowhere while I was on an assignment in Spain. You could've knocked me over with a feather. No one but Antonin was supposed to know I was there so I knew something was not right. We were on the coast in Barcelona and we rented a boat under an assumed identity and got off shore to talk. That's when she told me what Ephrem was doing and that she wanted out." He took a deep breath into his chest and let it slowly escape in a sigh. "That was a little over a year ago."

"And Jenco?"

"I introduced them. He was a hell of a soldier and a hell of a guy." Mitri squeezed his left fist in his right hand as he fought off the emotions. "I'd give anything..." He choked on his own words and his jaw muscles rippled as he gritted his teeth.

"I know." Laura kept her hand on his arm as he looked upward and blew out a gust of air in an attempt to dispel the grief that was torquing his chest into a knot.

"I guess I just needed to tell you...that's all."

"Mitri, I'm sorry and I understand, but I have to ask you this."

He knew what she was going to ask and he knew what she needed to hear, but there was no way he could promise her that.

"We don't have much time and I need you, but can you do this objectively?"

Without any hesitation at all and with every trace of sadness evaporated from his demeanor he replied, "Absolutely not. I will completely and subjectively annihilate anyone or anything that attempts to stop us from obtaining every last bit of the virus and Alexander. And if I just so happen to get my hands on Ephrem Goldman, then all the better."

She gave his arm one last squeeze before letting go. "Well, as long as we're on the same page, your subjectivity is good with me."

He gave her a nod of respect that conveyed not only his gratitude for her ability to listen and sympathize with his grief, but to maintain and help him maintain their mission bearing. As he stood to rejoin the others he knew in his gut that they were in great hands. With Laura on point they were going to deliver a knockout to the Gush Emunim and the Nephilim.

37

Alexander was beginning to feel the effects of the virus in every extremity. The pain from his broken ribs and arm were merging into the raging fever that was now coursing through his body. He knew it wouldn't be long before the vascular hemorrhaging began which would be followed by the sensation that every bone in his body was being slowly crushed under the weight of a steam roller. Yet amongst this torturous circumstance was an ember of joy was glowing just beneath the veneer of agony.

"The crown doesn't make the king." His voice was raspy and dry.

Ephrem's vitriolic pleasure prevented him from absorbing this bit of wisdom. "Your time on earth is very limited unless you give me something other than riddles." He held a syringe aloft. Presumably this was the vaccine necessary to reverse the effects of the virus.

Alexander was soaking in his own sweat and the top of his head was throbbing with every heartbeat providing a searing sensation that radiated down his spine. Yet, he was smiling as he said, "I am the Stone of David, Ephrem. Like those before me and those that will follow, we are born to slay the giants."

The weight of comprehension still had not pressed into Ephrem's consciousness. Paralyzed by the hypnotic aura of certain victory, he was still riding high on his confidence. However, as the clouds of delusion began to fade, he broke into a sweat and Alexander continued.

"It's never been the actual Stone. The only ones who assign it any value other than its historic significance are those who value possessions over human life. Rehoboam did not understand that which is why Solomon sent the Stone to be hidden away. Herod didn't understand it either. He was so convinced that if he could get his hands on the Stone, he would be accepted as the true king of Israel. It drove him to murder hundreds of innocent boys in an attempt to possess it. For millennia those who have sought the Stone and its secrets have been willing to murder and destroy in the name of something they couldn't possibly understand. The creative life force within humanity is more powerful than any destructive force that can be brought to bear against it. There are stretches of history during which it seems this is not true, but long after your bones and the bones of those like you have turned to dust, the goodness and creative beauty of humanity continues forward."

Ephrem began rubbing the back of his neck as the horrific pain overtook him. He dropped to his knees and held his face in his hands. Alexander watched him crumple further and further until he was on his side on the floor of the van. "What's happening to me?"

"It's not the Stone that killed Goliath, it was a teenage boy. A boy with more courage than the entire army of men standing behind him and before him. The crown doesn't make the king; the Stone doesn't make the warrior."

Ephrem's body was now shaking in feverish chills just as Alexander's. He looked positively dumbfounded at this turn of events and he could barely get the words out. "What...is...happening...to me?"

"When you broke into the laboratory in Tehran you actually stole an inert sodium chloride solution. You have inoculated yourself with saline solution."

"You fool! We'll both die."

"Well..."

The back door of the van rolled up. Standing with his arms stretched above his head still holding the door was an exceptionally tall man of Ethiopian descent. He wore a loose fitting traditional linen outfit in all black that seemed anachronistic compared to the technologically advanced and alien looking eyepiece he wore over his right eye. Alexander recognized it as what must've been the fruition of a joint development project from several years prior. If it was what he'd worked on so many years ago, then an almost unimaginable amount of information was being gathered, compiled, synthesized and distributed amongst the others wearing a similar device regardless of where they were on the planet. The amount of data and the speed with which the human brain was capable of processing once it was appropriately engaged was staggering. For now though, he would settle for a dose of the actual vaccine that he was hoping his ebony skinned colleague had in his possession.

Alexander was unable to move his head any further backward to see the source of the East Indian accent that spoke to him, "Greetings, Mathias."

She stepped into the van with a small nylon day pack and withdrew an IV bag, line and transdermal patch. She lifted his shirt, exposed his belly and began the process of administering the lifesaving drug.

"Thomas my old friend, what were you two waiting for? I feel like hell."

She smiled but said nothing as she continued her work. The large Ethiopian man replied on her behalf, "At least you have maintained the consistency between your feel and your look."

"Thank you, Matthew. You are too kind." Even with the tremendous pain and pressure of the virus bearing down on him, he managed to smile at the presence of these two longtime friends.

Ephrem's symptoms had really only just begun but he was writhing in agony nonetheless. "Please, please." He was breathless as he spoke. "Give me the real vaccine and

I will make all of this disappear. Teach me your ways and I will use my influence to support you. My daughter did it, I can help too."

Mentioning Ana was a mistake. Matthew and Jenco had been close friends and therefore he was friends with Ana by association. When he folded his long frame sufficiently to step up into the van to cut the duct tape from Alexander he might have ignored Ephrem. However, with the reminder of their deaths and especially *how* Ana had died burning freshly in the pit of his stomach, Matthew used his long powerful leg to push Ephrem completely out of his way and up against the side wall of the van. He held him there for a few seconds longer than was necessary grinding the ball of his foot into the ailing man's chest.

"You have nothing to offer us." His deep, booming voice and melodic tone reso-nated in his cavernous chest. When he was in battle mode, his colleagues had often remarked that he had the voice of an avenging angel. "Sparing *your* life would add nothing to the human landscape that is not already present."

He removed his foot and jerked a knife from its scabbard that hung around his neck. Ephrem's eyes widened in fear as Matthew leaned into his face, "You...will *not* be missed."

Matthew whirled around so rapidly that Ephrem violently jerked as he did. In his mind, his throat had just been slashed. In reality, the avenging angel had simply turned his focus to removing Alexander from his bindings. As he worked, he looked Alexander in the eyes and offered some final words of wisdom to the dying Ephrem Goldman. "People like you simply do not under-stand, it's not the arrow, it's the Indian." His face lit up with a brilliant smile as he gave Alexander a wink. Alexander experienced a rush of amusement, sadness and surprise at this comment as he'd had no idea that Matthew had known Jenco.

Thomas on the other hand shot Matthew a sardonic look, "Some sorts of Indians do not use arrows at all."

Matthew laughed, "You are correct. Some have a tongue sharp enough for the task."

He moved Alexander as gently as if he was working with an injured child and his incredible upper body strength made it seem as effortless. He felt the slight and unnatural movement in his ribcage right as Alexander winced. Though Alexander had not complained, Matthew worked with even greater care after this.

"You are getting too old to let those giants get so close to you, my friend."

Alexander made an obligatory groan as Matthew hoisted him into a fireman's carry, "Tell me about it."

Thomas threaded the padded backpack strap onto Alexander's left arm and secured it with a belt strap across his back and then between his chest and Matthew's back. She then unfolded a portable rolling cart and loaded the remaining crates of ARAs onto it.

"You can't just leave me here to die! That makes you no better than anyone else in this war. No better than a cold blooded killer."

Matthew turned back to Ephrem and laughed so genuinely deep that the echoes from the empty parking garage vibrated the sides of the metal van with amazing force, "I never claimed to be."

With his free arm he reached up and slammed the van door closed.

If he'd missed anyone at all from the old days, surely it was Matthew, "You are one cold son of a bitch."

"I have indeed had that specific training."

Thomas rolled her eyes and spoke as though she was speaking into a communication device though none was visible, "Package secure. We are in route."

"It appears our friend back there had a backup plan." Matthew said this in reference to the intel data he was obtaining through the eyepiece. They continued across the cavernous space and up a ramp. "Looks like a fierce firefight up there."

Alexander reasoned they must be further underground than he'd first imagined. If there was a fierce firefight anywhere close, it was completely inaudible. This thought was relatively short lived though as an enormous explosion rocked the building above.

"Shit!" Matthew was nearly toppled over with Alexander on his shoulders but he managed to remain upright. He looked into space as if he was seeing something in the distance, but he was actually viewing the scene at street level.

"Unmarked choppers and an assault team of the big boys just joined the party."

"Nephilim?"

"Yes."

"An assault *team?*"

"*Yes!*" Matthew seemed impatient with Alexander's questions.

"Something's not right. They don't fight like that...too much exposure."

"Well, it seems they're not overly concerned with that at the moment. They're apparently also hitting the Alliance headquarters in Rome as we speak."

Alexander thought for a second. "Is this Israeli or Palestinian?"

"What do you mean?"

"This building...was it built by the Israelis or the Palestinians?" He looked around to see if there was an indication of which floor they were on as Matthew accessed some data.

"Palestinian. Why?"

"And how many floors below ground are we?"

"Two."

"We need to go down then."

"Down?"

"Down."

38

The ZEHST dropped out of the upper reaches of the atmosphere with such intense velocity that those monitoring Israel's airspace were taken completely off guard. As the pilots switched from the ramjets to the turbojets to bring them to jump altitude, Laura and the team stood by on either side of the fuselage. Mitri would be taking over as Aquilas team leader in Ana's place. It was not a sympathy promotion and no one viewed it as such. Mitri was an extraordinary warrior and covert operator. When Ana came on board he had voluntarily removed himself as a squad leader of another team to take on the special assignment of infiltrating the Gush Emunim. Some egos couldn't have made such a move but anyone that knew Mitri knew that for him, the mission always comes first. Subjectively he may have wanted to continue leading his own team, but objectively his support of a greater mission took precedence. In much the same way, his subjectivity of wanting to get his hands on Ephrem Goldman would take a back seat to the objectivity of getting their hands on the virus, the Auto Robotic Arthropods and getting Alexander out alive.

They'd been briefed in flight regarding the situation on the ground. They learned of the switch Alexander had pulled on Ephrem and how it had led him to essentially commit suicide. A few high fives and cheers went up when they heard it. Laura tried to keep them focused and hold off on the celebrations till later but she had a hard time not jumping up with them. She had to admit, it was a stunningly brilliant tactical move even if it did nearly get him killed. Of course he wasn't out of the woods yet. She knew from the intel reports coming out of Rome before the Alliance headquarters had been attacked that Matthew, Thomas and he were still in the underground garage, that he had a couple of pretty bad injuries and that he was still experiencing the erosive effects of the virus.

Matthew and Thomas had their tactical teams on the ground, but two Saraph helicopters, also known as Apache Longbows, were keeping them pinned down as not one but two assault teams of Nephilim closed in on them. Laura's and Mitri's teams would be doing a Low Altitude Low Opening jump which meant they would not have the benefit of the element of surprise but would be able to deploy more rapidly.

The ZEHST slowed to jump speed and dropped to a dangerously low 500 feet. Aquilas, led by Mitri was the first of the two teams to deploy. Mazza, Garo, Pane and Di Nola followed him out the door on the green light. Their designated drop zone was to the west of the parking garage and behind one of the Nephilim assault teams. This would put them between two buildings secured by Thomas' team and would pincer the Nephilim from three directions with resistance from Matthew's team on top of and surrounding the outside of the parking garage.

The second of the Nephilim assault teams was making their way from the south on a street bordered by one of the secured buildings and an unsecured PLA building. On any given day there would've been at least a dozen IDF soldiers in and around this area but on this day not one could be found. Even the PLA soldiers were keeping out of sight. It was obvious that this private battle was going to be left alone by the resident authorities even though they all had a tremendous amount of vested interest in the outcome.

The Orion team, once again led by Laura, jumped in behind the Nephilim that were moving north toward the intersection toward the southeast corner of the parking garage. Asa, Montalto and Russo followed her out the door as the ZEHST banked from east to south. This put both of the Nephilim teams at a distinct disadvantage. Now, instead of outnumbering Matthew's and Thomas' teams and pushing in on them from two sides, they were outnumbered and surrounded on all sides. The bad news for Orion and Aquilas was that the path of least resistance for the Nephilim was a retreat into their positions that the two Apaches were now circling around to hit. They had hit the parking garage with two Hellfire missiles and were coming about to make another strike when the Orion and Aquilas assault teams dropped out of the sky. One chopper banked north and then west in preparation to come up behind Mitri and his team and the second obviously planned to hit Laura and her team in their turn to the south.

Laura knew they would be hit with either the M230 Chain Gun or with any number of Hydra 70 rockets. Either way, they didn't have the necessary armaments to take on the choppers. Matthew's team had the best vantage point and the most prescient data available thanks to the eyepieces. They were relaying the best potential cover to the ground teams when the Apaches came in low and fast from the west. They opened up the Chain Guns and a steady stream of 30mm rounds began plowing up the asphalt behind Laura's team just as they engaged their cloaking suits and scrambled to either side of the street to take cover. The Nephilim used the opening to push back toward them but were bewildered by their sudden disappearance.

"Orion 1 to Aquilas 1, they're pushing hard your way. Take cover. Repeat. Take cover."

"Roger, Orion 1." Mitri split his team and took cover up against the backs of the one secured building and the PLA building.

Laura didn't know any of the call designations for the other friendlies but needed to know immediately if they had an RPG or any other surface to air armaments to combat the Apaches.

"Orion 1 to Friendly, over."

"Esche'tu...Orion 1."

"We need those birds taken out. You have the tools for the job?"

"Negative Orion 1 our intel didn't account for Mossad."

"Mossad?"

"That's our best estimate."

One of the choppers broke to the south to engage the Aquilas team while the other remained stationary searching for traces of Orion. Laura knew they wouldn't keep looking for long and would begin lighting up the area with everything they had. Survivability would be minimal.

The Nephilim kept pushing back toward them but no one could fire without giving their position away. Soon both insertion teams would be corralled into the kill zone with the Nephilim behind them. Instead of having the Nephilim surrounded, the Nephilim would have them surrounded. The objective though was to get the virus and the ARA carriers which meant the Nephilim had to be taken out no matter what.

"Orion 1…Esche'tu. We're going to engage the Nephilim. Push into the target on my mark." She wanted his team to enter the parking garage as soon as they had nailed the giants.

Both the Esche'tu team leader and Mitri knew she was ordering the deaths of both Orion teams so that Matthew's and Thomas' teams could get inside the parking garage and retrieve the virus stores Ephrem had with him and the data detailing where the remainder was being kept. As soon as the Orion teams opened up fire on the Nephilim the Apaches would have them zeroed and take them out, but it was the only way.

"Orion 1…Aquilas 1. Choose your shots and fire when ready. We've only got one chance to get it right."

There was no hesitation on Mitri's part, and no bold statements or commentary. Antonin Carafa had assembled and trained some of the finest warriors she'd ever seen. They were courageous and understood that their lives would likely be cut

short as they fought for a cause hidden from most of the world and that would ultimately save the world. Their names would never be known and their stories never
told. Even when their skirmishes and activities occasionally showed up in the public
eye, it was quickly dismissed or assigned to more innocuous engagements between
drug lords, terrorists groups or tribal leaders. They were all very likely about to die
and Laura had come to realize that they had all accepted that fact a long time before
this day. Their deaths would not come at a time of their knowing, but would come
at the time of their choosing.

Mitri's one word reply came back as calmly and resolutely as if he was affirming a
trip to the grocery store, "Roger."

They lifted their weapons and using the heads up displays of their helmets took
careful aim on the heads of the Nephilim that were moving cautiously back through
their ranks. Each HUD communicated to the other which enemy combatant had
been targeted so that there was no duplication. The choppers hovered in anticipation of sending a barrage of Hellfire missiles and Hydra 70s down as soon as the
Nephilim were clear. As soon as the Orion and Aquilas teams opened fire however,
their jobs would be that much simpler.

Laura, Asa, Montalto, Russo, Mitri, Mazza, Garo, Pane and Di Nola had nine
of the twelve Nephilim in their crosshairs. The remaining three would be taken
out in a scramble hopefully right before the destruction from above came raining
down. They squeezed their triggers with near perfect synchronization. Nine of the
Nephilim dropped to the ground like giant trees being felled by power saws.

The M230 canons of the Apaches whipped onto target as soon as the shots had been
fired. Overhead, a sound rending the air with a violent scream caused everyone to
turn their attention to the clouds. The ZEHST was coming in low, very low. With
the precision of computer controlled timing, the ramjets shut down and the rocket
engines, normally reserved for atmospheric flight, fired and exploded with the heat
of three suns. A vapor cone, looking like an ethereal satellite dish formed around
the plane giving them all the last visual contact they would have with it before

disappearing. With his comm link open so that the assault teams could hear him the pilot simply said, "Bye-bye you rotor head motherfuckers."

With that, the hyper sonic jet was gone, but as it went, it left the violent sonic boom that is the signature of crossing the sound barrier in its wake. Every window in the vicinity exploded in flying shards of glass. More importantly though, the two Apaches that had been directly beneath the waves of the boom could not compensate for the downward force and were sent plummeting to the ground in an uncontrolled autorotation. The rotor blades caught nearby buildings then dug into the concrete and asphalt as they hit and flipped onto their sides. Everyone on the ground took cover as shrapnel and debris blew outward in every direction from the explosions.

The remaining three of the Nephilim, two in the corridor next to Mitri's team and one in the intersection ahead of Laura's were taken out before they could recover from the violent and unsettling commotion. With all vitals registering within normal ranges, Laura breathed a huge sigh of relief and then ordered her teams to close in on the parking garage. With the Nephilim taken out as well as the choppers, they were free to move in on the target.

At the entrance to the garage, the Orion and Aquilas teams disengaged their cloaking suits but kept their helmets on. The Esche'tu team leader greeted Laura at the front of the building.

"I am Tewfeeq."

"Laura." She shook his hand.

"That was very close."

Laura just nodded in agreement. She had one objective in mind and an after action report was not it. She turned to enter the building but Tewfeeq stopped her.

"I am afraid the area is infested with these robotic mosquitoes. You are not inoculated."

"These suits will protect us." She pushed past him and entered the garage amongst the rubble caused by the two Hellfire missiles that had been fired earlier.

A contingent with representatives of each assault team remained behind to secure the entrance as Laura, Mitri, Tewfeeq and the rest of their teams made their way down the ramps to the box van. They checked the van carefully before approaching or opening it in case it was rigged with explosives. All of their monitoring devices indicated that it was safe. Tewfeeq grasped the latch of the rear door and rolled it up.

"Empty."

Laura and Mitri looked at each other as the hair on the backs of their necks stood on end. The crates of ARAs were gone, they had anticipated that, but there was no sign of Alexander, Matthew, Thomas or Ephrem Goldman.

"Matthew, do you read?" Tewfeeq got no response.

"Thomas?" Still, nothing.

Laura tried to contact Rome but she also got no response. She then turned to Tewfeeq, "They didn't come out at some point during the firefight did they?"

"No, we would have seen or heard from Matthew. His data link is also not responding. Something is very wrong."

39

"Every building in the West Bank constructed by the Palestinians is connected to an extraordinary and ancient network of caves. Most of them have been in use since the Copper Age, in all about seven thousand years. About ten years ago, after an operation conducted by the Israelis in Bethlehem, the Palestinians began fortifying and preparing the caves for long-term survival." As they made their way through the very network Alexander was describing he had to ask Matthew to stop occasionally for a break. His broken bones and remnant effects of the virus were making the journey difficult but the brief respites of lying on the cool cave floor gave him time to recover enough to continue.

"I am not sure I understand why we are making use of them." Matthew checked Alexander's IV bag as he said this.

With his good arm, Alexander reached around to the small of his back and pulled Ephrem's iPad from his waistband. "This is why we're taking the somewhat less than scenic route."

"Does that belong to the soon to be late Mr. Goldman?"

"It does. I slid it away from him when the effects of the virus dropped him to the floor. These are not the only stores of ARAs and virus he has and I'm betting everything we need to know about where they are is on here." He slipped the iPad back into the waist of his pants and indicated he was good to go again. "It's not much further."

"Where does this come out?"

"The Church of the Nativity. It eventually leads to the traditional birthplace of Jesus Christ."

After another half hour of walking, that was exactly where they were standing. Surrounded by silk brocade drapes, ornate filigree hanging lamps and white marble it was a strange juxtaposition to his surroundings over the previous twenty-four hours. Over the years, he'd visited this particular cave a half dozen times. Whether this was or was not the actual birthplace of Jesus, just being there had the effect of engulfing his conscious thoughts with reflections on the mysteries of his faith. As a priest, he'd celebrated those mysteries but had a terrible time convincing other believers that living with those mysteries, living with the questions, was the key to deeper spiritual understanding. Certitude closes the mind and eventually leads to the persecution of others, to wars and to death. At the heart of the conflicts between the three Abrahamic faiths was this kind of certitude.

In fact, the only belief system Alexander had ever encountered that seemed immune to that kind of certitude was represented by the three priests who were now waiting to greet them. Meerab, Jumerd and Virop were not just any Zoroastrian priests, they were Alexander's mentors and closest friends since the day he'd been recruited by Walter Trowbridge. Their distinctive influence over the politics within the culture of Iran had given them easy access to the vaccine supplies in Tehran to make the switch. There had been no communications between them since the operation to make that switch, yet they had known where to find Alexander as this part of the operation was complete. He was not surprised to see them, but as usual he was amazed at what he could only describe as the prophetic clairvoyance they seemed to possess.

They were dressed in long white robes and wore matching round, flat topped hats. Their faces were covered from the bridge of their noses to below their chins with decoratively embroidered veils that gave them the appearance of 19th century surgeons. Matthew eased Alexander down from his shoulders and onto the floor where he helped him to prop against the cave wall. Without a word the three priests

270

gathered around him, placed their hands on the top of his head and remained in silence for several minutes. Alexander closed his eyes. Matthew and Thomas stepped back and watched in awe as the ritual continued.

Jumerd knelt beside Alexander and held his broken arm in his hands. Virop knelt on the other side of him and placed his hands over his broken ribs. Meerab kept his hand on the top of his head. The silence continued.

Meerab eased Alexander forward, removed Ephrem's iPad and placed it on the floor. They then began assisting him with the removal of his clothing. They neatly folded each garment and placed them in a large white canvas bag. From another bag they withdrew a robe, hat and veil that matched theirs. After dressing him, they placed a pair of leather sandals on his feet and helped him to stand. They each gave a solemn nod toward him then turned to Matthew and Thomas who knew they had just witnessed something beyond their comprehension.

Meerab broke the silence with his gentle voice, "Your mission is complete and you will find your people waiting for you at the car park."

Thomas began to lodge something of a protest, "It is our mission to return Mathias and these items to the Alliance."

Meerab bent down, picked up the iPad, handed it to Thomas and smiled. "Your mission is complete."

Alexander gave them a silent nod of assurance. They hesitated for a brief moment more then turned and pulled back the drape through which they'd entered. They were about to reenter the network of caves when Meerab spoke once more, "AmhaSelassie."

Matthew whipped his head around to face him. His full name had only been used by his mother and only when he had been a small child. His shock was evident and his mouth opened to speak but no words came to him.

271

"Mercy is the most powerful demonstration of strength."

Meerab, Jumerd, Virop and Alexander then turned and walked single file down the narrow corridor leading out of the cave and back up into the church that had closed its doors unusually early on this day of violence in the streets that surrounded her. Matthew and Thomas began their walk back to the parking garage with the black cases in tow and without a word between them.

The walk back took considerably less time since they didn't have to make the frequent stops that Alexander had required. Thomas' earpiece suddenly returned to life after having mysteriously stopped at the same time Matthew's eyepiece had stopped functioning. There was a flurry of chatter between the various teams as they dismantled the van and were sweeping the entire area for clues. Her voice stopped all of the chatter though when she made contact. Laura was the first to respond.

"What is your location?"

"We're close, about to arrive with the cases and Ephrem's iPad."

"Is Alexander with you?"

Thomas hesitated before replying as she didn't quite know where to begin. "Well, no..."

"No?" Her exasperation was evolving into anger.

"I'll do my best to explain." Matthew and she emerged from the level below just as she said this. She approached Laura who was standing at the back corner of the van with her helmet off now that the area had been cleared of the remaining ARAs.

"Where is he? And where's Goldman?"

Thomas and Matthew looked into the empty van then back to Laura. Matthew was still brooding over their encounter with the Zoroastrian priest and was not feeling talkative. Thomas waited for him to explain but continued when she saw he was going to remain silent.

"We left him here when we evacuated through the tunnel. Alexander knew about this network of caves and passages that led us to the Church of the Nativity."

Laura looked back toward the ramp where Thomas and Matthew had emerged. Thomas understood her line of thinking clearly.

"He's not there."

"Then where *is* he?" Her patience was completely gone.

"It's difficult to describe but essentially there were these three...men." She didn't quite know what to call them. "They tended to Mathias' injuries, dressed him as they were dressed, in all white and a veil then he left with them."

"Are you *kidding* me? How could you allow them to take him? Where were they going? Who were they?" She was firing off questions faster than Thomas could respond.

"He seemed to know them...really well. He also seemed to want to go with them. It was..."

"Holy." While it wasn't the word she was searching for, Matthew's word was actually more appropriate. He spoke it with humility and reverence and just a little fear.

"What do you mean, 'holy'?"

He removed his eyepiece and looked at Laura whose countenance was still ridden with anxiety. "I don't know. There was just something. He's OK though." Matthew's expression melted into a confused look as if he couldn't believe his own thoughts. "And..."

"What?"

"You're going to see him soon."

Thomas looked at Matthew as neither of them could understand precisely where those words had been formed. Thomas then looked back to Laura.

"We need to go now."

"Look, I don't know what happened back there but I need to see him now and I need to know where Goldman is and I need to know where the remaining stores of virus and ARAs are. If you can't help me with that, then give me what you've got and get out of my way."

Matthew felt an odd mixture of the feeling that he might be losing his mind and the calm of knowing the words he was about to speak were true. "Our mission is complete."

With that he motioned for his team to join him. Thomas did the same and they all walked out of the garage together in silence. Those that had been standing guard at the garage entrance were already sitting on a bus that had pulled up on the curb. Montalto stepped down and out of the bus.

"We're supposed to go with them."

Laura stepped up onto the bus and was warmly greeted by the driver. "You are Laura?"

"Yes."

"We are to go to the Old City."

She stuck her head back out and used a head nod to indicate that her team should follow. After sweeping the bus inside and out for anything suspicious they were off toward Jerusalem.

40

On the bus they discovered that each of them had a duffle with a change of clothing, the necessary identification for making their way out of Israel and 1800 Israeli New Shekels. After a half hour ride, the bus pulled up near the southeast corner of the Old City in Jerusalem. The driver stood and looked at Laura.

"They're expecting you."

Laura stood and made her way to the front of the bus. Mitri rose and began to follow but the driver held his hand aloft. "Only her."

"No, I'll be going with her."

Laura gave him an appreciative look, "I'll be OK. You get these folks back to Rome and find out what's going on there. We won't be far behind."

She stepped off the bus and faced into the setting sun that was caressing the sky with brilliant hues of pink, purple and orange. Shops were beginning to close and streams of tourists and religious pilgrims were making their way out of the gate as she entered. Directly ahead of her was the al'Aqsa Mosque, the Dome of the Rock and the Western Wall. She stood in silent reverence. It was the first time she'd ever visited this hallowed and violently contested piece of earth. She couldn't quite find the words to describe the feeling. Perhaps it was the enormity of the history of this place or the way the setting sun cast its gaze on the ancient stones. Whatever 'it' was, she felt something stirring within her that she'd never felt before. Then a familiar feeling washed over her. It was one she'd felt countless times before, the same feeling she'd had when Robert Cox had shown up at their cabin. Someone was watching her.

Laura turned around and looked up to the top of the ramparts of the Old City walls. He'd removed the hat and the veil but still wore the white tunic and robe of a Zoroastrian priest. His face seemed to glow as he observed her finally noticing him. He looked over toward the entrance steps and then back at her. She understood, bounded up the stone stairs and then wrapped him up in her arms before she stopped to consider his injuries. She let go as quickly as she'd embraced him.

"Oh, I'm sorry. Are you OK?"

He reached out and pulled her to him and in a quiet almost contemplative voice said, "I'm fine."

"What happened back there? I mean, one minute we're in the fight of our lives and then the next it was over. Ephrem was gone, you were gone. And what's this?" She plucked at the sleeve of his robe.

Alexander looked out over the Western Wall where a scattering of devout Jews stood in prayer. "I have a prayer in that wall you know. I can show you right where it is too."

Laura turned her attention to the wall but was not pleased with his refusal to directly respond to her questions.

"I once told you about my son, that he died as a teenager and that I couldn't discuss it with you until another time, if ever."

Her frustration melted away as she remained silent in his arms.

"He was a little boy when we came here together. We walked down to the wall wearing our borrowed paper yarmulkes and after explaining the significance of the Temple and the wall I asked him if he would like to put a prayer into one of the crevices."

A solitary tear ran down his cheek that Laura gently brushed away.

"He said he wanted to pray for the whole world to love each other and to take care of each other. I told him that was the best prayer I'd ever heard. I don't think he believed me, but it really was. To love each other and take care of each other. Everything else kind of just falls under those two basic tenets."

Alexander looked away from the wall and back to Laura. "I spent all of my time back then fighting to keep people like Ephrem Goldman from destroying the world. It ruined my marriage..." He had to stop and catch his breath. "It cost me my son."

Laura remained silent and pulled him closer.

"He was 15 years old when I was abducted and thrown into Tilanqiao. He was having trouble in school, we think he was into drugs and if he wasn't he was definitely running around with some rough kids who were. Anyway, when he learned that I'd been thrown into a Chinese prison he overdosed and died three days later. Walter came to the prison to tell me. If I could've gotten my hands on him I would've snapped his neck right then. I carried that anger and hatred of Walter for a long time. I blamed him for David's death. While I was battling the demons that roamed the earth, my son was battling his internal demons that I gave him...and he was battling them on his own."

Laura buried her face in his chest and held him as tightly as she could. Her tears soaked into his tunic as his baptized the top of her head.

"I'm so sorry...I'm so, so sorry."

"I forgot who I was for a while because I wanted to forget. I wanted to bury that life and leave it in the past so that I wouldn't have to face the pain. The only thing that kept me going in that prison was the promise I made to myself to tear Walter Trowbridge apart piece by piece"

He stopped talking and stared into the distance. The sky was darkening into shades of deep blue as the day continued giving way to night.

"And then I met you. It was brilliantly sunny that day, but as I walked into the light, the darkness that consumed me was more bleak than anything within those walls. We hear it frequently but it's no less true because of being over worn; vengeance and hatred will absolutely destroy the soul. Once we give it ground it is the most tenacious cancer within us. But you came along, and of course I now know it was intentional on Walter's part, and you began pulling me out of a deeper prison than Tilanqiao."

Laura looked into his eyes and knew that something had changed within him. He was different even from the last time she had seen him and made love to him in Rome. His body seemed to have healed miraculously fast and she would definitely ask him about that later, but she was sensing something far more profound. It had always been he who had an uncanny understanding of her inner life but now it was as if his heart was now open to her. Moreover, if she had to put it into words, she would've said she could hear his soul speaking to her as they stood in silence, and it was beautiful. The anger, hatred, vengeance and guilt, things she hadn't even known were there before, had evaporated. In their place was a sense of tranquility and an unshakeable foundation of wisdom that comes from facing and defeating one's demons.

"Over the years of fighting these Nephilim and those they've recruited and manipulated into their service, I've only experienced despair twice. No matter how often it seemed my life was about to end it never really bothered me, but I very nearly allowed David's death to kill my spirit which is a far worse thing than physical death. In you, I'd found the peace and beauty in which I wanted so desperately to live. Then, when Walter came back into my life that morning at our cabin, I felt my new life crumbling. The problem was that, what I'd built around us was not true. I created a fortress that was impossible to defend. At the time I didn't see it as a lie or a deception, but it was."

He looked once again down at the Wailing Wall and the place he'd stood with his son so many years before. She followed his gaze for a moment then turned back toward him, watched his face and finally recognized what it was that had changed. Alexander had found peace with his own life.

"I never intended to deceive you, Laura. I just wanted peace. The problem, was that I'd built a fortress and the enemy who would bring it crashing down was inside. The true enemy was inside me in the form of lies that I'd told myself."

Laura sensed the remorse and the buildup to an apology, "Alexander..."

Instead of continuing she decided to kiss him. There was a warmth and power that cascaded over her as their lips met. Tears began streaming down her cheeks, but they were not tears of sadness or even of joy. They were tears of knowing.

"How are you doing that?" She whispered this in short breaths drawn through the most beautiful tears she'd ever shed.

Alexander smiled through his own tears of knowing and responded to her question by returning her kiss. "There is much to say and much to hear and we will have time for both, but for now you need to go."

"Go? Go where?"

She hadn't observed his approach but standing only a few feet away was a man dressed almost identically to Alexander with the exception of a round, flat topped hat and an embroidered veil. Meerab reverently nodded his greeting.

"This is Meerab. He will take good care of you and you'll want to listen to him. He has much to offer."

Laura didn't want to let go of Alexander. "Can't you come?"

"For now, no." He understood her hesitation. They'd been apart too much and in the midst of horrific violence, but it was necessary for Meerab and Laura to talk privately. "The discussion you need to have will not take long and I will be nearby and waiting for you when you're finished."

He could tell she was not pleased with this momentary and unexpected further separation, but with all that she'd seen, heard and experienced recently he also knew that she understood. Once she emerged from the conversation with Meerab, her understanding would deepen and she would discover new aspects and truths of the path that had brought her this far and the one that lay ahead. She was a true Daughter of Enoch and her time to assume that role had come.

41

"One does not learn the wisdom of the ages in a single lifetime." Meerab spoke his first words to Laura after they'd walked in silence to the Dome of the Rock. They stopped just short of an archway. The illuminated gold dome and exquisitely detailed mosaic facade glowed majestically against the night sky. "Reincarnation is not a tenet of our faith; however we do believe that through particular trials and triumphs, joys and sorrows, one incline d to grow may live several lifetimes in a solitary moment."

He produced a beautifully woven headscarf and presented it to her. "In our faith tradition, we deem women to be equal with men. Also, wherever God is worshipped, regardless of whose place of worship, we cover our heads." He further extended the scarf toward her. Laura graciously accepted his gift and adorned her head. They then passed through the arch where they were greeted by who appeared to be an Imam, *"As-salaam alaikum."*

Meerab embraced the man and replied, *"Wa alaikum assalaam."*

Laura observed every detail of her surroundings. The gilding, faience, mosaics and marble work were absolutely breathtaking but perhaps the most impressive sight of all was the rock itself. The most contested piece of real estate on earth was this monolithic common thread of the three Abrahamic faiths. For Muslims it represents the place of Muhammad's ascent into heaven where he prayed with Abraham, Moses and Jesus. For Jews it is the place where Abraham prepared to sacrifice Isaac. For Christians it is the place where Constantine's mother built the Church of the

Holy Wisdom. It had been the flashpoint for global upheaval, enmity and warfare for millennia with no peaceful solution in sight. They continued around the rock and came to a marble archway with two Corinthian columns on either side that served as a passageway to a granite staircase. Meerab and the Imam stood on either side of the arch.

"We believe at the basis of the universe is a struggle between the energies of truth and falsehood. Truths are the natural coalescence of energy. Falsehoods are the manipulations of that energy to serve another purpose. Some falsehoods are relatively harmless and in many cases helpful. The three legged stool for instance is a falsehood, a reformation of energies to create a human comfort. Within the stool is a tree that has been transformed into something it was never meant to be. A goat herder who sits upon the stool to milk his livestock never considers the tree. Conversely, we teach ourselves to cleave an atom," he looked down the passageway into the Well of Souls "and we reform a beautiful, foundational truth into an abysmal annihilation."

The Imam remained at the archway as Meerab and Laura descended the steps. "Our prophets, your prophets, their prophets," he removed his sandals at the foot of the stairs as did Laura, "these were and are people who see energetic truths and falsehoods the way most people observe everyday objects. Most people see only the symbol while the prophets see the greater reality to which the symbol points." He reached into a naturally created indentation in the cave wall hollowed out by thousands of years of erosion before it was covered by generations of worship structures. It was a recess about ten inches in diameter and sank about as equally deep into the rock surface. Meerab held out his hand. In it was a smooth rock about the size of a plum. "The Stone of David."

Laura's eyes widened at this declaration. If this was indeed the actual Stone of David it was difficult to believe how unguarded and easily accessible it was. He offered it to her with a nod and a slight pushing forward of his hand. She took it with some trepidation.

"This stone is a truth. It was a coalescence of energies in the universe that produced the material of its creation. It was an application of the un-manipulated energies of

284

time, water, wind and motion that reformed it into the small thing you now hold in your hand. However, when it became The Stone of David, it became a falsehood. When it was loaded into a sling, sent through the air with great velocity and imbedded with great force into the skull of a giant warrior, it then became a falsehood. It became something it was naturally never meant to be, an instrument of death."

He took the stone back from her and placed it back into its resting place. "Your Alexander, our Mathias has been the Stone of David for many years." Laura's heart sank and began to ache as she absorbed what Meerab had just said.

"He has been the stone which we have loaded into our sling time and again and sent into desperate situation after desperate situation. This role amongst the 12 has traditionally been the most difficult and destructive to those who have fulfilled it. A truth is reformed into a falsehood. We are a coalescence of energies not intended to be instruments of death. Yet at times, prevailing circumstances dictate otherwise."

Laura looked at Meerab with a growing sense of concern. "Difficult and destructive" was perhaps too great of an understatement. Alexander's life had been completely dismantled by his role as Mathias and when he'd tried to rebuild a life out of the ruins, it too had been dismantled over the course of just a few days. She was forming a litany of protest and defiance against his further involvement in this role when Meerab interrupted her thoughts.

"Alexander has completed his journey as Mathias. It is time for another to assume those responsibilities. Because of his abilities and his willingness to apply them with such brilliance and fervor, we enjoyed a greater span of peace between truths and falsehoods than at any other time in history. However, the landscape is shifting once again. Those who see beyond symbols knew long ago this day was coming. Walter Trowbridge in his role as James was a tremendous prophet. He saw more broadly and with more depth beyond the symbols than anyone I've ever encountered. He saw this day coming, he saw you, Daughter of Enoch." Meerab paused and took in his surroundings; he stopped speaking as if he needed rest before continuing. "He also saw something horrific, a coalescence of falsehoods so violently destructive that humanity will once again be utterly destroyed."

"Once again?"

"Humanity's greatest conceit has always been that they are the highest order of consciousness at any given point of their trajectory. In reality, in the vast expanse of time, we are but the great-grandchildren of mere infants. It is that conceit that always leads us to destroy ourselves rather than face this truth. We are not even the most advanced generation of humanity that has dwelt upon this earth."

Laura straightened up at this comment in a posture of disbelief. "You have evidence of this?"

With a gleam in his eyes and a smile, Meerab held his hands in an open gesture toward her and took and held her hands suspended between them. "My dear, Laura, *you* are the living evidence of this reality. You are the proof you require." He released her hands and placed his own in a prayer like form in front of his lips then dropped them just slightly to speak. "In time...in time you will see. You are one of an extraordinarily small number of people whose heritage predates this generation of humanity. Once you learn to access it, your genetic wisdom will guide you and assist you in ways you cannot begin to imagine. Certain energies possess what we would call memory. Our genes possess a form of this memory. We are genetically predisposed to behave in particular ways because of our genetic memory. *Your* genetic memory is eons older than nearly anyone else on the planet."

"If this is true, wouldn't I have become aware of it in some way over my lifetime so far?"

"Have you ever had a dream that seemed to be a dream within a dream and when you awoke, you *knew* you had been in those places and had engaged with those people? However, as you regained consciousness you simply dismissed it as an intense dream."

286

She considered what he was saying and realized the intensity of her dreams had often caused her a tremendous amount of distress at times and elation at others. Whenever she had shared those dreams or had tried to describe them she was always greeted with some form of disinterest or dismissal.

"Zoroaster, Moses, Jesus, Muhammad, The Buddha, they all experienced transcendent engagement with a reality beyond the comprehension of others."

Laura was a bit shocked that a priest of an individual form of religion would make a truth claim that included so many other prophets of other systems of belief. She didn't have to articulate her thoughts for Meerab to respond.

"Zoroastrians predate every other known religion. We are at much greater ease with the belief and worship structures of others than they are with us or each other." He smiled a warm smile before returning to his instruction.

"Laura, the Nephilim are an ancient race. Their dreams are nearly as old as yours and their genetic memory combined with their predilection for violence and desire to manipulate truths into falsehoods makes them the greatest threat to humanity. They are now emerging into a greater visibility than anyone can remember ever having happened before."

"What exactly will that look like? How will it take shape?"

"You may recall the quote attributed to Admiral Yamamoto following the attack on Pearl Harbor, that he feared they had awakened a sleeping giant. Of course, as the quote is used he is referring to the provocation of the United States and the ensuing carnage from that act. However, the quote is misattributed to Yamamoto by film makers. It was actually a statement in a communication from Emperor Hirohito to Adolf Hitler well after December 7, 1941 expressing his concern that their arrangement with the Nephilim might well have been a terrible mistake. It now appears that the Gush Emunim have made the very mistake their own enemies made over 70 years ago. They have aroused the sleeping Nephilim. The attempt to distribute the biological agent was only another sad chapter in the feud between the children of Abraham. What will follow will be an absolute war on all of humanity. It did not matter to them whether the efforts of the Gush Emunim were successful or not, putting that plan into motion was simply one of the logistical necessities in a much larger and more complex strategy."

Meerab walked to the foot of the stairs and put his sandals back on and extended his hand in a gesture for Laura to follow. However, she found her feet unable to move as she continued to process all he had told her.

"It is important now for you to rest while we attempt to recover the Palermo Stone. It is the next and most vital step of your education and why we could not allow Ephrem Goldman to die."

Laura's streams of thought were shattered by this statement.

"He's alive?"

"He is and he must remain alive as he is the only one we have access to who might know where the Palermo Stone is being kept. The underside of the fake has been rubbed smooth. However, the genuine stone that was safeguarded in the presidential palace has the original text intact. It is not a listing of Egyptian Pharaohs and gods. It is instead, if you will pardon the expression, a genetic cookbook. Humanity is on the verge of great advances in genetic manipulation that already existed many thousands of years before. If these recipes are followed, so to speak, a group of extremely bad individuals with horrifying intentions will be unstoppable."

"It doesn't sound like I need to rest, it sounds like we need to regroup and go after this Palermo Stone."

"No."

Laura and he ascended the stairs to where the Imam was still standing at the arch.

"But if what you say is accurate, surely our time is limited. As with missing persons, it's paramount to begin searching as soon after the incident as possible."

"Laura, there are more people than you are aware of working against the Nephilim. For now, you need to rest your spirit and allow your tired body to recuperate."

"But what if they are already utilizing these recipes to advance their plans?"

"The entirety of our lives is lived along a pathway with an infinite number of other pathways that we may choose or be forced to follow. Said another way, we live amongst the 'what ifs.'" He held his hands in a gesture of silent resignation. "But if you are not prepared with the rest and the knowledge you need, then we will have failed before we begin."

She looked around at the ornate surroundings and pondered his wisdom.

"Alexander has a new role to fulfill. He will be with you along your path and will take you to those who will continue your instruction. Laura," he stopped walking and faced her, "you will be tempted to share the knowledge with him that you are about to gain. Do not."

Laura didn't quite understand why this admonition hit her so negatively but she was not in the habit of keeping secrets from those she loved and trusted.

"You are a Christian by tradition, no?"

"I am."

"Shortly before his death, Jesus told his closest disciples that there were things they could not yet bear to hear. In your role as Daughter of Enoch you will learn things that only you should know and because of who you are, you alone will be able to accommodate and process that knowledge. He will never ask you to reveal your knowledge and even if you feel the fate of the world hangs in the balance and that the revelation of the things you know is the only thing that will save humanity, do not. Because you must trust me when I say, it will not."

As they emerged from the Mosque, Alexander was waiting for them. Without a word, Meerab and the Imam continued walking. He took her hand, "It's time to go."

She blew out a breath of exhaustion, "Where?"

"To see our friends Robert and Antonin."

"Thank God they're OK."

"And they can't wait to see you."

42

The four of them sat at one of the café tables in the courtyard of Antonin's ancestral home. The reunion in Genoa had been both joyous and tearful as they took the opportunity to celebrate the victories of their operation and to mourn the losses.

"So what happened in Rome when the Nephilim attacked the Alliance headquarters?" Laura posed the question but Alexander was equally curious.

"It was unbelievable! Every warrior has pondered the circumstances when the enemy of his enemy becomes his friend." Antonin was as animated as any had ever seen him. "I still do not know how they discovered us, but I will find out one day and let me tell you..."

Robert had to cut him off, "I think we can all assume that you will exact your vengeance upon the Nephilim, Antonin. *I'll* tell you what happened. Judith and Jorah saw them closing in on us on their surveillance monitors and sounded the alarm. We transferred all of the data to secured storage facilities and then began an auto-destruct sequence for everything."

"Everything?" Alexander had come to appreciate the technological accoutrements of their underground facility and was disheartened to hear this news.

"Everything." Antonin resumed his story after shooting his old friend Robert a withering look. "Then, when we made our exit who should we encounter, *not* the Nephilim but the Spada."

This time Alexander looked apprehensive, "The Sword of St. Peter? The Pope's own Delta force?"

"Yes! And I tell you it was at first a most unpleasant encounter. However, we were then pleasantly surprised to learn that, with Boniface in seclusion after his resignation, some Cardinal in Buenos Aires had ordered them to intercede when the Swiss Guard intelligence division detected the movements of the Nephilim in the city center. They were very happy to have us on their team."

"I bet." Alexander didn't seem too fond of the thought that the same guys that had tried to gun him down on the Vatican grounds were now fighting alongside his team.

Like a proud father Antonin continued, "So when the Nephilim saw that they were outclassed and outgunned, they cut their losses and disappeared."

A set of double doors opened on the opposite side of the courtyard and a stream of men and women came out carrying huge trays of the famous kosher Northern Italian cuisine Robert was always gushing about. Antonin's attention span became like that of a child at the sight of home cooking, "Oh thank God, I am starving!"

He hopped up from the little table to join the rest of the enormous family at the long dining table set up along the gallery. Robert followed closely behind but Alexander and Laura remained for a few moments longer.

"We have a long road ahead."

"Yes, we do."

"We're not going back to North Carolina are we?" Her question hung in the air between them for a few seconds.

"No, not for a very long time."

"So what's next?"

His expression told her she should probably have held that question for another time. "Rest, Laura. Rest and healing. Because believe me, they're already suited up for battle with us and more specifically with you. Your role has changed and the battlefield is now broader and more deadly than any you've ever stepped onto before. As a Daughter of Enoch it is essential that you are eliminated. Once you assemble the necessary facets of knowledge, you will represent the greatest threat to the Nephilim in six centuries."

"Is this really my tough guy who's known for taking on Hell and half of Georgia talking?" She smiled, leaned across the table and gave him a big kiss. "Let's eat." She then stood, turned and went to join the others.

Alexander watched her walk across the cobbled piazza. He then brought the entire scene into focus. He considered all of the people at the table. He pondered his life before, his life between and his life now. The people in his life seemed to scroll through as they entered and left, lived and died. He knew that his new role would be the most challenging of his life. Balancing the tasks Laura had ahead of her with the tasks of those who would serve as her system of support would be daunting. The difficulty was exacerbated by the fact that he would often be in the dark regarding specifics of certain operations. It was an unenviable task, but looking at Robert, Antonin, Mitri, Jorah and Judith all gathered at the table, he knew if there was a group of people on this earth that were capable of making it a functional system, these were the ones.

His thoughts then turned to Walter. During his time in Jerusalem, Meerab had made only one comment about the two of them, "There is a fine line that separates love from hate. Crossing that line in either direction is always a matter of choice."

Alexander's thoughts ascended to a plateau of both clarity and uncertainty. He could sense the horizon but couldn't quite envision the fullness of its reality. Walter had continuously warned that if a member of the 12 was assassinated it would initiate a chain of events leading to the most catastrophic wars in recorded human history. Now, there were at least two of them gone. The Nephilim were moving into a position of exposure and vulnerability which meant they were already accepting the risks of doing so. The pawns, the nation states enlisted in previous wars, were now obviously of little consequence if any at all. An age of death was now at hand that Alexander had always assumed would come long after his time.

Gazing across the piazza, he absorbed the energetic presence and life of his friends. He was with them, but was no longer of them. His days of being bloodied in battle were now over, yet the more difficult and heart wrenching days lay ahead, those in which he would have to send his friends, his family into the crucible of violence.

"Hey, are you going to sit over there thinking about food or are you going to come eat?" Antonin wanted his entire family at the table and it was not complete without Alexander.

He got up and walked to the table burgeoning with food, conversation and laughter. As he sat Antonin stood and raised his glass of wine. "If we live in hatred, we die in hatred. If we live in love, then we die in love. May this day and every day be days lived in love. Salute!"

The others lifted their glasses and returned Antonin's toast, "Salute!"